HAUNTED A LOVE STORY

Emmaline Givens

Emmaline Givens Author House

Copyright © 2021 Emmaline Givens

The characters and events portrayed in this book are fictitious. Any similarity to real persons, living or dead, is coincidental and not intended by the author.

No part of this book may be reproduced or stored in a retrieval system, or transmitted in any form or by any means, electronic, mechanical, photocopying, recording, or otherwise, without express written permission of the publisher and author.

First Edition 2021

Cover Design: Emmaline Givens (Canva)

To contact the author or for more information, please visit my website at www.emmalinegivens.com or find me on Facebook.

Have a blessed day!

Let's stay connected!

I love hearing from my readers. Follow my Facebook Author Page (Emmaline Givens) or my website (www.emmalinegivens.com) to see what I'm up to behind the scenes and to take part in special promotional offers.

DEDICATION:

For my sister, Theresa.

CONTENTS

Title Page

Copyright

Dedication

Haunted: A Love Story

PROLOGUE	1
CHAPTER ONE	4
CHAPTER TWO	15
CHAPTER THREE	39
CHAPTER FOUR	58
CHAPTER FIVE	80
CHAPTER SIX	107
CHAPTER SEVEN	149
CHAPTER EIGHT	178
CHAPTER NINE	211
CHAPTER TEN	235
CHAPTER ELEVEN	267
CHAPTER TWELVE	304
CHAPTER THIRTEEN	324

Other books by this author:	341
About The Author	343
I want to hear from you	345
	347

HAUNTED: A LOVE STORY

PROLOGUE

NOBODY SAID IT was going to be easy. The words her mother recited almost daily while Kate was growing up had never rung truer than right now and for the first time in fifty-seven years, she found herself pondering the meaning.

Maybe her words were meant to be foretelling of things to come.

Maybe it was because her mother grew up during the forties and life was just harder.

Maybe it was her mother's four failed marriages that caused her to be so jaded.

Maybe it was that her only child chose to stay in the same small town she was born in, never to explore the world.

Maybe she was just born mean.

"Why the *hell* are you still sitting there?"

Kate continued to stare out the window even though she knew doing so would only provoke additional comments. On any other day she would have shut it down by playing along and not giving her ammunition, but in this moment, she welcomed the distraction. No, she *needed* it if she had any hope of getting through the next few hours without falling apart.

"I've been watching you for the last five

minutes and you haven't touched that coffee. It's got to be ice cold by now. And look at those bare legs... you don't even have your pantyhose on yet."

"I'm not going to wear any, mother. It's too humid."

"Have it your way... I'm not going to preach about it. It's your choice if you want to give those old hens something to chatter about for the next week."

She's right.

While she welcomed the distraction, Kate was too tired to engage in the banter her mother was trying to reel her into... it also wouldn't be any fun for either of them. At eight-two, Fiona's mind was as sharp as a tac and this morning, Kate was having trouble remembering if she brushed her teeth. Yesterday, when her physician found out she had barely slept since getting the news about Matthew, he had called in a sedative. Thankfully, she had *not* listened to her mother when she suggested that she take two, but instead opted for cutting one pill in half.

Hopefully by the time they got to the church she would feel normal, though, she didn't believe that she would ever *truly* feel normal again.

"If you don't move your ass, you're going to be late for the service."

Kate pushed her chair back and tossed her folded napkin onto her untouched piece of toast.

"It's not like they're going to start without me."

Using the table as support, she stood up and glanced at the clock on the wall before turning to leave the room. Her mother was right again, and she needed to get going. Their friends and family coming to pay their last respects were probably already inside the church or pulling into the parking lot, and she didn't even have her shoes on. As she walked down the hall toward the bedroom, the image of *the walk* she would have to make through the rows and rows of people waiting for her caused her stomach to roll.

Just thinking about being on display gave her anxiety and she made the decision to call Father Mike when she got into the car. She'd ask that he meet them at the side door where they could easily slip into the front rows. Having a plan helped her to move a little more quickly and as she bent down to pick up her sandals, her mother once again called to her from the kitchen.

"Kate, are you ready yet?"

I'll never be ready for this.

"Yes, mother... I'm coming."

CHAPTER ONE

WATCHING HIS FAMILY move about the room like he wasn't even there had taken some getting used to. But his confusion had started the night before when he found himself in front of the fireplace, staring at his living room. He had no idea how he got there or where he had been. He remembered the fire, but not much beyond the flames and smoke... or *the nothing* that came next.

The first night after he returned, he hadn't been able to move about the room. He was trapped in the same spot even though his body seemed to move normally. But each time he tried to lift his legs to change position or even turn around, it felt like his feet were glued to the floor. It hadn't been until the next morning when sunlight began to stream in through the window and move across the room that he discovered what the problem had been.

His feet were missing.

Or rather, everything below his ankles had blended into the basketweave rug Kate had purchased a few weeks before to bring the items in the room together. Oddly enough, it hadn't freaked him out. Like his extremities, his emotions seemed to be missing and having no other choice, he waited patiently to see what would happen next.

ONE MORE DAY. One more day to have the house filled with the familiar sounds of being overcrowded in the small cottage that her and Matthew purchased thirty years ago. One more day and the kids would be going back to their lives, and she would be alone. It amazed her how the home she felt was too big for them just a few weeks ago, now felt small.

But she loved it.

Over the years, she had brought up the conversation of making some improvements and perhaps adding a sunroom in the back or an extra bedroom, but Matthew would shake his head and shoot down the idea. He was not willing to throw good money away by fixing something up guaranteed to be demolished by their children.

So, for twenty-five years, their four kids rotated between two of the three available bedrooms and single beds and bunkbeds shuffled back and forth between the garage and the house to accommodate the design choice of the personalities sharing a room.

Ava was the first to move out when she left for college, and it was not a surprise when she chose to stay in Oklahoma City rather than return home. Her brother and sisters were thrilled at the idea and put their heads together agreeing on a bedroom solution that didn't change again until four years later when Victoria left for Nashville to pursue her music career. For the next two years the house was still full, but fairly peaceful.

Jackson was the next to cause drama in the house. The day after he turned eighteen, he informed them that he had enlisted in the Marines and would be leaving for basic training in three months; just two days after graduation. He had been offered a full scholarship to play football at the University of Tulsa, but without even talking it over with his parents, he chose to follow his passion for service in the military.

The next three years were mostly quiet again, but the months seemed to march by far too quickly.

Matthew had finally agreed to begin the renovation and after thirteen months of dust, plastic sheeting, weeks of takeout, hammering and sawing, they had renovated every room, expanded the main bedroom and added the sunroom Kate had talked about for years.

With only one child left in the house, they filled their free time with volunteering within their community: Kate at the local animal shelter and Matthew at the Linvalle Fire Department. Before long, between operating the hardware store that had been family-owned for two generations and the volunteer work, somebody always seemed to be coming or going and most of their free time was gone.

But only Matthew had been surprised when Charlotte graduated from high school and announced that she was marrying the boy she had been dating since freshman year. Kate knew it was coming before her daughter even got up the courage to sit her parents down and give them the news. Their youngest child reminded her so much of herself, and when they tried to talk her into waiting, she successfully countered their argument with the fact that they too had married the summer after high school.

It had worked out for them, and they had given in.

Having the kids home for Matthew's funeral had transported her back to the days when the house was overflowing with loud music, toys, dirty laundry, and never-ending trips to the grocery store. Ava stayed only one night, making the excuse that she needed to get back to her law practice and reminding her mother that she had already taken two days off from work to help her make the arrangements.

Charlotte hadn't spent the night but lived only eight blocks away so every morning she would return in time to help with breakfast and was the one to lock the front door at night when she left to go home to her husband.

It had been the worst five days of her life, but it had brought her family together.

"Mom, how long is grandma staying?"

Kate turned to find Jackson taking a seat at the table. She had been so lost in her thoughts that she hadn't heard his flip-flops against the wooden floor. Looking at him sitting in what had been Matthew's chair, she realized how much he looked like his father and the tears came without warning.

"Don't get up," Kate whispered, as she slipped her fingers under her reading glasses to wipe away a passing rain shower of emotion. "I'm fine... really." Sniffling, she walked over to the table to take a seat across from her son... her little boy who was all grown up.

"Mom, I'm sorry."

"Oh, hunny. It's not your fault," Kate whispered, reaching across the table with her hand to cover his with her own. "I sprung a leak because it hit me, looking at you just now, how much you look like daddy."

She could feel him clench his hand beneath hers as he fought back his own emotion. How many times over the years had she witnessed those little hands ball up into a fist as he tried to show her how tough he was?

"I don't want you to be alone."

"I'll be fine. Have you forgotten... in a town the size of Linvalle, it's impossible to be alone? Besides, Charlie is just up the street and grandma will be here until Friday... unless I ask her to leave before then." Kate smiled in response to her success in making him grin.

The dark mood that was threatening to overtake them had been pushed back once again.

"Have you been down to the store?"

"No," Kate replied. "Pete told me to stay away until the full report is in. Apparently, our insurance requested an arson investigator, and he couldn't get down from the City until Wednesday."

"An arson investigator? Dad would never-."

"Jack, it's going to be okay," Kate replied. "The building was a total loss... we have to let the process work itself out. You guys haven't gone down there, have you?"

"No," Jack quickly replied. "Well, Tori and I drove by when we picked up the food last night, but neither one of us could look at it. Are you going to rebuild... after everything is worked out?"

"Oh, I don't know, Jack. That's a lot of work and I'm not sure I want to do it without your dad."

"Charlotte lives in town. Why can't she help you?"

"What are you volunteering me for now?"

Jack turned around to find his youngest sister had returned from running her errands but was surprised to see that she didn't seem to be annoyed with him talking *about* her rather than *to* her. Being the youngest in the family, she usually had her guard up about everything. She was often referred to as the baby of the family, the spoiled brat, dad's favorite, or the one who didn't have to work... and walking in on a conversation about her, usually started an argument.

"It's nothing sweetheart," Kate replied. "We were just-."

"We were just discussing," Jack said, interrupting his mother, "the store and how since you live in town, there isn't a reason you can't help mom sort through the details of rebuilding."

"Rebuilding?" Charlotte replied, looking toward her mother. "I didn't know you had decided that."

"No decision has been made. We were just talking about what happens next."

"Mom, you know that if you decide that another store is what you want... I'll help you," Charlotte replied, pulling out a chair and taking a seat at the table.

"Charlie, maybe *now* would be a good time to tell Jack your news and not wait until tonight."

"What news?" Jack asked, watching the

looks pass between the two of them. "Let me guess... this time you want to be a yoga instructor."

Charlotte laughed at the image his words provoked in her mind. "No, but more flexibility might come in handy."

Kate smiled, understanding the joke but could see that Jack was not amused as he pulled his arm away and sat back into his chair.

"You're gonna be an uncle," Charlotte announced, reaching for her stomach.

Immediately, Kate could see tears begin to fill her only son's eyes. He didn't have to tell her what he was thinking, she already knew. It was the same reaction she had two days before when Charlotte shared the news with her. The person who had been hinting about being ready to be a grandpa relentlessly for the last year, was going to miss it.

"Don't start," Kate said, pointing toward her son. "I'm tired of tears."

"Nope, no tears here," Jack replied, rubbing the palms of his hands into his eyes. "So, when's the big day?"

"The end of the year," Charlotte replied, waiting for the reaction she knew would come.

"Ha! Your *favorite* time of the year and you're gonna be waddling around. I love it!"

"Shut-up, jerk."

"No tight little dresses for you this year," Jack laughed.

"Oh, they'll still be tight... just not so little." Charlotte replied, grabbing her breasts that had almost doubled in size over the past month.

Kate sat back and smiled but looked toward the entryway after she heard the front door open. She expected to see Victoria come around the corner, but was surprised to see her mother trailing behind her as well. Fiona always stayed at a hotel when she visited, and rarely showed up before noon when she could be sure that any neighbor with the energy to mow their lawn, finished before she arrived.

"What's so funny?" Victoria asked. It was the first time she had heard laughter since coming home for the funeral.

"Does Tori know?" asked Jack.

"Know what?"

"I see you finally told him," Fiona said, putting her purse down on the table.

"Told him what?" asked Victoria again, becoming annoyed that she was being ignored.

"Your sister is knocked up."

"Really, mother?"

Fiona scrunched her face and looked at her daughter. "What? Like they haven't heard *that* before."

"It's not the term, mom... it's," Kate sighed. "Oh, never mind."

Kate relaxed into her chair and watched Victoria high-five her brother before reaching down to hug her little sister; the three of them chatting away about how excited they were that a baby was on the way.

"Who emptied the coffee pot again?"

Shaking her head, Kate pushed herself up from the chair not surprised that Fiona had managed to bring the attention back to her.

"Give me a minute, mom. I'll make some more."

HE WAS GOING to be a grandpa. He felt like he needed to sit down but he knew he'd simply fall through the floor again and end up back in front of the fireplace. Over the course of the day, he had figured out a few things about his new existence. He didn't stand on the floor, he hovered just above it. He could move through the interior walls but had not yet been successful in going outside. He could pick up small objects but doing so weakened his energy to the point he nearly disappeared. He could speak but not loud enough for anyone to hear him, and his sense of smell had become so muted it felt more like a memory.

But what he was hearing as his family sat around the kitchen table felt like it took the breath in his lungs that no longer existed away. Even before Charlotte got married, he had begun talking about grandchildren. Ava, who was not here to celebrate the news with the rest of the family, had been married the month after she graduated law school and that was the first time the thought of chasing a little boy or girl around the back yard entered his mind. But unfortunately, her marriage ended after his son-in-law abruptly quit his job at the bank to take over his uncle's horse ranch. Ava decided she'd rather be married to her work than someone who had no ambition to climb the corporate ladder with her and his hopes of a grandchild were put on hold.

Kate had masterfully reminded him that he was only fifty-five years old and that there was plenty of time. Nobody could have predicted what would happen to him, but for the first time in their marriage, his wife had been wrong.

CHAPTER TWO

THE RETURN DRIVE from the City took her forty-five minutes and with each mile marker that Kate passed, the level of anxiety that she felt ticked up. While she was relieved that the morning had finally arrived that her mother would be returning home to Tampa, she understood it would come at a cost when she pulled back into her driveway.

Fiona had stayed for ten days, spending every night except the last at a hotel and had guests she deemed obnoxious not checked in for a pre-wedding celebration, she wouldn't have stayed with Kate at all. When Kate asked her what the other guests had done to be so disruptive, Fiona mentioned something about using the ice machine after five o'clock but beyond that, hadn't elaborated.

Their last evening together had been pleasant, even though Kate found herself looking at the clocks around the house more often than was necessary and rather than order takeout again, Fiona offered to make a meal that had been a staple in their household growing up... ketchup meatloaf. It actually tasted better than Kate remembered and for a little while, she hadn't focused on the clock marching closer and closer to when she would have to face being alone in the house for the first time in her life.

Coming up on familiar landmarks that identified her exit was approaching, Kate moved into the right-hand lane and a few minutes later was following the curve of the offramp that would take her into downtown Linvalle. But today, she turned right two blocks before she hit the downtown area and took the long way home.

She hadn't driven the streets that led to the school in as long as she could remember... maybe not even since Charlotte graduated. Her mother had caught an early flight and as Kate drove down the dogwood lined trees, she began to see familiar faces stepping out of their homes to begin their day. She waved at a few before putting on her sunglasses so she could avoid making eye contact that might invite a conversation. She'd had enough of the *'how are you doing'* and *'if there's anything you need'* comments to last the rest of her life. Her neighbors and friends meant well; she knew that. She had said the words herself over the years to other people who had lost a loved one, but the understanding of how hollow the words sounded when you were the one hearing them... she had no experience with until now.

Other than her father, she had never lost someone close to her. But at two years of age, she was too young to remember what it felt like to *have* a father let alone to lose one. Kate had glimpses of a memory when the police officer came to the store to tell Fiona that her husband had been killed in a car accident, but she hadn't been allowed to attend the funeral and her mother never spoke of it over the years. Instead, she threw herself into managing the general store her husband had just opened the year before.

Kate spent most of her free time in that store and three years after her father died, it had been Fiona who made the decision to move toward selling only household hardware and paint, and Thompson Hardware was born. Her mother also remarried when Kate was five, but she was clever enough to have the foresight to not let the new men in her life interfere or get involved with her business dealings. It was a good thing too. By the time Kate was nineteen, Fiona was divorcing her fourth husband. They had all been decent men, just not strong enough to handle her mother's independent and unbridled personality.

When Kate was twenty, she married Matthew and that same year Fiona swore off dating men who were looking for a wife.

Kate continued to work with her mother at the store, her own children playing in the same office space that had been her playground, and when Fiona stepped back to recover from an unexpected ankle surgery, instead of coming back she spoke with Matthew and Kate about the possibility of buying the store from her. Ten years later, the name changed to Chapman Hardware and Fiona left Oklahoma and retired to Florida.

Matthew was the visionary behind growing their business. Kate wanted to keep things the way they were. But unlike Fiona's move to specialize in one area, he expanded their inventory to compete with the big-box stores and make it easier for the people who lived in their town and surrounding communities to buy locally.

Although they both had grown up in Linvalle, Matthew was one who became involved in the Chamber of Commerce and pushed the members to reinvest in their community. Under his leadership and persistence, the two parks in town were updated with safe playground equipment for the kids to enjoy and he arranged weekly and monthly events so the community would come together to mow the common areas and have potlucks and barbecue. A few times, there was an organized effort to convince him to run for mayor, but Matthew had no interest in becoming a town officer and somehow managed to refuse yet gain even more respect from his friends and neighbors.

The same friends and neighbors she now desperately wanted to avoid.

Pulling into the driveway, Kate turned off

the ignition and stared at the house. A few days before the accident, they had removed the shutters and screens to get the house ready to be painted. The last time they touched the outside of the house was ten years before and for the last month, Kate had been training a new volunteer at the shelter to take her place so she could step away from her responsibilities for a few months to focus on the final step of their rehab project. Matthew had wanted to hire somebody to do the work, but she had insisted that they do it themselves since they weren't taking a vacation this year... it would be *their* time to be together. But now the unopened buckets of paint, folded drop clothes and stacked shutters and screens felt overwhelming.

Leaning over to grab her purse sitting open on the passenger seat, Kate stopped when she noticed the tip of a white envelope poking out. Pulling her purse onto her lap, she reached inside and found a sealed letter from Fiona. Holding it, she rubbed her fingers over the hand-written name before bringing the envelope to her nose and inhaling the scent of the ink. Fiona was obsessed with fountain pens and scented inks. She collected them and kept them in a locked antique secretary desk; the one item she took with her when she walked away from the store. It had been a gift from her first husband and the only thing from her past that she cherished.

Kate was about to open the letter to see

what words of wisdom her mother had left her with, but a glance in her side mirror alerted her that she was not alone. Lilly, her friendly but incredibly gossipy neighbor who lived across the street was standing on her front porch staring at her car. Pushing the envelope back into her purse, Kate reached for car keys before pulling on the door handle and stepping onto the driveway. Even before she turned to acknowledge her, she knew Lilly would be frantically waving to get her attention as soon as she turned around.

"*Woo-hoo*. Hi, Kate!"

While still facing the house, Kate closed her eyes, took a deep breath in through her nose and smiled before turning around. She didn't want to do this, but she knew she had to... if not for herself, for Matthew. He would hate that she was putting up walls to keep everyone away.

"Hello, Lilly," Kate said as she pushed the car door closed. "I didn't see you standing there."

"Oh, that's okay," she called out, stepping off her front porch to walk toward the street. "It's my choice of wardrobe today... earth tones tend to make me blend so I almost disappear."

Kate watched as Lilly giggled and shrugged her shoulders.

"I wish," Kate replied, still smiling as she took a few steps toward the back of her car.

"What's that, dear?" Lilly asked. "I didn't quite catch that."

"I said, nice shoes." Kate replied, looking

down at Lilly's neon-colored sneakers.

"Oh, thanks for noticing. I'm trying to break them in." Looking first left and then right, Lilly took a step off the curb to stand in the street. "Ed and I are going on a cruise next month, and we're supposed to dress up like we were back in high school. It's going to be loads of fun."

"Make sure you take lots of pictures," Kate said to her as she took a step toward the house. "I'm sorry I have to run, but mom thinks she left her glasses here and I told her I'd look for them as soon as I got home."

"I didn't mean to keep you. But if you need anything, you know where to find us."

Nodding her head, Kate turned back toward the house and forced herself not to run. As she stepped onto the porch, she turned back to Lilly and waved a final time before disappearing into the house.

WATCHING HER FROM the window he could see how uncomfortable she was and desperately wanted to run outside and help her, but he still hadn't figured out how to get the doorknob to work. Every attempt to grab onto it failed as his hand moved *through* the metal as if it wasn't even there but if he attempted to push through the outside wall, instead of moving through it, he was immediately transported back to the front of the mantle.

It didn't make sense and he failed to understand what he was doing wrong.

He had already managed to pick up an object even though the act of doing so caused him to feel lighter… somehow weaker. But how he could feel any lighter than he currently was made no sense either. He was air. No, he was *less* than air, and the only thing he knew for sure was that he didn't understand any of it.

Unable to bear watching her struggle any longer, he moved away from the window and waited for her to come to him.

THE SIMPLE ACT of shutting out the world

behind her brought a sense of peace, and Kate leaned back against the door, closing her eyes to take the moment in. It was only eight o'clock in the morning, but she felt like she could go back to bed and had almost convinced herself to do just that when her phone rang. She didn't have to look to know who it was, the ring tone she selected gave it away.

"Hello mom... yes I made it home... no it didn't rain again... wait why hasn't your flight left... how long of a delay... well that's not too bad you'll be home before supper... yes I found your letter... no I haven't read it yet... I will... I will... okay I'll talk with you later... get home safely... bye."

Ending the call, Kate stepped away from the door and walked into the kitchen. She would love to turn the phone off but hesitated to do so in case the kids needed to get a hold of her. Before this week, the only one who called on a regular basis was Charlotte, but ever since Victoria and Jackson left, they had begun texting her regularly to see how she was doing or just to say hello. Tossing her purse onto the table, she walked to the cupboard and reached for the bag of ground coffee and filters. Five scoops and eight cups of water... her muscle memory guided her to the amount she made, and it wasn't until she stood in front of the fridge that she realized she had made too much. It was the amount her and Matthew had always made in the morning and until today she hadn't been forced to think about adjusting it because there was always someone in the house looking to fill a cup. She began to think about how much coffee she should be making now that she was alone but gave up when none of the ratios made sense.

I'll worry about it tomorrow.

Grabbing the half and half, she walked back to the counter, but the coffee had only begun to drip into the carafe, so she placed the carton down and decided to wait in the sunroom. Passing the kitchen table, Kate reached into her purse and grabbed the note left by her mother. Adjusting her position in her cushioned wicker chair, she chuckled after she turned the envelope over to discover clear tape over the folds. Her mother refused to lick an envelope and had she been at home in Florida, she would have had access to her envelope moistening pen that resembled a bingo dabber. But here, she had to settle for Scotch tape. Slipping her index finger into the edge of the seal, the scent of lavender was released as she ripped open the top edge.

> *Kate,*
> *I'm sorry that I couldn't stay longer, but you know that town doesn't fit my personality. I'm sure that you weren't expecting to become a member of the Widows Club so soon, but the best*

advice I can give you is to not hide but embrace it. People are going to want to help you and even though you are strong enough to go this alone... don't. The sooner you let them in, the faster you can show them that you are fine, and they will give you your privacy back. Besides, you can't keep hiding inside your house and spend your days cleaning. I could have eaten off your floor...

I'll be back in a few weeks. By then the insurance nonsense with the store should be cleared up and you'll have a decision to make. I also need to think about what I want to do with my old house. The town wants to buy the property to use the building for some sort of community space since it's close to the school. But I will admit, the thought of a bunch of little kids running around on my oak floors with their dirty shoes makes me cringe, but so does finding new renters. The family in there now have bought that gray ranch house up the street from you and I'm getting too old to be a landlord.

If you clean up the guest room, I may even consider staying with you and not going back to that hotel. If you ask me, the new owner is letting his son-in-law run the place into the ground... and now that it would be just the two of us, I wouldn't feel like I was intruding on your life. And don't take that the wrong way! You know I loved Matthew and I would prefer that he was still there to push you... but he's not, and now you need to learn how to push yourself.

If you need a suggestion on what to do first... pick up a paintbrush and start with the shutters.

> *Talk with you soon,*
> *Mom*

Kate placed the letter onto her lap and stared out into the yard. Her mother's harsh delivery didn't change the fact that she was right... again. If she kept pushing people away, they would only keep coming back or worse yet, the whisper and gossip train would gain momentum.

From the other room the coffee maker began to beep, and Kate sighed as she pushed herself out of the chair. Reading her mother's words had been motivating, but now she needed the coffee to do *its* job and wake her up. The telltale signs that she was not sleeping had settled in under her eyes, but she was having trouble breaking the cycle of surviving only on catnaps.

It had been eleven days since the fire, and she still hadn't been able to lay down in their bed.

After the kids left, Fiona showed up with a bedspread and set of sheets thinking something new might make the difference, and when Kate opened the shopping bag, she felt optimistic that it would. The bedspread that her mother chose was a cheerful garden print, but by the time she pulled on the second yellow pillowcase, Kate could feel the sadness begin to take hold as the memory of their Sunday morning routine bubbled to the surface. Fiona had recognized the change in her expression, but to her credit, instead of dwelling on the disappointment she must have felt, she left Kate alone in the room and returned to the kitchen to start the meatloaf.

But maybe today would be different.

Maybe today, she would walk through the house and not be reminded of how much she missed him.

Maybe today, when she went to collect the mail, her box would once again be full of junk and not condolence cards.

Maybe today, she would open their closet and not smell the lingering scent of his cologne.

Maybe today, she would finally wash the coffee cup carefully hidden under the sink... the one he used the last morning they were together.

Maybe... but maybe not.

The sound of the doorbell pulled Kate out

of her wishful thinking but instead of running to the front door to see who was there, she remained seated at the table and finished her coffee. Whoever or whatever it was, could wait. After a few more minutes of sitting, she could feel the caffeine begin to work its magic and she reached for her purse to find her phone. She was supposed to meet Charlotte for dinner, but she didn't feel like going out again and texted her to cancel. After she sent the text, she didn't set her phone down but waited for the call she knew would come.

"Hello Charlotte... yes her flight was delayed an hour but I'm sure she's in the air by now... everything is fine I was just thinking about getting started on painting the house today... no I have everything I need... I will... I will... talk to you later... bye."

Placing her phone on the table next to her purse, Kate picked up her empty mug and walked over to the sink to rinse it out. From the window, she could see the hydrangea and sweet alyssum bushes that lined the brick path leading to the back gate and she couldn't remember the last time they had given her so many buds. In another week or two, her yard would smell like honey. Placing the mug in the dish rack, she turned around and leaned against the sink. She wanted to go outside but she didn't want to work in the front where she would be out in the open and vulnerable to people passing by. Making the decision to start with the shutters instead of the house, she decided to move the project to the back patio. After returning to the table, she reached for her phone and stopped, pulling her hand back.

Matthew's reading glasses were on the table next to her phone.

How did they get there?

Reaching down, she picked them up and held them in her hands. She hadn't touched them since the day Matthew died after she found them on the kitchen table when she got home from the hospital. That night, after Charlotte fell asleep on the couch, she had returned to the kitchen and carried them into their bedroom where she placed them on his nightstand. She was sure that they had remained in the bedroom the entire time since then because each night that she sat in the chair, she could see the reflection of the moon in the lens.

Maybe mom used them this morning?

That possibility made the most sense. The only opportunity she would have had to write the letter would have been this morning while Kate was in the shower, and she probably grabbed the glasses so she could see what she was writing. Only Fiona would be that bold. Picking up the glasses, she walked back toward the bedroom to put them back where they belonged.

HE WATCHED HER through the patio doors as she relocated the shutters from the side porch to the back of the house and it calmed him somehow to see that she had managed to keep the tears away. The the only other time he remembered seeing her eyes so consistently red and puffy had been following the loss of their dog, Birdie.

But as he continued to observe her on the other side of the glass, three words kept replaying in his mind... life wasn't fair. They had sat together for hours looking through numerous fan decks before settling on Robust Orange, Sap Green and Wimborne White as the colors for the door, trim, and the house. How many arguments had they worked through before finally agreeing on those colors? And whose idea had it been to change the colors in the first place?

His.

They were supposed to be painting *their* house together.

Still at the stage in his transition where

anger was eager to dominate his emotions, he turned away from the window and began to pace. For some reason, being in motion helped him keep an even keel of how he was feeling.

While he was still struggling to control the rollercoaster ride his emotions were on, he glanced down at his feet and was reminded that he had discovered a few perks to this existence.

For instance, he no longer had the need to use the bathroom, shower, breathe, sleep, eat, or worry about what to wear. While he could no longer see his reflection in a mirror, at least he knew he would be comfortable walking around for the rest of eternity in his favorite pair of jeans, flipflops and the U2 t-shirt he had been wearing the day of the fire.

That day... his last day, was still mostly hazy.

He had made a quick run to the store for something but when he tried to focus and bring his mind back to what happened, he only succeeded in falling into what felt like a black pool of nothingness. It wasn't a sense of fear that he felt when he tried to go back... more like a sense of falling through darkness.

Maybe he really didn't want to remember the details of what followed in the footsteps of his struggle to breathe as thick, black smoke filled the space.

Don't go there!

Not knowing how much time he would

have with her, he desperately wanted to learn how to communicate. Through trial and error, he figured out that moving through any physical object, like a wall or a chair, came at a cost. While he never grew physically tired, coming in contact with *anything* zapped his energy and he would begin to disappear.

He needed to figure out how to make this work before he ran out of time.

TAKING A STEP back to look at her handywork from a different angle, Kate was satisfied with what she had accomplished. While it had taken her longer than she anticipated, she made good progress for it being her first day working on a project this big all by herself. For the first three hours, her goal had been simple… keep moving and focus on what was in front of her.

And for most of the afternoon, that strategy worked.

She started with a single shutter, refusing to focus on the unfinished stack leaning against the wall behind her and stopped only because she ran out of available space for the painted ones to dry. By the time she decided to begin cleaning up, the stacks were even; six completed and six remaining to be painted.

It was when she stopped painting to clean the brushes that her thoughts drifted back to pick at the scab that was beginning to heal. This would be her first night alone in the house and while it had been easier this morning to push that truth out of her mind, as the sun dropped lower in the sky her optimism fell too making room for the doubt to return. Looking around the patio and deciding her clean-up effort had been adequate, Kate walked to the slider and pulled the door open but paused before stepping inside. The house looked warm and inviting, but she dreaded going in.

Stop being a chicken shit!

The classic line Matt would say to her every time he felt like she was letting fear hold her back popped into her head. The memory so vivid, it felt like her thoughts were shouted out loud and he was standing next to her, motivating her to shake it off.

"You can do this… don't be chicken poop."

Taking a deep breath, she stepped inside.

SHE HEARD HIM. There could be no other explanation for what just happened. But instead of turning toward him, she had entered the house and left him standing there as she continued toward the kitchen. He tried to repeat what happened, but nothing worked.

Not shouting.

Not whispering.

Not even swearing.

Nothing he tried could penetrate the barrier that existed between them and for now, he gave up and decided to simply observe. She looked so much more relaxed than in previous days, and it was the first time he had seen her sit down, put her feet up and enjoy the sunset from the room she designed.

Something inside of him began to *ache* and he couldn't turn away, so he slowly began to move backwards to put some distance between them. When he heard a *clunk*, he turned around and discovered he had moved *through* the coffee table, knocking over a bronze sculpture in his path. Fortunately, it was still intact. They had found the piece in a little art gallery on Federal Street in Nantucket two years ago when they took a road trip to celebrate their thirty fifth wedding anniversary. She said it reminded her of the summer street dances they used to attend before the kids, before they took over the business, before life got too busy.

The entire twenty-seven-hour drive home, she kept it on her lap.

He preferred the woods, but Kate loved the beach and with so few opportunities to get away, he always let her pick the place. It was easy for him to take a few hours in the early morning or evening to hike or fish in the nearby lakes and woods, but getting her to the ocean took more planning. Lost in his memories, he failed to hear the approaching footsteps and it wasn't until he looked back down toward the table that he realized Kate had come up behind him and was reaching *through* his leg to pick up the sculpture.

Even then, he felt nothing.

He wasn't sure what he had expected should they come in contact with each other... the thought that they would touch again hadn't even entered his mind until now. But now that it happened, his imagination wasn't letting it go and he couldn't get the thought out of his head that there should have been *something*. Heat, cold or even a mild tingling sensation, like a limb that had fallen asleep.

But the fact that he felt nothing, left him feeling alone.

Moving free of the table, he continued forward until reaching the back corner of the room and by the time he dared to look at her again, she had picked up the sculpture to inspect it briefly before setting it back down. He continued to watch as she looked around the room to try and find a source that could have caused the sculpture to fall over and when her eyes settled on the corner that he occupied, he suddenly felt exposed. When she shivered and squinted her eyes, peering deeper into the corner, he moved farther back. And when she began slowly creeping toward him, he moved even farther and farther until finally he disappeared into the wall behind him and found himself in the bathroom.

It was then that he began to feel like a child.

He had spent the last forty-eight hours trying to figure out how to get her to notice him and when it appeared that she finally did, his instincts had been to flee. He was a ghost, incapable of being harmed yet he had been afraid. What if the moment she saw him, *really* saw him... he disappeared into the nothing from before again? Had it been his fear that he would cease to see her and be near her that had driven him to leave? He wished that he could do it again and have the courage to stay, letting the natural course of what was supposed to happen next, happen.

Then a heavy feeling began to set it. What if he had blown his chance? What if he had been given one opportunity to see her and he wouldn't get a do-over?

No.

His life, their life wasn't meant to end this way... with him hiding in a bathroom, too afraid to tell her to be strong and that he'd see her again one day.

He wouldn't let it.

IT HAD BEEN the noise of something falling over that brought her into the living room to investigate the sound. But the familiar yet foreign sensation she felt after picking up the sculpture had sent a tingle up her spine. Her eyes had been slow to make the adjustment from a bright to a dark room, and after she fixed the sculpture, movement drew her attention to the back corner. But as she studied the room to get a better view of what she was looking at, familiar objects began to come into view.

For a moment, she had thought she was looking at Matthew, but her eyes and wishful thinking had been playing tricks on her and what she thought was her husband turned out to be an artificial plant in the back of the room. Feelings of both relief and loss began to battle inside her. What she would give to speak with Matthew again if only to be able to say goodbye.

CHAPTER THREE

ANOTHER NIGHT SPENT in the chair, but at least this time she had managed to sleep for almost a five hour stretch. It was two o'clock in the morning when she had finally shut off the television and walked into the bedroom, but like the night before and the one before that, she didn't even attempt to lie down in the bed. Instead, she didn't waste time and grabbed the afghan off the end of the bed, settling into the chair. The effort to drag the ottoman in from the living room had paid off. Being able to put her feet up seemed to have made the difference in sleeping for more than thirty minutes at a time.

When she left the bedroom, initially her thought had been to push the ottoman back to where it belonged, but after folding the blanket, it made more sense for her to just leave it. She knew the more comfortable she made herself, the harder it would be to lie down once again in the bed, but she did it anyway. She was at the point of being so exhausted that finding a way to sleep took priority over working through *why* she didn't want to sleep in their bed in the first place. Eventually she would have to face the why, but she convinced herself it would be easier once she had more energy. But for now, she had a lot of work to get done outside and to make that happen she needed to be able to recharge her batteries.

Figuring out how to sleep in her bed once again could wait.

Walking out of the bedroom she heard the garbage truck as it jerked and rumbled down the street, reminding her the trash bag was still next to the sliding door. She had meant to run it out to the curb last night and toss it in the bin, but it was still early, and she didn't want to risk running into her neighbor again. The last time she had made the mistake of rolling her bin to the curb while it was still light outside, and it opened her up to Lilly seeking her out to start up another conversation. But while she cowardly waited for the evening hours to dwindle away, she become engrossed in a Netflix series her daughter had mentioned and completely forgot about it.

Trash day had always been a part of Matt's routine. Every Tuesday evening, he would walk around the house and gather up the garbage from the bathrooms, laundry room and kitchen and the next morning he would take the garbage can to the curb on his way to the store. Before the fire, if he forgot to collect the garbage in the house, he would toss it into the back of his truck and take it with him; the bins in the alley were picked up every day. Even if she had the desire to leave the house, the inspector was in town today and there was no way she would be caught anywhere near downtown to observe the rubber necking as vehicles passed in front of the rubble that was left of their business.

She'd worry about it later. Right now, she needed coffee and for the first time in almost a week, she was hungry.

WHAT WOULD SHE do? Unlike Kate, he no longer had the need to sleep and had been up all night figuring out how he could make this new existence work for him. Unsure if she would continue to be able to see him like before in the living room, he avoided finding out by making sure he was not in the same room. It was in the process of avoiding her that he discovered he could now move through the exterior walls without ending up back in front of the fireplace.

While hiding out in the bedroom, she suddenly entered the room pushing an ottoman and, in his haste, to get out of her way he stepped backward through the wall and found himself outside on the patio.

He still hadn't figured out *how* it was possible or *what* had changed, but he decided he would no longer waste time pondering why things happened the way they did and stayed outside in the dark where he would be safe from running into her while he came up with a plan.

It was while he was outside that he noticed the bag of garbage leaning up against the wall and instead of thinking that there was no way he would be strong enough to move the garbage, he focused and picked it up. He held onto it for about fifteen seconds before carefully lowering it back to the ground. He repeated that motion over and over until he no longer had to focus on the action... he just did it.

He also noticed that his energy or whatever it was that was allowing him to exist, seemed to be building up resistance against the side effect of fading away when he came in contact with physical objects. Something had changed since he knocked over the sculpture or maybe it was from when Kate touched him, but he continued to push away thoughts of *how* any of this was possible to focus on what he *wanted* to be possible and today would be the day that she saw him.

No matter what happened after that.

And he waited patiently for her to discover what he had done.

KATE POURED HER first cup of coffee moments before there were two loud thuds from the direction of the front door. Her first thought was that it's too early for an Amazon delivery and she thought about ignoring it, but the sleep she was able to catch up on had lightened her mood and she decided to investigate what it was. Setting her cup of coffee down on the counter, she slowly walked toward the table. Reaching for her sweater hanging over the back of the chair she heard Charlotte call out from the front porch.

"Mom! It's me... open up!"

"I'm coming, I'm coming."

Quickening her pace after hearing her daughter's voice, Kate opened the door just as she was lifting her leg to give the door another strong backward kick.

"Charlotte Frances Chapman, stop kicking my door."

The young woman turned around and that's when Kate noticed the cup of coffee in each hand and the paper bag clenched between her teeth. Reaching forward, she took the bag and couldn't help but smile at the scene. Though the smile soon faded after she looked back toward the door to find two wide, black scuff marks from her daughter's combat boots.

"You couldn't wait ten seconds?" she asked, turning back toward her daughter.

"Sorry. But I almost spilled the coffee all over *this* stupid box," Charlotte said, motioning with her leg, "when I tried to ring the bell. So, I had to improvise."

"Box... what box?" Kate asked, looking down at the wall. "Oh, I completely forgot there was a delivery yesterday."

"Well, step out of the way and I'll kick it inside," Charlotte said, grinning and pretending to get into position.

"There will be no more kicking," Kate replied. "Just go inside and I'll get it."

Stepping aside so her daughter could pass, she leaned down and gripped the top of the box, picking it up with one hand. It weighed next to nothing, and she struggled more with trying to remember what she had ordered than getting it inside.

Entering the house, she set the box down inside the door and followed Charlotte into the kitchen to find her already removing two plates from the cupboard.

"You made coffee already?" Charlotte asked, peeking around the cabinet to look at her mom.

"Are you still not sleeping?"

"Actually... I'm making progress with that."

"Good," Charlotte replied, placing the plates on the table next to the paper bag. "Well, I hope you haven't already eaten something 'cuz I brought bagels and coffee just the way you like it."

"Your timing is perfect," Kate replied. "I was just going to make myself some toast. Go sit down...I'll grab the silverware."

Removing the bagels and small plastic containers from the white paper bag, Charlotte looked out the window onto the back patio. She could see the stack of painting supplies that had been previously stored on the side porch had been moved.

"I see you've started painting. How's it going?"

"Well, after I moved everything to the back to keep out of view of *you know who*, all I managed to get done was start with the shutters. But I guess progress is progress."

"I'm proud of you, mom. I know it can't be easy being here."

"I wish I could take all the credit. When I got back from the airport, I found a letter from grandma suggesting I get off my *ass* and step back into the world of the living."

Charlotte sat down and pulled a cinnamon raisin bagel from the bag. "I guess I need to call Fiona and thank her then." Smiling, she reached across the table and took the butterknife from her mom. "You look better... the circles under your eyes aren't as bad as they were the other day."

"No thanks to you," Kate joked, watching her daughter take her first bite.

"Excuse me?"

"I was up until after one o'clock in the morning binge watching that Netflix show, Bridgerton."

"It was good, right?"

"*Different* from what I expected," Kate replied. "But I did end up watching the whole thing."

"You finished it?"

"I did," Kate replied, walking to the microwave to warm up the coffee Charlotte handed her.

"Well, then... I'd say you liked it," Charlotte replied, turning around to follow her mother. "It's been picked up for season two you know."

Kate watched her daughter shove another piece of the bagel into her mouth as she thought about how nice it had been to have her stop by. When Matt was alive and they had the store, Kate didn't have time for impromptu breakfast dates... life was too busy. Grabbing her coffee, she refused to let herself think about the fact that her life had to be turned upside down in order to stop and enjoy a quiet, unplanned breakfast with her daughter.

Even if it was for only twenty minutes.

"I hate to eat and run... but our car is overdue for an oil change and Ben wants me to drop it off this morning."

As Charlotte stood up to leave, Kate remembered the garbage bag was still outside and walked toward the patio door.

"I'll walk you out. I have to bring the bin back in."

"Already done. I passed the garbage truck on my way here and pulled it in for you," Charlotte said, reaching for her purse. "Honestly, I was surprised to see it there... I thought you'd forget again."

"I didn't remember everything," Kate replied. "The bag from the kitchen is outside on the patio. I meant to take it out but got sucked into that show."

"Well, since it's my fault," Charlotte said, reaching for the door, "I'll grab it for you."

"You don't have to do that."

"Did you leave it by the porch door?" Charlotte asked.

"No," replied Kate, stepping outside. "I left it right... there." Kate looked down at the empty ground next to the door. In her mind, she could clearly remember opening the sliding door and leaning the plastic bag against the wall.

But it wasn't there now.

"Oh, well. Hey, it looks like you'll have another great day to continue your painting project."

Kate continued to search the patio area even after Charlotte stepped back inside to grab what was left of her coffee.

"Okay, I'm off... Mom, I'm leaving."

"Thanks again for breakfast... it was nice. Wait, don't you want to take the rest of the bagels with you?"

"No. They'll have a better chance of getting eaten here than in my house." Approaching the door, Charlotte reached for the handle and looked down at the package leaning against the wall. "Don't forget you have a package here."

"I won't, I won't." Kate stepped through the doorway and watched her daughter walk to her car. As she began to back out of the driveway, she raised her hand and waved. "Talk with you later."

She continued to watch until her car disappeared down the street, but when she heard the garage door open across the street, she quickly stepped back inside and closed the door.

FROM HIS VANTAGE point, he only had a clear view of the kitchen table and when Kate walked across the room to enter the kitchen, he knew she would be coming outside soon. But a few minutes later when he saw her walk toward the front of the house, he was both delighted and surprised to see Charlotte.

It was good that his daughter hadn't let too many days go by between visits. Kate needed to be pushed to socialize before it became *too* easy for her to just stay home by herself. He felt at peace watching two women he loved very much enjoy time together. Kate looked more relaxed than he had seen her in months... years really. And for the first time he let himself think about how much he was going to miss her when it was time for him to go.

The way she raised her left eyebrow before a snarky comment.

The way she tucked her hair behind her right ear.

The way she folded her paper napkin instead of crumpling it up before throwing it away.

The way she tapped *Fur Elise* on the top of a table when she was thinking.

He was lost in his memories but when he heard the glass door open, he managed to move through the potted boxwood at the edge of the patio. He hated the topiary plants she insisted they buy to act as a natural divider between the patio and the lawn, but they gave him cover today.

He watched as they looked at the spot where the garbage had sat and while it wasn't quite the reaction he had hoped for, he knew it would get her thinking and he planned his next move.

AFTER HER DAUGHTER left, Kate picked up the sealed box and brought it into the kitchen. Turning it over to read the shipping label, still didn't shed any light on what was inside. Knowing that it was likely something Matthew had ordered, rather than open it up and once again get sidetracked from projects that needed to be completed, she decided to wait until later and placed it on the table. Opening the cupboard, she reached inside and grabbed a travel mug to transfer the coffee now sitting cold on the counter that she had poured prior to Charlotte's arrival.

No reason to let it go to waste.

Putting the insulated mug inside the microwave, she began to search for the canvas shoes she had worn yesterday and finding them by the glass door, she slipped them onto her feet just as the microwave behind her began to beep. Walking back to retrieve her coffee, her mood became energized with the thought of going outside into the sunshine. She was determined to get the shutters finished today and perhaps even start on taping up the windows so she would be ready to start the trim in the morning.

Grabbing her coffee, she walked outside and took a moment to breathe in the fragrance of summer before reaching into the back pocket of her phone to open Apple Music. She needed to look for something appropriate. Something that would fit her current mood and help keep her motivated to stay on track.

Eighty's Summer Hits... perfect.

Finding an option that would work, she pressed play and set her phone down on the picnic table next to the row of potted topiaries and got to work.

HAVING SLIPPED BACK into the house, he watched her as she began to nod her head from side to side to the beat of the music. It hadn't begun to hurt yet to watch her even though each day he hung around, he could see that she was learning to move on without him. Together, they had watched plenty of movies about ghosts that hung around to haunt their homes for years... decades really, but he had no insider knowledge even though he had passed over to the other side that the same fate would happen to him.

It had been nearly two weeks since the fire and having no idea how much time he would have; he knew he had to make a move.

Moving away from the patio, he turned to look at the box on the table and after glancing at the label, he knew instantly what it was. It was a surprise he had ordered to celebrate that they had finally finished the house and he hoped when she opened it, she wouldn't let herself slip back to the bottom of the hole she was only just beginning to climb out of.

While the thought crossed his mind that perhaps he could make it easier if he moved the box to the trash bin and possibly save her some pain, the selfish side of him *wanted* to see her face when she opened it. As he moved around the house, he looked over the items they had collected during their life together.

The living room wall full of family

portraits, graduations, and vacation moments.

The mismatched dishes and mugs that Kate had collected at garage sales over the years, piece by piece replacing the expensive boxed sets they had received for their wedding.

Her spot on the couch when they sat back for the evening to watch a movie or reruns of Seinfeld.

The reading glasses that could be found in every color and in every room.

The heavy old bookcase that no longer matched the décor since the remodel, but Kate would not part with it because it was the first piece of expensive furniture that had been delivered and not pulled out of a box in a hundred pieces needing to be put together.

And as he stood in front of the watercolor painting Kate did while they were in Nantucket, he couldn't look away. She had taken a day class to pass the time while he went fishing and spent her morning painting by the water. When he got back to the dock, he had been so excited to show her the fish he had caught but when he spotted the painting behind her he forgot about the fish and could focus only what he felt was the most beautiful painting he had ever seen. He had encouraged her to pursue classes when they returned home, but too quickly they fell back into the routine of their busy life, and it never happened.

When the patio door opened, it wasn't until

he turned around that he became aware of how dark the room had become. Time had stood still as he got lost in his memories and as Kate walked into the house looking down at her phone, he slipped back into the shadows at the back of the room and waited.

PLEASED WITH THE progress that was made outside, Kate pulled the patio door closed behind her and walked into the living room to turn on the central air. The cooler temperature from this morning had been steadily replaced by warmer and more humid air as the day progressed with blue skies giving up their position in the sky to the storm system moving in. By the time she stopped for the day, all the shutters had received their second coat of paint and she had relocated the supplies into the garage for safe keeping. She had hoped to get started on taping the windows so tomorrow when she got up, she could begin painting the trim, but the frequent stops to dance around the patio prevented that; the music had done its job to keep her mood up but slowed down the progress she hoped to make.

After giving her eyes a moment to adjust, she walked to the kitchen and turned on the recessed lighting. On a clear day, there would still be plenty of natural light streaming in from the sunroom this time of day, but the gloomy skies overhead made the lighting in the house feel more like fall than the beginning of summer.

It was almost five o'clock and she had forgotten to take out something to make for supper again, but she didn't want to grab takeout, so she walked to the refrigerator to see what her options were. After spending a minute looking over the contents and throwing a few items that were well beyond the sell-by date into the garbage, Kate pulled out a loaf of bread, butter and American cheese, and set them on the counter. Tomorrow she would have to get to the store and that meant tonight she would have to make a list.

I need wine.

Spinning around, Kate once again opened the door to the refrigerator and pulled out the last bottle of Kendall-Jackson chardonnay. She was hungry, covered in paint, her feet hurt, and she could use a shower but right now she *wanted* a glass of wine more than anything else. It was after she reached into the cupboard that she spied the box on the table. After opening the bottle, she filled her glass, grabbed a pair of scissors, and walked over to the table.

Country Homes Done Your Way.

Looking at the label failed to help her recollect any order that would make sense, so she placed the glass down on the table and positioned the box to cut through the heavy tape when her phone rang. For a moment, she thought about ignoring her mother's call but instead placed the scissors on the table and answered the call.

"Hi mom... I'm fine... I was going to call last night but after paint-... yes I started painting yester-... just the shutters... the color looks good... anyway like I was saying I was going to call you but I started watching a series on Netflix that Charlotte recommended and lost track of time... no you wouldn't like it... because everyone talks with an accent... an English accent... that's what I said... no I still haven't slept in my bed... I'm sure the new bedding will be comfortable... I know... I know... but I did manage to sleep for five hours last night... yes in the chair... my neck is fine... then I'll get a new chair... don't worry about it... yes I've seen her we had breakfast this morning... she's fine... she might help me paint... yes outside only... yes I painted again today... yep still working on the shutters... I just came in a moment ago... yes I put everything in the garage... mom I am aware that it's going to storm... yes all the windows are closed... yes I have candles and batteries... no I haven't heard anything... mom the inspector was just here yesterday... I'm sure that Pete will call when he has some information to share with... he was just here yesterday mother... I will... I will... yes if I haven't heard anything by Friday I will give Pete a call... I know... mom I know that... I'm not upset... I know I'm fine... yes I have something to eat... no I haven't eaten supper... because I just came inside five minutes ago... I will... I will... okay you too... bye."

After hanging up the phone, Kate took a long drink from the wine glass. Her mother meant well but her directness was not always easy to tolerate. Her stomach growled and she took another drink from her glass before setting it down on the table. She had only eaten an apple and a few crackers for dinner and the wine was going to her head quicker than usual, so the contents of the box as well as the grocery list would have to wait until she ate something. She had just turned on a front burner of the stove when she heard a faint clap of thunder in the distance, and she reached for the cheese and bread.

CHAPTER FOUR

EVEN BEFORE SHE turned off the water, he left the bedroom, moving through the wall and into the living room. He couldn't watch her while she got dressed. It wasn't that he hadn't done it more than a thousand times, something about watching her when she didn't know he was there made it feel wrong.

But that would change tonight.

Tonight, he would reveal himself to her and face the only thing he still feared, her reaction. Would she freak out and run from the house or would she have a hundred questions that he couldn't answer; either one could end in a disaster.

But at least he could stop hiding and start trying to reach her.

He had known for a full day that he could reveal himself to her. Yesterday afternoon, she had seen him in the shadows, but his own character failed him, and he had fled from the room rather than face her. He had spent the night thinking about what his first words to her would be.

Hi, how ya doing?

Now don't freak out.

I know this is weird.
Yes, it's really me.
Breathe.

All the scenarios that ran through his head sounded stupid... juvenile even, and he wished he had paid more attention when they watched the movie, *Ghost*. From what he remembered, Patrick Swayze had done a pretty good job convincing Demi that she wasn't seeing things and that it was really him, but he would have to wing it.

Hearing the fan in the bathroom turn off, he stepped back into the shadows and waited.

SHE WAS UPSIDE down, still trying to get the dampness out of her hair when the blow dryer suddenly shut off. Standing up, Kate flipped the switch back and forth to make sure she hadn't shut it off while jiggling the dryer around, but it was after she looked toward the nightstand and didn't see the blue illuminated numbers coming from her alarm clock that she realized the problem was not the dryer or the outlet.

What the heck?

Placing the blow dryer on the counter, she adjusted the towel wrapped around her and stepped out into the bedroom to peer into the living room. The nightlight plugged into the outlet in the hallway was dark as well, confirming it wasn't a blown fuse from the bedroom; the entire house had lost power.

Great.

Retracing her steps, she walked over to her dresser and pulled out her PJs. The room was growing darker by the minute and without being able to turn on the light in the closet to see what she was grabbing; she would be dressing for bed earlier than usual. Letting the towel drop to the floor, she pulled the cotton top over her head and saw the first flash of lightening through the bedroom window illuminate the back yard. She could tell that this storm was going to be bad... not only because of the alerts and warnings that had been coming across her phone over the last few hours, but because that was her luck of late. As she stepped into her bottoms, she looked to her left to see if her phone was on the dresser. Not finding it, she tied the string around her waist and began feel with her hands over the length of the bed, but it wasn't there either.

Where, where, where?

Failing to find her phone in the bedroom,

she returned to the bathroom to feel her way around the counter but only found her empty wine glass. Stopping for a moment to think about the last time she remembered using her phone, another weather alert came in and she followed the buzzing glow to Matt's pillow.

How did it?

Still trying to rationalize how her phone ended up where it did, she shoved it into her pocket and made her way around the bed to wait out the rest of the storm in the living room. In anticipation that she might lose power, she had pulled out the lantern from the pantry along with a lighter she found in the junk drawer and placed them on the kitchen table before she jumped into the shower. Entering the hallway, a loud clap of thunder shook the house and made her jump causing her to almost drop the glass in her hand.

Get a grip!

Shaking off the tingle she felt between her shoulder blades, Kate walked into the living room to grab the lighter she had placed on the table and carefully set the empty glass on the counter. As she maneuvered around the living room furniture, another flash of lightening lit up the back yard helping her find her way and as she reached for the candle, her phone rang. The sudden sound of *Hit Me With Your Best Shot* blared from her pocket causing her to jump back, knocking into the table behind her. While steadying a wobbling lamp, she pulled out the phone and answered Charlotte's call.

"Hello... oh I'm fine but I'm changing your ring tone... because it just freaked me out and I almost knocked over a lamp... yeah mine is out too... about five minutes ago... no I don't want you to come and get me... I ate supper already... well don't open your fridge too much we don't know how long the power is going to be out... I imagine five or six hours if you try to keep your door closed... do you have candles... make sure... make sure to blow them out before you fall asleep... okay... well thanks for thinking about me... let's hope... yep... talk with you tomorrow... love you too... bye."

Hanging up the phone, she made sure to place it on the kitchen table where she could easily find it again and walked back into the living room to light the candles on the mantle and the coffee table. Another boom of thunder shook the house. She had looked at the weather app before she put her phone down and the larger cell from the storm hadn't even reached them yet.

It was going to be a long night.

After letting her eyes adjust to the candlelight, she made her way easily back into the kitchen and the detergent on the counter reminded her that the dishwasher was still full. At least her plan to wait and start it *after* she finished her wine had worked in her favor and she wouldn't have to worry about the dirty dish water funk from being stopped mid-cycle. Accepting the cards that the universe had dealt her, Kate opened the fridge to grab the bottle of wine and carried it along with her empty glass into the living room. Taking a seat on the oversized chair next to the couch, she placed the glass on the coffee table and filled it half full, leaving the bottle open when she put it back down.

Except for the rain drops that had just begun to hit the roof, the house was quiet. Too quiet and she welcomed the sound of the approaching storm to break up the silence.

Relaxing into the chair, she raised the glass to her lips and took a long drink as more thunder crashed over her head. This was the first time since the remodel that a storm had knocked out the power, but not the first time she had sat in the dark in this room. Taking another drink from the glass, she smiled as the memory of their first night in this house bubbled to the surface. After a very long day of moving, she had finally gotten Ava to sleep and they were sitting on the carpeted floor that smelled like the bottom of a shoe, eating cold pizza.

When they did the walk through, they hadn't been told or perhaps they forgot, that it was no longer a functioning fireplace and the chimney had been sealed years before to prevent birds from nesting. It was after the pizza was gone and he opened the last beer that Matthew noticed the logs she had collected and stacked in a wicker basket that he got the bright idea to light a fire. Just like tonight, she had sat back smiling, watching him with a goofy look on his face as he proved his manliness. Within minutes, smoke had begun to fill the room and the three smoke alarms they had purchased were beeping loudly on the kitchen counter while little Ava was screaming in her crib. Kate leaned her head back, closing her eyes to listen to the sounds of the storm gathering strength outside as a single tear escaped from her eye.

"Kate."

Catching the next breath in her throat, she opened her eyes to stare at the ceiling and listened, but heard only the steady *ping pang, ping pang* as rain fell onto the steel gutters. The combination of alcohol, sitting in this dark room and her memories had made for a perfect storm to help her imagine the comfort of his voice. After a minute more of stillness, she exhaled and lifted her head, pausing to stare straight ahead where her eyes began to focus on a shape emerging from the darkened corner behind the couch. Rather than turn away, she held her gaze on the image that seemed to be moving from the back of the room and *through* the couch. In the past when her tired eyes played tricks on her, facing down the impossible allowed her the time it took for her to focus and find the true image...

the plant she forgot was there, the coat rack with her summer hat perched on the top, the sweater hanging on the hook behind the door.

But this time the image wasn't fading or morphing into something she recognized... it was holding steady and becoming clearer to her even though what she was looking at wasn't possible.

"I've missed you."

She wanted to speak, but she couldn't even remember how to release the air she was holding in her lungs let alone get her vocal cords to function. The tears began to flood her eyes and blur her vision. It was then that she found her voice as she blinked rapidly, forcing her eyes to move the liquid clear, only to return. She couldn't see him and began to panic as the pain of loss began to sink hooks into her chest once again, but choking as she tried to catch her breath, she called out his name.

"*Matthew?*"

"I'm here. Kate, I'm here. Sweetie, close your eyes and focus on the sound of my voice... you have to calm down."

"But if I close my eyes, you'll leave me again."

"Trust me." He could hear the pain in her voice, but she listened to him and put her head down. "Think about something else... think about the time we were shooting off fireworks in the back yard and Ava got mad at us for making so much noise and locked us out of the house. Think about when Jackson brought the weird looking spider in from the garage and when he dropped it, all the babies spread out across the kitchen floor. Think about when Charlie took the scissors and cut her own bangs and how we laughed about it for a week every time we looked at her. Think about how many times I walked into the old patio door until you put a big yellow happy face sticker in the same spot that I would smash my face into the glass."

It was then that she smiled and gathered the strength to raise her head to look at him. "You're still here."

"No place I'd rather be."

"But... how?"

He was there and yet he wasn't. Even in the dark she could make out the couch and the picture hanging on the wall directly behind him. Maybe she was dreaming and any minute she'd wake up. But it didn't feel like a dream. She could smell the scent coming from the vanilla candles on the mantle and hear the branches from the maple tree slap against the house from the wind that had begun to pick up outside. Another crack of lightening lit up the room, giving Kate the first opportunity to get a better look at him. He was wearing the same clothing he had on when he left the house that last morning and the hair on the left side of his head was sticking straight up like it did every morning because of the way he slept.

"I don't know how to answer that question, Kate. Where I was before I wound up in the living room is kinda fuzzy."

"How long have you been here?"

He laughed at the normality of the question... like he had been gone all day fishing, and she was excited to see him and wanted to know when he got home. His mind wanted to drift to the depressing alternative answer, but he wouldn't let it. Instead, he answered her question and focused on what was happening right this minute.

"The night before Charlie told Jackson he was going to be an uncle."

He heard her sharp intake of breath and watched her bite her lower lip as she struggled to keep from crying, the same trick he had watched her use many times over the years; replace one pain with another to refocus your mind.

"No more tears, Kate... not tonight. If I only have enough time for you to see me... so I can say goodbye... I don't want to waste it being sad."

It was as if she had stepped back in time. He had used similar logic the last time she was with him... that morning before he left for the store. They had just finished breakfast and were about to start painting the trim. She had become annoyed that he forgot to bring home the extra stepstool they kept behind the counter at the store, but he remained calm and told her not to worry. It would take him five minutes to hop in his truck, run down to the store and grab it. Just like then, he had calmed her down and walked out the door, calling out over his shoulder *'back in a bit'* as the door closed behind him.

She hadn't watched him leave the driveway that day like she usually did. Instead, she went to the porch and began dividing up the shutters into two piles so that when he returned, they would be ready to go. She had been so absorbed in the task, she failed to notice the black smoke rising in the sky coming from the direction of downtown. She failed to notice the neighbors gathering in the street to get a better view as the smoke grew thicker and darker a moment before red and yellow flames became visible over the treetops. It was only after the town siren went off that she realized he had been gone much longer than he should have, and she put down the brush and walked out into the street to join her neighbors. But the moment she realized where the smoke was coming from, she knew.

Even before she saw Pete's truck turn onto her street, she knew.

"You're doing it again."

Wiping the tears from her cheeks, Kate placed the wine glass on the coffee table in front of her. "You're right, no more tears. I've cried enough over the last two weeks."

"Good, because I'd much rather talk about what you plan to do now... with the store, with the house... with the extra time you'll have on your hands."

She looked up at him astonished that nothing had changed... he said he wanted to take the time to say goodbye, but instead he *still* felt the need to push her. *Make a plan.* Three little words that had been the driving force behind her and the kids for more than thirty years. Always moving them forward. Always pushing.

Pushing her to take on more responsibility at the store.

Pushing her to decide on a house.

Pushing her to have another child so Ava would have a companion.

Pushing the kids to join sports and finish what they start.

Pushing her to volunteer at the shelter when Charlie started school.

Pushing her to get a mammogram when she turned forty.

Pushing her mother to think about retiring.

Pushing the kids to go to college.

Pushing her to take vacations.

Pushing her mother to sell them the store.

Pushing her to expand the store.

Pushing her to continue painting.

Pushing the remodel even though the kids were long gone.

Push, push, push.

And here he was again from beyond the grave, still pushing. She was about to tell him to stop and push back like she always did... but instead, she paused to think about what would become of her without him pushing. Would she just stop moving forward? What exactly would she have accomplished if he hadn't been behind her, beside her, pulling her forward with him... always pushing her to be better, do better and want more?

"I see your mind working again... they were simple questions to keep you from standing still. You can't stand still, Kate."

"You may be right, but I don't have to make any decisions right now."

"Sure, you do. You're going to hear from Pete any day and you have to make the decision about what you want to do with the store."

"Why? Why do I have to do that now? Why can't it wait?"

"For several reasons. But let's just focus on the easy one... the town. The chamber and the mayor aren't going to want to have a burnt-out building sitting in the middle of main street. They are going to want to have it replaced, either with a new store that you occupy or with someone else wanting to move into the space."

She hadn't thought about that. For almost two weeks, everyone in town who drove down main street has had to look at the crumbling and burnt structure that reminded them of the tragedy. Not to mention, it *was* an eyesore. The Chamber of Commerce as well as all the other businesses that lined the three blocks that made up downtown had great pride in keeping their historic buildings in tip-top shape. Matthew himself had been a part of the committee ten years ago that pushed all the existing businesses to paint and repair the historic buildings which resulted in a boom when it came to their visiting revenue stream. For those business that needed help, he had created a fund that they kept active by putting on rummage sales, carnivals and chili cook offs to help those businesses that needed it come up with the extra cost to refurbish some of the structures.

"I didn't think about that," she replied.

"Look, I'm not saying you need to decide right this minute or even within the next few days what you want to do. The cleanup will take a week or two which will buy you some time."

Her neck was getting sore from looking up at him. "Can you sit down?"

"Actually... no. I tried a few times, but I kept slipping through the furniture and floor only to end up back in front of the fireplace."

"Show me."

"What?"

"Show me... sit on the couch," Kate said, pointing behind him. "I want to see what happens."

"You want to see what happens?"

"Yep."

She watched as he took a few steps

backwards and slowly lowered himself toward the couch. Outside a flash of lightning lit up the sky at the same time he slipped through the cushion and disappeared. She scooted forward to the edge of the chair, her hand covering her mouth as she stared at the empty couch. Another flash outside and she looked toward the fireplace to see him begin to appear in front of the mantle.

"Told ya."

"*O--kay*," she replied, standing up. "That was weird. But how can you stand but not sit?"

"Ya got me. The first night I showed up, I didn't have any feet... it was like I was a part of the rug, and I couldn't move."

"You didn't have any feet!"

"They showed up the next morning."

"And you always end up back in front of the fireplace?"

"I think it has something to do with this," he replied, moving to the right to give her a full view of the gold metal urn behind him on the mantle.

Bringing the urn front and center served as a stark reminder that while she was speaking with him and he seemed like the same old, Matthew, he really wasn't. It was more like an illusion of who he was... something borrowed that had to be returned.

"I can see you start to drift back to the dark side and I'm going to ask again that you don't," he said.

"Then distract me."

Frustrated, she snatched her empty wine glass off the coffee table and turned her back to him as she walked toward the kitchen. After opening the door to the refrigerator and not finding what she was looking for, she placed the glass on the counter and exhaled as she closed her eyes and leaned forward.

Stop being stupid.

"Looking for this?"

Opening her eyes, she watched as he came toward her holding the bottle of wine that he placed gently on the counter.

"You can't sit, but you can hold stuff. How does this work?"

"Like I said before, I have no idea what the rules are. I figured it out a few days ago through trial and error. My first few attempts... my hand just passed through what I was trying to grab. But then I saw you outside talking to Lilly, and I could tell that you were getting upset and bumped into a chair and it moved. Then I began to *practice*. The first thing I moved were my reading glasses and then your phone in the bedroom earlier. I watched it fall off the dresser while you were in the shower and I knew you'd never find it in the dark, so I put it on my pillow."

"I found your glasses on the table when I got home from the airport, but I thought mom had moved them when she wrote her note to me."

"Ah, the letter... one of the few times I've agreed with what Fiona had to say."

"You read it?"

"Looking over your shoulder when you were sitting in the sunroom yesterday." He watched as she crossed her right arm in front of her chest to reach up to touch her left shoulder. "Did you feel me standing next to you?"

After shaking her head, no, she reached for the bottle and emptied what was left into her glass.

"It's my fault."

"What is?" he asked.

"The reason you're not *really* here."

"Why would you think that?" he demanded, his voice becoming louder.

She couldn't look at him but knew by his tone and the way he annunciated each word that he was becoming angry. She had only seen him lose control a handful of times in her life and he was on the edge of doing it again now. The last time Ava missed her curfew. The morning after a house fire claimed the lives of an entire family. Five minutes after Jackson informed them that he enlisted. The day Birdie got hit by the car.

"Kate. Why did you say that?" he asked again, softening his tone.

"I forgot to note the delivery of the lamp oil in the red book."

The red book was a notebook they kept on the counter where they wrote hazardous items received but not yet put away. It was a system that Matthew had put into place after he began to volunteer at the fire department and was forced to watch videos about common household items that can fuel a fire. She hadn't yet spoken with Pete as to the cause of the fire but was sure that her carelessness had played a role in how quickly the fire engulfed the structure.

"Lamp oil?" he replied. "Is that what you think happened?"

"What else could it have been?"

"Oh, Kate," he whispered, lowering his head. "It wasn't the oil. It wasn't because of you at all... the fire was *my* fault."

"You're just saying that to make me feel better."

"No... I'm not."

"How could it be your fault?"

"It was my stupid mug warmer I kept under the counter. I forgot to unplug it when I closed the store on Saturday. I took a call as I was locking up and just got out of my routine. I smelled the smoke as soon as I opened the door that morning. I *should* have stayed outside and called it in. But like an idiot, I went in just to have a look. It was a small fire... isolated to the shelf under the counter and without a second thought I walked past it to get the fire extinguisher on the wall. Then there was an explosion behind me, and I got knocked to the floor. Then there was a second explosion, and the shelves came off the wall and I couldn't get up."

Even though tears were blurring her vision,

she couldn't take her eyes off him and watched him move from side to side before leaning forward, bracing his hands on his thighs as he bent his head. It looked like he was trying to catch his breath, but before she could move toward him, he popped back up and his face looked calm.

"After the smoke, I don't really remember anything... then I was here, standing in the dark."

"I'm sorry," she whispered.

"You don't have anything to be sorry for, Kate," he said. "It was my decision to go back to the store and it was *my* decision to ignore my training and walk toward the fire. The only thing you get to own is how you move forward."

"*How* are you so calm?"

"I guess it's because I've already lost everything that matters to me, and I don't want to lose the last chance I have to make it easier for you... and on that note."

As he moved toward the kitchen table, she wiped her eyes and finished the last of the wine in her glass. When she looked at him again, he was looking at her and seemed to be waiting for her to join him.

"Do you know what that is?" she asked.

Nodding his head, he motioned with his hand for her to come over. "I ordered it a while ago, but it's something we've talked about getting for years... open it."

Opening the junk drawer, she reached inside to grab a pair of scissors before joining him. After cutting through the brown package tape, she placed the scissors down on the table and glanced at him before she opened the flaps. He was totally focused on what was inside and grinning from ear to ear. Everything about him seemed so normal even though she could see straight through him and into the living room. The fact that he was this happy about whatever was inside the box foreshadowed it would bring her sadness, but she pulled back the flaps anyway. After she pulled out the brown packing paper and let it fall to the floor, the box looked empty when she peered inside. But as soon as she reached in and felt the smooth, cold stone beneath her fingertips, she knew what it was.

Even in the low light, he could see her eyes begin to brim with tears and wished he could pull her in close to comfort her. "Well... take it out! I want to see it."

His prodding was rushed, and he knew it, but he needed to push her past the sadness she was feeling. He had spent hours looking through all the different sizes and styles available to choose from until he settled on the one that he knew would be perfect. As he watched her reach into the box, he silently sent a request to the heavens that everything was spelled correctly because he knew if it wasn't, Kate wouldn't follow up to make it right. She'd keep it in the shipping box and stick it up on a shelf in the garage. When he saw her smile, he knew it was perfect and shifted his position to look at what she was holding.

"The Chapman's."

"Aww, it turned out great!" he said and smiled at her as she read the words. "It'll look awesome hanging on the wall by the side porch door."

"When did you do this?"

"The day you stopped fighting me about the renovation," he replied. She went quiet and he didn't need her to speak the words to know what she was thinking. "This is still the Chapman's, Kate. You're here. The kids still consider this to be their home and *hell*, even when the day comes that you no longer own it... it will *still* be known as the Chapman house."

"You think awful highly of yourself."

"Of *us*, Kate," he replied. "I think highly of us. We made a difference in this town and people won't forget it."

You made a difference.

"It's nice," she replied.

"It's nice?" he asked, surprised by her less than enthusiastic interest in the effort he had put into finding just the right sign. "That is hand-polished black granite, with hand carved lettering, highlighted with weatherproof paint that you are holding in your hands."

She laughed at the passion he was trying to

interject to help soften her mood, but it was the familiarity of him trying to prove a point that did the job. He was gone. And even though he was standing in front of her, she knew it wouldn't last and she'd be alone again... but somewhere deep inside of her, she also knew that she'd be okay when he had to go. That's when it dawned on her, that perhaps he was here because he wasn't ready to let go and not the other way around... that she had to help *him* move on... be the one who did the pushing this time.

This time, she would have to help him.

CHAPTER FIVE

THE NEXT MORNING after she opened her eyes, it took her a few seconds to figure out where she was. The power had still been out when she returned to the living room to sit on the couch. She hadn't intended to fall asleep there, but should have known the minute she put her feet up on the coffee table that sleep would find her.

She couldn't remember the last time she had slept on the couch, but it was the first night she had not slept in the bedroom chair since losing Matthew. Bits and pieces of their conversation began to come back to her, and she stared at the fireplace and wondered where he was. When she last saw him, he had been standing on the other side of the coffee table looking down at her, and the last thing she remembered were her eyelids feeling heavy.

But he wasn't there now, and she wondered if he had ever really been there.

Maybe last night had been a dream.

The microwave beeped again, alerting her that she needed to set the time and she flipped the knit blanket off her legs. Even before she reached up to touch her hair, she knew it would be a mess, but she gathered most of it successfully on top of her head before leaning forward to stand up.

"The paper is at the end of the driveway. I was going to get it for you, but *Miss Nosy Pants* was already out in the front yard watering her roses."

She was surprised to hear the soft voice from somewhere behind her but not startled. *Miss Nosey Pants.* That was how Matthew fondly referred to Lilly.

"It might have been worth it to see the look on her face as the paper lifted off the driveway and floated through the air."

"Don't even joke about that. It's hard enough to avoid her when I go out," she replied, walking towards the kitchen. "If you did that, she'd probably camp out on the front lawn."

"I think you might be right about that. Remember that time Fiona stayed with us."

"You mean the *last* time my mother stayed with us," Kate interrupted.

"Fiona swore that she saw her watching us with binoculars from across the street and that's why she went outside in her robe and flashed her."

Kate rolled her eyes and looked over at Matthew, who was doubled over laughing. "It was not funny."

"It was *hilarious*!" Matthew replied, still laughing.

"Oh, yeah. It was a real knee-slapper. Mom

left the next day to go back to Florida and Lilly went around town telling *everybody* about what happened. People were afraid to come to our house... they thought we were a couple of swingers."

That reminder of what followed only made him laugh harder and a few seconds later Kate caught the giggles and was laughing alongside him.

"What did I miss?"

Startled to hear another voice, she turned around to see Charlotte standing in the open door holding the newspaper in her hand. Kate quickly turned to her left in time to catch Matthew slip through the living room wall.

"Hi, hunny... what are you doing here?"

Walking into the living room, Charlotte handed her mother the paper. "I came over to make sure your power came back on. What were you laughing about?"

"You know, I can't remember," Kate replied. "What time did your power come back on?" she asked, trying to shift the subject away from herself.

"Around one o'clock. Are you *sure* you're, okay?" Charlotte asked, glancing around the room, and noticing the open box on the table.

"Yes. Yes, I was just thinking about something, and it made me laugh."

Kate watched as Charlotte walked over to the table to pick up the house sign.

"This is what was in the box, huh?"

"Your dad ordered it."

"I like it," she said, turning toward her mother. "It will look great on the side porch... that's where you're going to put it, right?"

"Yeah, that's the plan."

"Well, let Ben know if you need any help hanging it. He'd be happy to help... all you gotta do is ask." Placing the sign back into the box, the young woman pulled keys from the front pocket of her sweater. "Well, I just wanted to check on you."

Kate followed her daughter as she retraced her steps to the front of the house. "And thanks for that."

Charlotte turned back and nodded as she stepped through the open door. "You bet."

She continued to watch until Charlotte's car was out of sight, only stepping back inside after her car disappeared down the street.

"That was close," she said, turning around. "But it got me wondering... do you think the kids could see you?"

"They couldn't see me before, but then neither could you," he replied, moving to be next to her. "We could try it the next time Charlie comes around if you want."

"Let me think about that before you test the theory."

He watched her move to the kitchen only to stop and stare at the bag of ground coffee after she removed it from the cupboard. He was about to ask her what was wrong when she turned to him.

"For the life of me, I cannot figure out how much coffee to make now that it's just me." He watched as she sat the bag back down on the counter. "I tried to half everything... half the coffee, half the water, but it just doesn't taste the same."

"Do you want my honest opinion?" he asked.

"Of course."

"If you are doing what you say... putting in half of everything equally, then it's in your head. It doesn't taste the same because you don't want it to."

"Well, how the *hell* do I fix that?"

"Buy a different brand of coffee. You never liked *Pete's* anyway... you learned to tolerate it because it was my favorite."

She studied him for a minute, not sure she wanted to admit that she hadn't thought about that simple solution. "That might just work."

Kate walked to the fridge and grabbed a magnetic marker to add an item to the whiteboard. When she returned to the counter, she made the same amount of coffee she had always made before turning around to face him. He was near the patio door, looking out into the yard... the look on his face revealing he was lost in his thoughts.

Last night, hours after the shock had worn off that he had somehow managed to come back and was really standing in the room with her, they had stayed up late talking about nothing and everything. The part of the conversation that had done the most good for her was knowing that he had no memory of pain or being scared. She had spent hours agonizing over how he felt in his last moments and knowing that he had no memory beyond the smoke filling the space, she felt herself moving forward... past the pain and anger.

"What's on the agenda for today?" he asked, turning around when he heard the coffee maker beep.

"Painting," she replied. "The weather has cleared up, so I need to move everything back out of the garage and into the yard."

"Are you still happy with the colors we picked out?"

"I think they'll be good. I've only just finished the shutters and they're that off-white, like the house will be... I guess the real test will be when I start the trim."

"You'll leave the attic windows for when you have someone else here to help, right? You shouldn't go up on the ladder to the second level without having a spotter here, Kate."

"I'm not stupid, Matt." She knew her reaction was harsh, but it had been only two weeks since he died, and she was *already* sick of people telling her what to do and checking up on her like she was a child. "Charlie and Ben are coming over to help me with the upper-level painting."

"Okay, okay... *God*, no need to be so touchy. It was just an observation."

"No, it wasn't an observation... it can't be an observation when it hasn't happened. Don't forget... I'm not the one in this relationship that took unnecessary risks." She knew that last comment was severe and the fact that he didn't have a sarcastic comment ready to shoot back at her, proved it landed like a grenade.

But he needed to hear it.

She was the one in their relationship who followed the rules and didn't take risks. She wore her seatbelt. She stopped at Stop signs instead of *rolling* through them. She didn't even tear the tags off their mattress. He was the one who let the kids drive the car the last block home even though they didn't have a driver's license. He was the one who sky dived. He was the one who rode a motorcycle without a helmet even though he had two of them on a shelf in the garage collecting dust. He was the one who volunteered at the fire department and got excited when the sirens went off or his pager beeped.

He was the one who lived his life as if he was invincible and look what it got him.

"I'm sorry. I know you're the careful one. It just hit me looking out at the ladder lying beside the garage that the kids only have one parent left." She watched as he turned his head to look back into the yard. "And I know it's my fault. I did this to our family... to us."

"You have to stop this," she replied, softening her tone. "For however long it is that you're going to be here... I won't keep stepping backward to revisit the same discussion we had last night."

In her opinion, they had gotten everything off their chest that needed to be said. They had dug through all the dirt that had accumulated over their life together until her fingertips were raw. They had laughed. They had shouted at one another. And she had cried. But when her eyelids grew heavy, it seemed like they had run out of things to discuss, and they both agreed that moving forward their focus would be on enjoying whatever time they had left and not rehashing the life that was behind them.

Refusing to let his lack of a response derail her mood, she put a period on her thought. "Look, if you feel yourself slipping back into wanting to discuss the past, slip through the wall instead and leave the room. Don't tell me why you're going... just go. I'll know why."

"Deal."

Opening the dishwasher, she reached for her coffee cup from yesterday and rinsed it out. She poured herself a cup of coffee and went to the fridge to grab the milk... when she turned around, he was gone. For a moment, she wondered where he was but shook it off and walked to the kitchen table to enjoy her coffee. She could see the birds outside flittering around the birdbath and walked to the patio door; the house was too quiet, and she welcomed the sounds from outside to fill the void. She half expected him to be there when she turned around, but he wasn't, and instead of searching for him, she returned to the table and picked up her coffee.

Her phone dinged, alerting her that she had a message and after she turned it over to read the text, she wished she hadn't. The message was from Pete. The fire inspector from Oklahoma City had faxed in his preliminary findings and he wanted to stop by later to discuss them with her.

Great.

She had too much she wanted to get done today to be worried about a visit from the town fire chief to talk about what happened at the store. Her reluctance to meet with him might have something to do with the fact that Matt already told her it was the hot plate that started the fire, and she worried that maybe insurance wouldn't cover the loss. If that were the case, she had enough in savings to live off for several years, but it would take the decision about whether to rebuild the store or not, out of her hands. And that part was a relief.

Something about having limited choices

appealed to her and she texted him back to stop by any time between noon and two o'clock.

TAPING OFF THE windows had taken longer than she thought, and it was when she ripped off the last piece of tape that she wondered if she had made a mistake. If another summer storm rolled through tonight, she'd be out taping all the windows again tomorrow. She had spent too much time worrying about things that were out of her control when she should have been excited to see what the green trim would look like on the house. It was one of the last things that her and Matt had worked on together, and it would be a disappointment if she hated the finished product.

As she finished painting the trim of the first window, Matthew reappeared. She could tell that his mood was subdued and not as upbeat as it had been, but he didn't appear to be sad... just quiet.

"Do ghosts get bored?" she asked.

"Umm, I don't really know how to answer that," he replied. "I guess if you get stuck somewhere long enough, it's possible."

"Stuck... is that how you feel?"

"I haven't had time to think about it, Kate. You missed a spot." He moved a few steps back and cocked his head, first to the left and then to the right. "I like it."

"Me too," she replied. "I think the green was a good choice. Better than the red and white color scheme you wanted to go with."

"*Crimson and cream*," he replied.

The grin on his face along with the accent he picked up whenever he spoke about his beloved OU football team, made her laugh out loud.

"Oh my, *God*... don't move," she whispered as the smile fell away from her lips.

"*Yoo-hoo*, Kate."

Across the street, a very enthusiastic, Lilly dressed in workout gear, walked-jogged toward her waving spastically with her right hand. Out of the corner of her eye, she could see he hadn't moved and anxiety gripped her breastbone tighter and tighter with each step her neighbor took.

"I thought that was you I saw bobbing up and down." Lilly said but stopped talking the last twenty feet to catch her breath before finally stopping a few feet away from Kate. "Whatcha doin' over here?"

Kate nervously looked to her left and side stepped in front of Matthew to block him from her neighbor's view. "Just freshening things up with some new paint."

"Are you alone?" Lilly asked, bending forward to scan the side porch. "I could have sworn from across the street, it looked like you were talking with someone."

"Nope, I'm alone. It's embarrassing, but I talk to myself when I'm working out what to do next."

"Oh, we all do that," Lilly said, taking a step closer. "Heck, some days if I didn't talk to myself, I wouldn't have anyone to talk to at all, and I'll deny it if you repeat this, but sometimes the conversations I have with myself are more engaging than when I'm talking with Ed."

Behind her, Kate heard laughter and turned around to see Matthew bending over holding his stomach. "Stop it," she whispered.

"What's that dear?" Lilly asked leaning forward.

"You better come up with something quick," Matthew said, still laughing.

"I thought I heard a bee behind me," Kate replied, taking a step forward.

"That was lame."

"I have no doubt! With all these pretty flowers, I'm sure that you have bees buzzing everywhere. I always say to Ed that you have the prettiest yard on our street and that I get the benefit of looking at all that beauty without having to do any of the work."

"That's actually a really smart way to look at it," Kate replied.

"Kiss ass."

Matthew breathing into her ear was annoying her and Kate stepped forward, getting closer to Lilly than she cared to, but needing to get away from him. Unfortunately, Lilly took the move as an invitation to ask the question that brought her across the street in the first place.

"I hope you don't take this as me being a nosy neighbor," Lilly said, lowering her voice to almost a whisper. "But have you heard anything about the store?"

Kate shut out the chuckling she heard behind her along with the chant of *nosy pants* he had begun. "Actually," Kate replied, pausing to take in a slow but deep breath, "I heard from Pete this morning and he's stopping by this afternoon to discuss it."

She knew it was a risk to tell Lilly what was happening because she was known to be a chatter box, but she also knew it would shut Matthew up. And it did. She had not told him about the text from Pete before now and this time when she glanced back, he was gone.

"Did he tell you anything about how the fire started?"

Kate shook her head, no. "I don't know anything yet."

"But you *are* going to rebuild, aren't you? Downtown just wouldn't be the same without a

Chapman Hardware store."

"Lilly, honestly I'm not sure what I'm going to do." Kate replied, glancing over towards the porch.

"I'm keeping you from your project," Lilly said as she touched Kate gently on the shoulder. "We can chat another day."

Kate watched as Lilly turned and began to walk toward the end of the driveway, surprised that the entire way home, she never turned around.

Not once.

BY THE TIME she stopped for dinner, Kate had painted all the trim along the front and both sides of the house. While she had spent the last three hours alone, focusing on not making a mess had provided the distraction she needed. Although she was not looking forward to seeing Pete, she did want to hear what the investigator had to say. Maybe if she hadn't already heard the account from Matthew about what happened she would look forward to finding out more... but she already knew. And now she needed to be careful to not challenge what Pete said if his findings were different from what her husband had told her.

But whether the official findings matched or not, she would finally have an answer regarding the options available to her even if she had no idea what she wanted to do.

After putting the cover back on the can of paint and wrapping her brush in plastic wrap, she moved the supplies to the back of the house. When she was finished with dinner, her goal was to finish the trim in the back, so tomorrow she could start on the foundation. She was surprised that Matthew hadn't yet commented on her painting strategy. Most people would paint the house first and then work out to the trim and the door, but Kate liked to get the harder, more detailed work out of the way first.

And she was excited to see how the new colors looked.

Walking toward the house, she didn't know what to expect when she went inside. Matthew had disappeared almost three hours ago, and even though she had expected to see him peek out of a window as she moved around the house, that hadn't happened. He was the one who returned from the dead to say goodbye. He was the one who wanted to spend whatever time they had left *together*, yet he was also the one who disappeared on her twice in the last twenty-four hours. She tried not to let it annoy her and instead, focus on how she might feel if the roles were reversed.

Dead, her body burned to ash and sitting in a shiny gold designer jar on top of the mantle.

Gone, but not really *gone*.

But not knowing when the *encore performance* of her life would end.

It was a *shitty* position for him to be in and while it presented a degree of uncertainty for her, how she felt couldn't compare to the thoughts that must be passing through his mind. She would hold it together as best that she could, for him. He was the one having to go through it and while she would be beside him and offer whatever support she could, ultimately it was a journey he would have to make alone.

Stepping in through the slider, she left the door open to allow some fresh air and the floral aroma coming off the gardenia bushes that lined the fence in the back yard enter the house. She grabbed the cup and what was left of her coffee from the counter and popped it into the microwave. The unopened box of crackers in the cupboard and her twice warmed coffee would have to do for dinner today. Removing a notepad and pen from the junk drawer, she placed them on the kitchen table just as the microwave began to beep.

Today would be a working meal. The crackers and a single can of soup in the pantry were the last of the food worth eating. She'd have to make a run to the grocery store in the morning and she hated shopping. That too had always been Matthew's job. He made almost an event out of going to the store. His lists were always well-organized, and he rarely went down the same aisle twice during the same visit. Kate was not as familiar with the layout of the aisles, so her shopping experience was always longer, but she made up for it by going early in the morning as the sun was just peeking over the horizon and the aisles were fairly empty except for the employees restocking the shelves.

As the items on her list grew, she tried to recall the last time she stepped inside the grocery store. It had to be sometime in March, before Easter. Jackson was coming home for a five day leave and she had wanted to surprise him with some Peeps. Matt had given her a hard time about buying their son Easter candy, but Jackson loved them and had eaten both packages in one sitting. If the girls would have cared about reliving their sugar-filled childhood, she would have bought something for them too, but only Jackson inherited her love of sweets.

"Getting anywhere with that list?"

She looked up to find him in front of the fireplace again. Ignoring his question, she asked him one instead. "Where have you been?"

"Has Pete been by yet?"

She put down the pen and exhaled audibly. "No. I answered your question, now you answer mine... where'd you disappear to?"

"I took a stroll around town?"

"You *left* the property?"

"I wasn't sure if I could, but after hearing that Pete was stopping by.... I sorta needed to put some distance between me and this place."

"You mean between you and *me*."

"No... I said what I meant," he replied as he moved toward her. "I didn't want to be around when Pete showed up. I didn't know if I could face him... considering what he was coming here to talk about. I feel like I let him down... you know, doing what I did."

"I'm sure he doesn't think that."

Out of habit, she reached out to touch him, but her hand moved through him like he was particles of dust visible in the sunlight. That was the first time she had even tried to touch him since he came back and when she looked up at his face, his only response was to tilt his head and raise his eyebrows.

"Did you feel *anything*?" she asked.

He shook his head, no, before moving closer to the open patio door. "Just another reminder that I'm *not* really here. I have no sense of touch or smell, and I imagine taste too... even though I haven't tried to test that theory yet," he said, smiling. "But I'm never hungry so that's a fair trade off, I guess."

"Not having a sense of smell isn't necessarily a bad thing," she laughed. "You *hate* the smell of gardenias, and they are in full bloom. I think the smell is wonderful, but you'd be closing the door instead of standing in it if you could get a whiff of what was coming in from the yard."

"Good point," he replied. "Remember when Charlotte went out there with a pair of scissors and cut a vase full for Mother's Day?"

"I do," she replied, smiling. "I also remember that every night after she went to bed, you stuck the vase in the garage and brought it back in the next morning when you left for work."

"Do you think she knew... that I did that?"

"I doubt it... that child slept like the dead... still does." He laughed at the reference that quickly became awkward. "I'm sorry I said that."

"Don't be... it was funny, except now I know the dead don't actually sleep."

Before Kate could respond, the sound of the doorbell interrupted their conversation. She looked over at Matthew, but he had already begun to move. She thought he was leaving again and for the first time since he returned, a sense of panic filled her chest, but she was able to calm down after she realized he was only moving to position himself in front of the fireplace. Pete rang the doorbell again and this time he began knocking.

"Coming!" Kate called out.

As soon as she opened the door, she found herself looking into the gentle eyes of Matt's best friend. They had all grown up together and even though Pete left to attend college out of state, he returned after graduation to take a teaching position at the high school. The two guys seemed to pick up right where they left off, but Kate had a toddler to chase after and encouraged them to go off and explore new fishing holes to get them out of the house.

Some days it felt like she had three toddlers on her hands.

That first summer, Matt got the brilliant idea to try and form a men's softball league and Pete helped him get people signed up. After a week of putting up flyers and making calls, they had enough interest to field three teams, then spent the next two weeks cleaning up the old softball field at one of the two community parks that would serve as their *Linvalle Men's League Softball* field.

While the two guys spent the summer catching up playing softball, Kate went to work playing matchmaker. After several failed blind date attempts, by the end of the summer she had finally made a match with Meg, a friend of hers who owned the local flower shop. That fall, there was a small wedding in the park and for the next ten years the two couples were inseparable. While they never had kids of their own, Pete and Meg were the godparents to Jackson and Charlotte. Unfortunately, the same year Jackson graduated high school, Meg died in a car accident and Pete avoided all future attempts to set him up. Instead, he threw himself into his job and joined the fire department as a volunteer.

It would be a few years later that he convinced Matt to sign up too.

"Hi, Pete."

"Did I catch you at an okay time?"

"Sure, come on in." Kate stepped aside to open the door for him and watched as he took a few awkward steps toward the living room. A few weeks ago, he had walked into the house without even knocking, but today he looked uncomfortable and fidgety. "Let's go sit at the table," she said motioning toward the kitchen. Turning to close the door, she glanced over her shoulder toward the living room to see if Matthew was still there.

He was.

She followed Pete over to the table and waited for him to take a seat before she sat across from him. It was uncomfortable, how awkward he seemed... avoiding eye contact and picking at a scab on one of his knuckles while his eyes darted around the room.

"Would you like some coffee?"

"Sure, if it's not too much trouble."

"No trouble at all," she replied. "I always have extra these days."

An awkward silence filled the room again. Reaching for a mug, she glanced at Pete to find him staring out onto the patio toward the grill and she suddenly became sad for him. He had lost his best friend and if she let herself think about it, he probably didn't have anyone to talk to about it except for Father Mike. Pouring the coffee, she realized that after all these years she had no idea how Pete took his; he always showed up with a travel mug already in his hand.

"Do you take any cream or sugar with your coffee?"

"Black would be great."

"Black, huh... I wouldn't have guessed that."

"I got used to it when I was in college," he replied as she set the steaming cup in front of him.

"Those late-night study sessions with all the pretty coeds, I imagine."

"Something like that," he replied with just a hint of a smile revealing itself for the first time since he arrived. "How's the painting going?"

"Good. I made a lot of progress today," she replied, taking a drink from her cup of cold coffee. "I did the shutters the day that big storm rolled through. They're still in the garage."

"Same color as the trim?"

"No. They white... *Wimborne White* is the actual name. The same color the house will be painted eventually."

"Sounds *fancy*," he replied, raising his left eyebrow, and smiling as he took a drink.

She returned the smile and looked over Pete's shoulder toward the fireplace. Matthew was staring toward them but had not moved an inch since taking his position in the darker part of the room. The expression on his face was neutral... vacant.

"It does, but at the end of the day, it's just another version of the color white."

"I bet you pay more for that fancy name though."

"Can't disagree with that," she replied.

"How was it having all the kids back under this old roof?" he asked, looking up toward the ceiling.

"Crowded... messy, loud, but good. I wouldn't have made it through without them all being here. I was so relieved when Jackson called and said he'd be able to make it. At first, we didn't think his request would be granted given the fact he was just home at Easter but in the end, it worked out."

She got up to walk to the microwave. As much as she wanted to warm up the coffee, she needed to move and change positions to try and stop the sadness from creeping back in more. She stared at the clock counting down... *seven, six, five*, to give herself a few more seconds to pull it together before rejoining Pete.

"So, have they started to tear down what's left of the store yet?" she asked, opening the door to grab her cup.

"Tomorrow. Now that the inspection requested by the insurance company has been completed, the town can move ahead with cleanup."

"Does that mean our insurance should cover the damage?" Pulling her chair back, she kept her eyes on his, anxious to hear what he had to say.

"The answer is yes... both property and life insurance policies should pay out the claim."

As she sat down, she realized that she hadn't thought about that until this very moment, that Matthew's life insurance might be in jeopardy. They had money in the bank to cover the funeral expense and none of the kids... not even her mother had brought it up, which was surprising because Fiona took her financial security very seriously.

"Kate, did you hear me?"

"Sorry, yes. Until this moment, I hadn't even thought about Matthew's life insurance policy. We both had one, but to be honest, I have no idea how much insurance was on the store or -."

Her sentence trailed off and he reached across the table to cover her hand with his. "I know this is hard and I'm sorry you have to go through this... it does get easier."

She looked at him then. Unlike the hundreds of people who had said similar words to her, he had experienced what she was feeling... he had gone through it. She smiled softly and slowly pulled her hand back to grab onto her cup and took a drink. She wanted to look over at Matthew but couldn't. She didn't want to see the look she knew she would find in his eyes.

"Ask about the findings, Kate?" Matthew said from across the room.

"What?" she asked, looking over Pete's shoulder once again.

"I want to hear what he says about how the fire started."

"Who are you talking to, Kate?" Pete asked, turning around to see if someone else was in the house.

"What did the inspector say about the cause of the fire?" Kate asked.

Pete turned around in his chair to face her, confused by what just happened. "I've only received the preliminary report, but it looks like a defective hot plate under the counter was the point of origin." His confusion only continued when she didn't seem surprised or curious about the information he was sharing with her.

"Okay."

"Kate, I have to say... I'm a little surprised that you aren't asking me more questions about what happened that day."

She thought about her reply carefully before she responded to his statement about how he expected her to feel. "Other than finding out if the insurance would be covering the loss, nothing else matters. Digging into the fine details of how Matthew died isn't going to make me *feel* better and it *damn* sure isn't going to bring him back."

She knew Matthew would be gone even before she glanced over Pete's shoulder.

"I'm sorry. I didn't mean to upset you."

"I'm not upset, Pete," she replied. "I was upset when Jack broke his ankle goofing around on the bleachers at the field. I'm beyond upset. I'm frustrated. I'm angry. I'm afraid. I'm confused and I'm alone. Finding out the details of what happened to Matthew in that store isn't going to help me and there is *nothing* anybody can do or say to make my feelings go away. Only time will help with that."

Reaching across the table, she grabbed his cup before walking toward the kitchen sink. *I'm not going to cry. I'm not going to cry. I'm not going to cry.* She turned on the water and began to wash the cups to distract her from stepping across the line. Out of the corner of her eye, she could see Pete sitting at the table watching her.

"You know, Pete, I really need to get back to painting before my brushes dry up." Shutting off the water, she reached for the dish towel to dry her hands and turned to look at him.

"I'll let you get back to it then," he replied, standing up and pushing the chair back under the table. "Do you want me to text you after the lot has been cleared so you can come downtown to talk about next steps?"

"How long do you think the cleanup will

take?" she asked.

"Clearing all the electrical, sewer and water lines, the debris... I'd say by the end of next week."

"Fine. Text me when it's done and we can go from there.

He studied her expression. "You aren't sure what you want to do with the lot are you?"

She hesitated before slowly shaking her head, no.

"I'll keep that to myself," he replied.

"Thank you. I appreciate that," she said, stepping away from the sink. "Let me walk you to the door."

"That's okay... I know the way and I've taken up enough of your time." He turned to walk to the door and as he pulled the baseball cap out of his back pocket, he called out over his shoulder. "Have a good rest of the week, Kate."

"See ya, Pete."

She continued to watch as he opened the door and closed it behind him without turning back and as soon as he was gone, she breathed in deeply and exhaled. Hearing his truck start up she finally felt a sense of relief and began to relax and when she glanced toward the living room, the space in front of the fireplace remained empty.

Matthew had disappeared again.

CHAPTER SIX

THE DAYS THAT followed seemed to fly by. The weather cooperated and Kate finished the trim and moved onto the siding. The boards were in great shape and after a little bit of sanding she was able to jump right into painting. Her forearms no longer ached like they had the first few days as her muscles got use to the repetitive motion of moving the brush from side to side and top to bottom.

Matthew had spent part of the time watching her work and strolling around the yard supervising like Mr. Miyagi from The Karate Kid. The first few times, it had been funny and made her laugh, but by the fifth time of hearing *'it's all in the wrist'* she wanted to throw the paint brush at his head. Instead, of letting him see her annoyance, she ignored him by putting in her earbuds and listening to the soothing lyrics of *Simon and Garfunkel.*

She turned around every now and then to see what he was up to and while he spent most of the day watching her, a few times he was nowhere to be found. She surprised herself by not worrying about where he was or freaking out that he might be gone for good. Instead, she refocused her mind on the task she needed to get done and concentrated on finishing the painting. By the end of the day, all that remained to paint were the areas located beyond the reach of her six-foot ladder and the doors.

And the timing couldn't have worked out better... she was sick of painting.

Charlotte and Ben were coming over tomorrow morning. Kate was making breakfast and Ben was going to help her reach the higher parts of the house while Charlotte's job was to pull the tape from all the windows and paint the doors. Even if she had to stay outside painting in the dark, this project would be finished tomorrow. She wasn't looking forward to going to the grocery store in the morning, but she was looking forward to seeing Charlie and updating her about what the inspector from the City found. She had yet to decide if she would share what caused the fire. The second Charlotte heard that a hot plate was involved, she would know what happened and Kate was afraid the sadness she was feeling would be replaced by anger; and she didn't want that.

But if her daughter asked, she wouldn't sugar coat the truth.

Putting away the painting supplies for next to the last time, she could feel the long days that piled up behind her and Kate felt drained. Looking up at the sky as she came out of the garage, she could see storm clouds once again approaching from behind the house. *Please, God, not tonight.* Throwing a prayer up to the heavens, she pulled the garage door down and walked toward the house. Matthew was just inside the open patio door and as she lifted her arm to wave, she caught a glimpse of the devilish expression on his face.

What is he up to?

When she stepped into the house, she cautiously looked around to see what had changed. In the past, whenever that sheepish grin crossed his lips, he had done something that made her want to scream in anger or laugh until she cried. Looking into the living room, everything seemed untouched and as far as she could tell nothing was broken. Turning her head toward the kitchen, the coffee cups were in the dish rack and her grocery list was still lying on the table, so nothing had changed there. But when she looked back at Matthew, he remained by the patio door watching her, like he was waiting for something to happen... anticipating it.

He did something.

"What did you do?" she asked, resting her hands on her hips.

"I didn't do anything," he replied, crossing his arms in front of his chest. "She followed me home."

"*Who* followed you?"

As she was waiting for him to stop smiling

and start talking, behind her she heard the distinct sound of tiny nails on a wood floor. She turned around to look for what was making that sound and didn't have to search very long. Her gaze shifted to the floor to find a tiny, skinny, chocolate lab puppy trotting out of the bedroom toward her.

"Oh, my *God*, Matt!" she said between clenched teeth. "A puppy!"

The only thing he had going for him right now was that Kate rarely yelled. It wasn't her style. She would talk and talk and talk, until you finally agreed with her or gave up, but she rarely lost her cool. He watched as the puppy finally made it to Kate's feet and immediately placed her tiny paws on her shoes, trying to gather shoelaces in her little mouth. Kate was doing her best to try and ignore her, but he knew if he could wait it out, that little brown fur ball would win her over.

"While Pete was here, I needed to leave. So, I started walking. I didn't have a plan, I just needed to get out of here. When I finally stopped to pay attention to my surroundings, I was in the back alley behind the store. Did you know that from the back of the building, unless you look *really* closely, you wouldn't be able to tell anything even happened there?"

He could tell he was losing her and needed to get to the point.

"Anyway, I was going to check out the inside

of the building when I heard a noise coming from behind the dumpster and when I went to check it out, I found this little gal."

"That's a touching account, Matt. But how did you get her home?"

"She followed me," he replied.

"The dog can see you?"

"Oh, yeah. Did I forget to mention that part?"

She watched as he crouched down to call to her. The puppy immediately flipped her little body around to get to him, falling off her shoe and tumbling to the wood floor. Shaking her head, she watched as the puppy ran toward him, jumped through him, collected herself and tried again.

The dog could definitely see him.

"How is this possible?" she whispered.

"I have no idea," he replied. "You know, I remember reading an article about animals and little kids being able to see ghosts... I guess it's true."

Grace walked over to the kitchen to get a small plastic bowl out of the cupboard and after filling it with water, she placed it down on the floor at her feet, but the puppy didn't seem to care. She was still trying to jump up into Matthew's lap to the point she was wearing herself out. Picking up the bowl, she carefully walked over to where the puppy was collapsed at his feet. The little thing didn't even have the energy to stand up. She just laid her snout on top of the rim and started to lap the water with her tongue. Water flew everywhere and Kate walked to the kitchen to grab a dish towel from the drawer.

"We can't keep her," she said, walking back over toward the dog.

"I know we can't... but *you* can," he replied.

She stopped by the table after the meaning of the words she used sunk in. *We can't keep her.* She knew that. Somewhere deep inside, she knew that. Even though her husband was still there, he was really gone and any day, any hour really... he could vanish and never return.

"She has to belong to someone," she replied, bringing the towel over to place under the bowl of water, most of which was now all over the floor instead of inside of the bowl.

"Kate, I found her by the dumpster in the back alley. How could she have gotten there by herself... downtown... and nobody saw her? And look at how skinny she is! It looks like the poor thing hasn't eaten in days."

He had a point, but there was no way she was ready to take on the responsibility of a dog let alone a little puppy who would require lots of training. She turned away from Matt and looked at the tiny creature now asleep on the wood floor. She was thin... too thin for her age. She looked to be eight or nine weeks old and should be round and fat, but Kate could see the ribs and hip bones peeking through the brown fur that looked dirty.

Looking up at the clock on the wall, she knew the shelter was closed. "It's too late to do anything about it now, so she'll have to spend the night. But I have nothing to feed her."

"Good thing you have a car then and that the store is only five minutes up the road," he replied. "You go get her some food and whatever else you think she needs, and I'll keep an eye on her. It looks like she'll be out for a while."

"I'm a mess. And I think I have paint in my hair."

His only reaction was to shrug.

Exacerbated, she reached for the grocery list on the table and yanked her purse off the edge of the kitchen chair. "I'll be back," she said, reaching for the keys hanging up by the front door. "Don't let her pee on my new rug."

He watched as she pulled the door closed behind her before turning his eyes to the puppy who remained asleep at his feet. "You heard her, no peeing on the rug." Crouching down again, he reached out to touch the soft fur but could only rely on a memory of how it felt as his finger passed through the little dog's body. "Don't you listen to a word she says... by tomorrow morning, you'll have her hooks into her. You're gonna love your new home."

SHOPPING TOOK LONGER than she expected and as she pulled into the driveway, she envisioned the mess that would probably be waiting on her new wood floors. The items that she had written down this morning, she found quickly, but before she even got to the pet aisle, her plan began to go south. Puppy food was the only item she had added to her list while stopped at the one traffic light she had to pass between the house and the store. But by the time she actually got inside, almost immediately her mind began to drift to other items that may make sense even though Kate was sure the dog's stay in her house, would be a short one.

She had no intentions on keeping the puppy.

But as she passed the aisle full of school supplies, the idea of picking up markers and posterboard so she could make *'lost puppy'* signs to put up on the telephone poles seemed like a good idea. Somebody had to be looking for this dog; it was just a puppy and probably had escaped through a fence or ran through a door that had been left open by accident.

Then something else began to burrow into

her heart.

If she was going to go through the effort of making signs, it would likely take a few days to track down and confirm the owners. She couldn't hand the puppy over to the first person that said it was theirs; they would have to prove it to her. That meant the puppy would be with her at least a couple of days.

Mentally, she began to chant in her head the items she would need from the pet aisle.

Food, bowls, bed, collar, leash, treats, toys... food, bowls, bed, collar, leash, treats, toys.

As she was wheeling the cart back to her car, she felt a drop of rain land on her bare arm and quickened her pace. By the time she transferred all six paper bags into the trunk of her Honda Civic, a soft and steady rain had begun to fall. During the short drive home, with each swipe of the windshield wiper, she could feel the adrenaline high she felt from getting the puppy get wiped away too.

Thankfully, the rain had stopped by the time she reached for her purse, and she took a second to gather her strength before pushing herself out of the car. Walking back to the trunk, it felt like she was wearing ankle weights. It would take her two trips to get all the groceries carried to the porch and that would give Lilly two opportunities to run across the street to inquire about what Pete had to say. After putting the first three bags onto the bench, she glanced across the street to look for any sign that Lilly was waiting but there was no evidence that she was even watching her through the window, which was odd. Gathering the last of the bags into her arms, Kate felt the first the few drops of rain and quickly closed the trunk. As she stepped onto the porch, the sprinkles quickly turned into a downpour and then pea-sized hail.

Her first thought was of the puppy. If Matthew had not found her, she would have been caught outside in this horrible weather, but she didn't have time to dwell on what could have happened when the porch door opened, and a little ball of brown fur came out to greet her.

Matthew watched from inside the open door as Kate smiled and got down on her knees to scoop the puppy up as she bit at her fingers and chin.

His plan was working.

TURNING OFF THE kitchen faucet, Kate could still hear the rain hitting the roof. Hopefully it stopped soon, otherwise her plans to finish the house tomorrow might be derailed. As she finished drying the supper dishes, she realized for the first time in weeks... she was relaxed. Whether it was the lack of sleep, long days outside in the fresh air, the wine, or a combination of all three she didn't know, but she also didn't care. Laying the towel down on the counter, she leaned over to peer into the laundry hamper next to her and smiled at the sight of the sleeping puppy.

After two hours of chasing after her to stop her from chewing on the rug, the legs of the chair and the plush throw hanging over the couch, she had given up and plopped her into the plastic hamper. She had forgotten how much work a puppy could be. Birdie had been a year old when they adopted her from the shelter and the transition to their home had been easy.

"Did you think of a name yet?"

"A name? No." Kate whispered as she looked down into the basket a final time before grabbing her wine glass from the counter and stepping into the living room. "I'm not keeping her."

"Then you better get to work on those posters you talked about making," he replied. "Although I can't help but notice the markers are still in the plastic bag hanging on the pantry door behind you."

Casually glancing behind her, she ignored the sarcasm in his tone and stepped through him as she made her way into the living room.

"Are you really trying to convince me that you don't want to keep her?" he asked.

"I'm not trying to convince you of anything," she replied. "I just think it's wrong to not even try and look for the family who might be missing her."

"I found her by the garbage, Kate," he replied as he moved into the room to join her. "And look at how skinny she is... she's been on her own at least a few days."

"That may be true, but that doesn't mean she doesn't belong to somebody."

"I didn't see any signs for a missing dog when I walked around town today," he said.

"Were you looking?"

"Well, not exactly," he replied, moving back toward the kitchen.

"I'm going to make a few signs before I go to bed tonight and tomorrow morning, I'll go out early. If I don't see any signs on main street, I'll put up one of my own by the post office and the library."

"And if nobody calls?" he asked.

"If nobody calls, I guess she can stay here," she replied, taking a long drink from her glass.

"Yes!"

She jerked forward and looked back at him with wide eyes and pursed lips, pointing toward the basket. Only after he looked inside and gave her a thumbs up did she relax back into the chair, shaking her head.

"I don't know what you're so happy about," she said, putting her feet up onto the coffee table. "I'm confident I will find her owners tomorrow."

Kate closed her eyes to listen to the sound of the rain hitting the roof. She thought about turning on the TV for a little while but decided against it. Quiet was better. The last thing she needed was to stimulate her mind and get her thoughts going again. If she was lucky, in thirty minutes she'd be ready for bed.

"Remember the first night we brought Birdie home?" he asked, his voice barely above a whisper.

"Uh huh," she replied, keeping her eyes closed. She couldn't see him, but she could sense that he was moving into the room to be with her.

"Maybe you should try to sleep in the bed tonight."

She opened her eyes and found him directly in front of her. "I sleep just fine on the chair."

"Do you really think you're going to get any sleep holding a puppy on your lap?"

"She's sound asleep and should stay that way as long as *nobody* wakes her up," she replied, raising her right eyebrow. In the distance, she heard a rumble of thunder and a few seconds later, the rain began hitting the roof with more urgency. "Great."

"At least you can't blame me if she wakes up. It'll be like fate."

"No, but I can blame you for bringing her here in the first place." She finished her wine and pushed herself up from the chair. "Well, I'm heading to bed."

He waited as she took a few steps toward the bedroom. "Aren't you forgetting something?" She stopped but didn't turn around and it looked like she was about to say something when a loud clap of thunder shook the house. Without saying a word, Kate walked across the living room and reached into the hamper to pick up the whimpering puppy. She turned around and walked past him and closed the bedroom door without saying a word.

Even though she could no longer see him, she could hear him laughing.

SHE WASN'T SURE if it was the whining or the kisses that woke her up, but either one would have been effective. The room was still fairly dark when she opened her eyes, so she knew the sun had not yet begun to peek over the treetops, but she needed to get up. Charlotte and Ben would be here in a few hours, and she not only had to get breakfast ready, but she also had to spend some time with the dog in the back yard. Sitting up, she pushed herself out of bed and stopped. After a quick, short intake a breath, she turned around and looked behind her.

She had slept in the bed.

After she went into the room and shut the door, she remembered sitting in the chair, putting her feet up on the ottoman and pulling the comforter up over her hips. The puppy played around for about five minutes, but then settled into a spot on her lap and fell asleep. She had no memory of moving from the chair to the bed, but it must have happened. In front of her on the floor, the puppy began to turn in circles.

"Oh, no you don't!"

Grabbing the little ball of fur, she sprinted toward the patio door. Outside the air was cool and a little damp, left over conditions from the storm that passed through the night before. Stepping across the patio in her bare feet, she put the puppy down on the grass and watched as it stepped around on the wet, cold surface unsure of what was happening and proceeded to step back onto the patio where she promptly squatted and peed.

"Not there!" she whispered to be considerate of her neighbors who probably were not awake this early on a Saturday. Kate continued to watch the puppy as she pranced around the patio leaving a trail of tiny paw prints behind her as she made her way back through the open patio door. "Where do you think you're going?"

Following the puppy inside, she found her at the pink and white ceramic bowl finishing what was left of the dog food from the night before. Walking over to put a little more food in the bowl, Kate could sense she was no longer alone and turned around to find Matthew in front of the fireplace, a smile on his face.

"And how was your night?" he asked.

"Better than I expected... I guess," she replied. "We ended up in the bed, but I have no idea how I got there."

"And no accidents to clean up this morning?"

"Not that I have found, but I haven't thoroughly checked out the bed yet."

He watched as she reached back to close and lock the patio door before turning to walk toward the bedroom. "I thought you were making breakfast for Charlie this morning?"

"I am," she called over her shoulder. "But I have to run uptown and put the posters up. I have time, they won't be here until about eight."

He looked down at the dog who had finished eating and now was sitting by the empty bowl, staring up at him. "Don't look at me." He chuckled as the puppy cocked its head to one side and continued to stare. "I think she's still hungry."

"Well, she'll just have to wait until I get back. It shouldn't take long," she said, reaching for the keys hanging on the wall. "If it looks like she needs to go to the bathroom, make sure you open that door and let her into the yard."

He watched as she left without turning around or even saying goodbye. Shifting his eyes to the puppy, she had moved over to the couch where she found one of the squeaky toys Kate bought at the store. She seemed content enough and he moved through the house until he passed through the front door. Outside, the morning sun was beginning to shine through the treetops and the driveway was still wet from the rain the night before. One of his favorite things about summertime was the way the mornings smelled after the rain had washed everything clean. Although he could no longer smell the freshness in the air, he could remember how it felt to be walking outside, spinning his key ring around his finger as he walked to his truck.

Across the street, his neighbor walked out of the house to fetch the paper at the end of the driveway. Matt continued to watch as Ed looked around before pulling out a cigarette and lighter from the front pocket of his shirt. After lighting the cigarette, he took a long drag and tilted his head back, releasing a series of perfect white rings that hung in the air like halos before slowly rising high above his head only to disappear into the pale blue morning sky.

Hearing a car approach, he turned to the left to find Kate's white Civic coming up the road. Across the street, Ed waved at her car before turning to go back inside and as she turned into the driveway, Matt moved toward the approaching car. As soon as the car door opened, he could tell that she wasn't happy. He knew there was no way she saw any *'lost puppy'* signs posted so something else must have happened.

Kate looked around as she stepped out of the car to make sure they were alone on the street before she spoke to him. "What are you doing? You're supposed to be watching the puppy."

"I've only been out here a few minutes. When I left, she was playing with her toy on the bed."

"The bed!"

"On *her* bed," he clarified. "She's in the living room chewing on one of the many squeaky toys you bought for her."

Without turning her head to look at him as she passed, she replied. "She better be."

"Did you get your signs put up?" he asked, following behind her.

"I did."

"Did you see any *'lost puppy'* signs?"

"I did not," she replied.

He continued to follow behind as she stepped onto the porch. "Kate, how long are you-."

The door in front of him slammed closed inches in front of his nose. If he were still alive, he might be offended that she could have broken his nose but instead, he moved through the oak barrier and continued where he had left off.

"How long are you going to deny that the dog will be staying right here."

She didn't reply, but after more than thirty years of marriage he had experienced the silent treatment before and it did not detour him. Experience had taught him if he was persistent and kept an even tone with his reply and listen to what she had to say, she would eventually get over whatever it was that he had done wrong. This morning, however, she was being unusually reserved with her replies and as he moved around the corner, he became aware of why.

The puppy had pooped on the floor.

He continued to where she was standing. "Hey, look on the bright side… she missed the rug. Easy clean up."

"You can clean it up," she replied, walking into the kitchen to start the coffee.

"*What*? No, I can't do that."

"Sure, you can. You've moved my glasses, a bag of garbage *and* I saw you carry the wine bottle the other night."

"Now, wait a minute. Those specific instances were different… special even. Think about what you're asking me to do. Do you *really* want me moving that," he asked, pointing toward the floor, "knowing I could drop it and make even more of a mess?"

"You know what... you're right. I think you've already *helped me* enough."

He moved forward and stopped next to the puppy in front of the closed patio door. They watched her move back and forth between the mess on the floor and the kitchen. He looked down at the puppy when she suddenly got up on all fours.

"I wouldn't if I were you."

Whimpering, the puppy sat back down.

MIXING UP THE batter for the French toast, she glanced over toward the patio door where the puppy had been sleeping for the past thirty minutes. The poor little thing had looked so sad sitting there, watching her clean up the mess she had made that Kate began to feel bad for her. But by the time she had everything cleaned up, her hands washed, and the trash taken outside to the garbage bin, the puppy had laid down and fell asleep. She didn't want to admit it, but the little thing was growing on her. As she reached into the fridge for the bacon, she heard a car with a loud engine pull up to the house.

Charlie and Ben had arrived.

"That boy still hasn't gotten his muffler fixed."

"I believe it's supposed to sound like that," Kate replied. "Your age is showing."

"My age has nothing to do with it. He's going to be a father soon," he replied. "He needs to grow up and swap that vehicle for something more practical."

"Funny that you should bring that up."

"What?" he asked.

"Their transportation situation." Kate reached into the fridge, pulling out the bacon and orange juice. "I was *thinking* about letting them have your truck, so they can trade it in for whatever car works best for them and still have two vehicles."

"My truck!" he replied. "I love that truck. I can't believe-."

"Knock, knock...Mom, we're here."

Still shaking his head in disbelief of what he just heard, Matt began to move out of the living room and toward the bedroom door. She was seriously considering giving his truck away. He loved that truck and had driven all the way to Tulsa to get it because the dealer in Oklahoma City didn't have the color he wanted. And she was willing to just *give it away*.

"Hi, hunny," Kate replied. "We're in here."

"Who else is with you?" Charlie asked,

coming around the corner and looking around.

Kate froze. She had become so used to having Matt around the house that she forgot that others can't see him. Glancing back toward the bedroom, she watched as Matt disappeared into the bedroom.

"Who else is here with you, mom?"

Before Kate could reply, a high-pitched growly bark could be heard coming from the bedroom and a few seconds later, the puppy came slowly walking out into the living room.

"You got a dog!" Charlie exclaimed, looking back and forth between her mom and the puppy walking towards her. "It's adorable," Charlie said, taking her purse off and hanging it on a kitchen chair before sitting on the floor. The puppy instantly flipped a switch and went from trying to be fierce to seeking affection, running towards her.

"I don't know if I'm keeping her."

"It's a female? When did you get her?" Charlie asked as the puppy jumped into her lap and began to lick her face. "Ben, look! Mom got a dog."

"She was found in the alley behind the store yesterday and like I said, I don't know if she's staying."

"Oh, how could you not want this *cute little baby*," Charlie said, as the puppy continued to assault her with kisses. "Wait," she said, looking toward her mom. "You went to the store?"

Kate did not lie to her children, and she wouldn't start now. Behind Charlie, she could see Matt slowly making his way toward the kitchen but staying in the shadows that clung to the wall. "Like I said, I didn't go into the store... she was found in the alley. I'm sure she belongs to someone. I put up a few posters today and am honestly expecting a phone call any time now."

"Hi, Ben," Kate said, waving toward her son-in-law. "I hope you're hungry because we're having French toast, scrambled eggs and *real* bacon."

Kate walked back to the kitchen, grabbing eggs and milk from the fridge. The sooner they made breakfast, the sooner they could get outside and finish the painting. "*So*, while I'm getting breakfast ready, I wanted to talk to you kids about something."

Charlotte looked at her husband and got up from the floor to stand next to him. "What is it? Did something else happen?"

"No, nothing else happened," Kate replied. "Charlie, you need stop worrying that every time someone needs to speak with you, it's because something happened. Both of you, come over here and pull out the stools... have a seat."

"Mom, you're freaking me out. Just tell us what's on your mind already."

"Your dad's truck."

"What about it?" Charlotte asked.

Over their shoulder, she could see Matt

advancing on them and he didn't look happy. "Your dad's truck," she replied, turning her attention back to the breakfast she was making. "While your father loved that truck, I have no need for it, and it doesn't make sense to hang onto something that'll just take up space in the driveway. Especially knowing you both could really use it."

"Mom, I don't know what to say."

"You don't have to make a decision today. Go home, talk about it in private and let me know what you decide."

"But neither of us drive a stick shift, so I don't see what talking about it will accomplish," her daughter replied.

"Charlie, I don't expect you to keep it. Trade it in on a car *or van* that will work for your family," Kate said. "If your dad were here, he'd be thinking the same thing."

As she dropped the battered toast onto the griddle, she glanced toward the patio door to look at Matthew. She could see his face had softened and the look on his face let her know he was okay with what she said. He was also pointing to the puppy who had begun to turn in circles.

"The puppy has to go to the bathroom... Ben, can you take her outside please?"

Charlotte laughed as her husband jumped up from the stool and ran to the door to grab the little dog. Through the open door, she could see him carry the puppy between his legs as he ran to the grass.

"He's so cute."

"He reminds me a lot of your dad," Kate replied. "You two will make awesome parents."

"Do you really think so?" Charlotte asked. "I'm starting to get really nervous about it."

Lifting the last piece of French toast from the griddle, she looked at her daughter. "That's completely normal to feel that way and it probably won't stop until after your holding your child in your arms." Kate handed the French toast to her daughter as she picked up the bowl of eggs and plate of bacon. "Bring that to the table for me, please?"

"Mom, were you nervous?"

"Extremely, but you have to remember the only point of reference I had was Fiona and although she loves to give advice about her life experience now... when I was your age, my mother was a completely different person."

Charlotte walked to the door to call her husband. "Ben, breakfast is ready. Can he leave the puppy outside?"

"No... bring her in," Kate replied.

"Bring the puppy with you."

A few seconds later, Ben walked through the open patio door holding the puppy by his chest. The aroma of bacon filled the space, and his mouth began to water. "Where do you want her?"

"You can just put her down and pull the screen door closed," Kate replied.

The puppy immediately ran forward to jump on the squeaky toy she spied on the floor and Kate motioned for Ben to join them at the kitchen table. A few times, she snuck a glance over Ben's shoulder to see what Matt was up to. The morning sickness that Charlotte had been plagued by for the past few months had finally passed and she was devouring the French toast. It was good to see her having a healthy appetite again. Between the morning sickness and her father's funeral, she had only lost a few pounds but on her small frame it had been noticeable.

"How are things going down at the shop, Ben?" Kate asked.

"Good," he replied in between bites. "Dad's thinking about adding another bay at the end of the building."

"Oh, wow," she replied. "That's great news. Business must be really good then."

"Oh yeah. Ever since I became certified to work on diesel engines too, business has really picked up... he's even thinking about hiring another mechanic."

For as long as she could remember, *Poverly Motors* had been servicing most of the local cars in town and the community as a whole had a high respect for the quality of work and the family. Ben's dad had taken over the business from his father and by the way things looked, he'd be passing the keys down to his son some day. It was a good, steady business and she had never worried about whether Ben would be able to provide for them. They complimented each other and soon they would be starting a family of their own.

They already owned a home so while they were quite young, they had a good foundation to build their future. Fiona had gifted them the very first house she had owned in town as a wedding present. It was only two bedrooms, but the house was situated on an almost two-acre lot and the rooms were very generously sized. The house needed a lot of work which to their credit, they insisted on doing themselves and after a solid year of saving up and doing most of the work to save on labor costs, they had a nice little house that had increased significantly in value. And if one day down the road they wanted to expand the footprint of their home, they had the land to do it.

Twenty minutes later, everyone had finished eating and while Charlotte cleared the table, Kate and Ben went out into the yard to discuss what they wanted to tackle first.

But he watched his daughter as she moved around the kitchen, the similarity between her and Kate making him both happy and sad at the same time. Of all their children, Charlie was the one he had the least in common with. Unlike her brother and sisters, she was not into sports and didn't care about what was going on at the store and that translated to the two of them spending very little time together while she grew up.

He watched his daughter with pride at the woman she had become. Not because of the way she washed the dishes, but because she chose to wash them even though her mother had only asked her to clear the table.

And he couldn't take credit for any of it.

NOT ONE CALL. The posters had been up for nearly eight hours and not a single call except for the person who had called the wrong number asking about a motorcycle for sale. But while nobody appeared to be missing her, the puppy was beginning to settle in quite well at the house.

By the time Charlotte joined them outside, Ben was up on the ladder painting the trim. The windows hadn't been taped but for the two windows that remained, a razorblade would have to do. Kate thought she would be the one going up the ladder, but Ben had convinced her that he could handle a paint brush and she was pleasantly surprised how well of a job he was doing. She had forgotten that he had done most of the painting of their current house, so he probably had more experience than she did.

While Kate and Ben chatted about unimportant things, Charlotte had gone around to all the windows and removed the tape, the puppy following her every move. When she moved to the front of the house, however, she made the puppy stay in the back yard where she would be protected by the fence. That was when Matt moved out of the house and onto the patio, doing what he could to keep the puppy entertained. For the first few minutes, Kate had been worried that Ben or Charlie may see him but after the first few minutes, it was obvious that they couldn't, and she began to relax. Ben had assumed the puppy was chasing after a fly and commented about how he wished babies were as easily entertained.

"Oh, they can be," Kate commented. "It was always the little things that you don't think of that trip a new parent up. The tiny rock from outside that hitched a ride into the house on your shoe. The paperclip you didn't even realize you dropped. The cap from a water bottle. That's why you have to watch them like a hawk, especially after they begin to walk."

"How did you get used to not being able to go out anymore, you know, after the baby comes?"

"Is that what you think? That once your

child is born you have to give up your life?" she asked.

"Well, sort of," Ben replied. "My mom all but said we better not think about dropping the baby off every weekend."

Kate laughed. "Well, not knowing exactly what the conversation was between you and your mom... she might have a point if you think that every Friday night you can pack up a diaper bag and drop your child off at grandmas for a few days like you don't have any responsibility." She held up her hand to shield the sun so she could see him. "Is that what you were asking?"

"Yes and no," he replied. "I know that our lives are going to change when the baby gets here. But my mom made it sound like we'll never be able to go away again... you know, just the two of us, until the kid turns eighteen."

"That's partially true, in my opinion," she replied. "Let me see if I can explain it a little bit. When you have a child, it'll be important that the two of you find time for each other but in the beginning, that'll be difficult. You'll be working so you'll need your sleep and that means a lot of the first few months will fall on Charlotte."

"That's what I'm worried about," he replied.

"Worried that she can't handle it?"

"No, not at all. Charlie is strong, but that's what I'm talking about... she doesn't like to ask for help."

She waited as he came down the ladder to

stand next to her. "Have you spoken with her about your concerns?"

"I tried, but she just shuts down the conversation." They swapped paint cans and as Ben put his foot back on the ladder, he turned back to her again. "Can you talk with her... maybe about what you and Matt did when you first had a kid?"

"I can try, but that doesn't give you get a pass to stop talking, to keep talking about it with her... it's important that you get her to engage to talk through this."

Kate didn't even realize what she was doing, but Matthew did.

As he stood back on the grass with the puppy, he watched as his wife began to lay the foundation of the man that Ben would become. He doubted that she even realized what she was doing, and he wasn't sure that he wanted to bring it to her attention either. Ben was where he had been forty years ago. A young man, still figuring out what kind of human being he was going to become but already responsible for keeping other people fed, sheltered, loved... safe. Out of the corner of his eye, he saw Charlotte coming around the corner carrying a handful of wadded up painter's tape. He almost missed the frown on her face as he focused on the barely noticeable bump protruding under her shirt.

She was beginning to show.

But something had happened on the other

side of the house while she was painting the doors to cause her to wrinkle her eyebrows in a way she only did when she was *pissed off*. The puppy also noticed her presence and took off running in her direction.

"Mom!"

Kate leaned back to peek around the boxwood planters. "Yeah?"

"Why didn't you tell me that Pete stopped by yesterday?"

Shit.

Lilly, when are you gonna to learn to mind your own business?

"It's not that I didn't tell you... it just hadn't come up yet."

"Well, it's come up now, so what did he say?"

"He said the investigator had faxed in a report noting the preliminary findings, that the fire was accidental and that the insurance companies should pay out their claims."

"Insurance companies?" Charlotte asked. "How many policies did dad have on the store?"

"One on the store and one on himself," Kate replied.

"Oh... right," Charlotte whispered. "Could he tell how the fire started?"

Kate felt the ladder move and looked up to find Ben looking down at her. "Yes." She couldn't look behind her to see if Matthew was still there or not, but for the first time, hoped he had disappeared. "The report said it was the hotplate that your father kept up by the register. Apparently, it had malfunctioned."

"Oh, daddy," Charlotte said, picking up the puppy at her feet. She needed something to distract her from crying, something she could hold on to that was alive before she asked the question she really wanted to know the answer to. "Did the report say anything else... like how dad died... was he in pain?"

"No," Kate said, replying quickly.

In her opinion, the response was not a lie. Charlotte had asked if the *report* noted how her father died, and Kate had not asked that question of Pete. Maybe someday she would tell the kids the details, but today was not the day. She could see her daughter physically exhale in relief which affirmed to her that she had made the right decision in keeping the details to herself.

"Lilly also said something about you making a decision about the store... that you told her that you weren't going to rebuild." The puppy began to squirm in her arms and wanted to be let go, so Charlotte crouched down and released her. "Is that true?"

"Do you really think that I would tell *her* before I talked with my children?" Kate looked at her daughter who shrugged her shoulders. "She caught me outside yesterday when Pete stopped by. She asked me when I thought the construction would start or something like that... and I told her I was still thinking about my options."

"Well, that's why she believes you're not rebuilding... you opened the door," Charlotte replied.

"And her imagination filled in the blanks," Kate replied. "Look, I'm fifty-fifty at this point. Part of me can't imagine not going down to the store every day... it's been a part of my life for as long as I can remember. But I also have enjoyed the past few weeks and the more time that passes, the more it feels like rebuilding the store would be going backwards."

"The store was like a child to you and dad," Charlotte replied. "If I'm being honest, I don't really get how you can just walk away from it."

"Charlie," Ben interjected, "I don't think you're being fair."

"Ben, it's okay," Kate replied. "I want her to express how she feels as long as she remembers that having a conversation, means that you listen too. Look guys, it's been a long day and while I'd love to have this conversation... how about we both sleep on it for a few days. Come back on Sunday for supper, and we can discuss it over a nice meal?"

"I'm in," replied Ben, as he stepped off the ladder.

"Eager much?"

Kate laughed as she watched her daughter walk over to her husband and give him a peck on the lips. "That settles it then. Thank you both, so much for helping me today and I'll see you back here on Sunday at... say five o'clock?"

"Sounds good," Charlie replied. "Do you want us to bring anything?"

"Just yourselves."

Kate walked the two of them through the side gate, making sure the puppy stayed in the back yard. As she locked the gate, she quickly scanned the area to see if she could see Matthew, but he was nowhere to be found. After making sure the latch was secure, she hurried to catch up with Ben and Charlotte.

"Hey, thanks again for coming over and helping me get the painting done." She turned back to look at the house. "It feels good to have finally finished it."

"I think it looks great," Ben said. "I like the new colors, and from here you can't even see the touchups you'll have to do on the trim around the doors."

"Jerk," Charlie said, jabbing him in the side with her elbow even though she knew he was kidding.

"The doors came out great," Kate said, reaching across to give her daughter a hug. "Thanks for doing them for me... and my wrists thank you too."

"Oh! I forgot the nail for the sign," Ben said. "I can do it before we-."

"Don't worry about it," Kate quickly replied. "I think I can handle that."

"Okay, then," Charlie said as she walked around the car. "We'll see you on Sunday."

"Drive safely."

Kate winced as Ben started the engine. Standing this close to the car, she had to agree with Matthew that it was quite loud. She waved as the car began to back up and continued to watch until the car was out of sight. Glancing across the street, she saw the curtain move so she knew somebody had been watching her. That made twice now that Lilly chose to stay inside and not say hello. In the back yard, Kate could hear the puppy beginning to bark and she turned to go to her.

Time to make that little alley girl something to eat.

Hey, that has a nice ring to it.

"Hi, Allie Girl!" Kate said, leaning over the closed gate to smile at the puppy. "Are you ready for some supper?"

CLOSING THE FRONT door softly behind her,

she crept across the small entryway toward the living room. As she peeked over the couch, she could see the puppy was still sound asleep on the cushions and breathed a sigh of relief. She had taken a risk by leaving her alone, especially after what happened the last time... but the crate was somewhere in the attic, and there was no way she was going up into that dark space tonight.

As soon as she named her, Kate knew she would be keeping the puppy. She also knew that she wouldn't be able to relax until the signs that she had put up earlier in the day had been taken down. She was hoping that Matthew would show up again before she left, but by the time the puppy fell asleep, he had still not turned up. Fortunately, having the dog spend most of her day outdoors had worked in Kate's favor and after feeding Allie Girl and making sure she had a chance to go back outside before she left, Kate didn't have to wait long for the tiny creature to curl up and fall asleep.

Slipping out of her shoes, she walked to the kitchen table and reached for the notepad. Tomorrow, she'd have to run back to the store again to grab more food now that she was staying, and she'd also have to think about what to make for Sunday's supper. She tried to concentrate on a meal plan, but looking up toward the ceiling, the thought of having to go up into the attic in the morning made her shiver. She hated climbing up into that space. The hatch was easy enough to open and the ladder was sturdy, but ever since she watched *The House On Sorority Row*, it had become Matt's responsibility to manage it.

"You're gonna have to get over it."

She looked over toward the fireplace to find him there again and leaned toward the right to scan the floor.

"What are you looking at?" he asked.

"Just checking."

He moved toward her. "Checking for what? She's asleep on the couch."

"Seeing if you brought anyone else home with you."

"Funny," he replied. "I see that you took the posters down. I guess you've decided to keep her then. I will admit... you held out longer than I thought you would."

He watched as she glanced up toward the ceiling before writing a few more things onto the paper in front of her. It had been harder than he thought watching her complete the task of painting the house without him. For the first time, he had also been happy that Charlotte had found a local boy to fall in love with and was still close to home. As she moved her face toward the light coming from the kitchen, he could see that her face had gotten some sun and he knew that within a few days, the tip of her nose would begin to peel.

"I would offer to help you in the attic, but

I haven't figured out how to get up there... it seems that I only have access to ground level activity."

"Don't you think that's strange?"

"You got me," he replied. "Hey, did you notice that Charlotte has started to show?"

"What?"

"Yeah, I noticed it when she came around the corner after talking with Lilly."

"She's showing? I missed it... ah, *dang* it," she replied. "I was so preoccupied with her asking about the store and what Lilly said... and with the painting, that it didn't even cross my mind that she could be showing already."

"How many months is she now?"

"Umm, let's see... the baby is due in December, so that would make her five months?" She put the pen down on the table. "I can't believe I missed it."

"You'll have plenty of opportunities to see it."

"That's true. They're coming back Sunday for supper." She picked up the pen again. "She wants to discuss the store and what my plans are."

"So, you've decided then?" he asked, needing to know the answer yet not wanting to hear her say the words.

"Not entirely, but I'm beginning to lean in one direction."

"And that direction would be?"

"I'm not prepared to say it out loud just yet."

"When do you th-."

From behind her, the phone began to ring. The song she chose as the ring tone gave away who the caller was, but after getting up, Kate looked at the clock hanging over the window in the kitchen.

Why is she calling so late?

"Hello... of course I'm at home... what's the matter... because it's after eight thirty there... you never call this late unless something is wrong... you're what... this Sunday like the day after tomorrow... no it's fine I just wasn't expecting you to come back so soon... I know you have your house to deal with... I didn't say that... I didn't say that either... of course you can stay with me... what time does your flight get in... no that's not too early I can pick you up... mom I can come and get you... okay fine take an Uber... I'm heading to the store in the morning so I can pick you up anything you need... just text me what you want before you go to bed tonight... I won't forget... I'm fine... everything is fine... they're fine too... I'll see you on... oh wait Charlotte and Ben are coming over for supper... yes on Sunday... no I haven't decided yet... I was working on that now... I don't need you to make supper... I don't need you to pay for delivery either... because I want to cook... okay have a safe flight and I'll see you on Sunday morning... you too... bye."

"Your mom's coming back... that'll be fun."

Kate looked over at him and rolled her eyes. She had already slipped once today when Charlotte showed up and she called out, *'we're in here'* and now her mother was going to be in the house all day with her.

"I forgot to tell her about the puppy."

Matt began to laugh. "I think the puppy will be the least of your worries."

Kate tried to ignore him and sat down to pick up the pen again, trying to focus on the list. Her mother was hopping on a plane and would be here the day after tomorrow. She could feel the muscles in her neck begin to tense even before she realized she had neglected to ask how long she planned on staying. If patterns with her mother were a clue, it would be a week or possibly two before Fiona packed up her bags again to head home.

Great.

"Hey, there *is* an upside to Fiona being here."

"What's that," Kate asked, closing her eyes, and taking a deep breath.

"Lilly will keep her distance."

He had a point. Lilly was scared to death of Fiona. "While that's true, Lilly has been keeping her distance ever since yesterday. The last few times I've been in the front, she has not even popped her head out to wave."

"She'll get over it." Hearing the puppy whimper, he moved over to the couch to have a peek. The puppy had spun around to change positions but was still zonked out. "My advice would be to take advantage of her leaving you alone... it won't last forever."

"I suppose you're right," she replied. "It is a little unnerving though, especially if I let myself think about what she might have told other people."

"So, what. If you decide to give up the lot, she will have done you a favor and got that rumor mill rolling... the sooner it starts, the sooner it stops. *If* on the other hand, you choose to rebuild, she'll be the one with egg on her face."

She hadn't thought about it that way, and of course he was right.

"You should make a roast for Sunday... easy one pot meal that everyone will enjoy."

She smiled at him and began to write down the items she would need at the store.

He was right again.

CHAPTER SEVEN

THE BLUE WATER of the Atlantic Ocean cooled her off immediately. After a long day of walking in ninety-degree weather exploring the shops and side streets admiring the beauty of the architecture from a different time, it felt good to end the day with the waves washing over her feet. After a few seconds, the cool ocean water soon turned into baby crabs snapping at her toes, but it was the real pain that she felt that pulled her out of the dream, and she woke up to Allie Girl biting her bare feet.

"And good morning to you."

It was a good thing she wasn't the type of person who liked to sleep in because it didn't appear that her new puppy would allow her to get away with it. Pushing back the covers, she grabbed Allie and placed her on the floor. She'd have to remember to push the ottoman closer to the bed tonight so she could get down by herself until she grew into her paws. If the old wives' tale proves to be true, before too long she'll be able to get up and down off the furniture all by herself just fine.

Pushing herself off the bed, she jammed her feet into her slippers and followed the path Allie had taken. She found her waiting at the patio door, her little tail flipping back and forth behind her, picking up speed as Kate approached. For such a young puppy, it was remarkable how well-behaved she was. After opening the door, Allie made her way toward the grass and rather than follow her, Kate decided starting the coffee was a better use of her time.

"You still going to go to the store this morning?" Matt asked, peeking his head in through the open patio door.

"That's the plan. Hey, would you keep an eye on her?" Kate asked. "I need to get caffeine into my system… that little monster spent half the night trying to tear into the pillows."

Matt turned to scan the yard and found the puppy sniffing the ground by the garage door. He was feeling a little bit of guilt. Perhaps, he should have stayed at the house last night to entertain the dog so Kate would have had a better night. After all, it had been his idea to force a puppy on her. Instead, the past few nights he had been leaving to roam the town taking a trip down memory lane. He didn't want to say anything to Kate, but yesterday morning he couldn't remember the name of the park that he played softball at two nights a week, and it had taken him several minutes to remember the way home.

He didn't understand exactly what was happening, but he assumed it wasn't good.

"Come on, puppy… let's go in the house."

Matt followed the little brown ball of fur as she bounced her way into the house. Once inside, he found Kate putting the cap on her travel mug and on the counter behind her, he noticed a new brand of coffee sitting on the counter.

"How is it?"

"How's what?" she asked, looking over the list a final time before heading out to the store.

"The new coffee?"

"Oh, it's not bad actually. Maybe it's all in my head, but your suggestion seemed to have worked."

My suggestion?

Picking up the list, she paused when she noticed the peculiar look on his face. "What's wrong?"

"Nothing... I was just thinking about what's going to happen tomorrow when your mother gets here."

"Oh, I don't want to talk about it," she replied, walking over to Allie Girl who was sitting next to her empty food bowl. "You behave... I'll be back in about thirty minutes, and I'll feed you then."

He moved toward the kitchen to clear the path she would be traveling to get to the front door and then followed behind her after she passed him. He couldn't shake the feeling that he had forgotten something again.

"Be back soon," she called out as she closed the door.

Rather than continuing to follow like he had been doing, he stayed inside and looked out the sidelight. He knew she'd be back but something about the way she left caused him to feel sad. Something was missing, something that would happen between them whenever the other left, but he couldn't sort out if he was *forgetting* what it was or if the moment itself had been lost. From behind him, Allie Girl began to whine. He moved to be next to her, but it only seemed to excite her more and she tried to jump up on him.

"I'm sorry," he said, stepping back, "but you heard her... you have to wait."

Outside, he heard a car pull into the driveway, but he wasn't concerned... he figured that Kate had come back because she forgot something. A few seconds later, he heard a knock at the door and Allie Girl began to bark.

Matthew began to move toward the door, but before he reached the entry way, he heard a key in the lock and froze. A moment later, Ava opened the door and peeked inside.

"Mom," she called out. Removing her key from the lock, she stepped inside the dark house and with laser focus, zoned in on the puppy. "A dog?"

The last thing she expected to see when she got home was a dog, let alone a puppy that was going to pull her mother's focus, energy, and time... everything that she *should* be investing in rebuilding the store. A distraction that served as an excuse to pull her time away from what she should be doing. Needed to be doing. *Actually...* when she thought about it, the last thing she expected to find after she opened the door was that her mother wouldn't be sitting at the kitchen table.

Stepping into the house, she flicked the lights on and sat her bag down on the back of the couch. It had been three weeks since the fire and the first thing she did when she got to town, was to drive by the store to see how much progress had been made. She was disappointed to see they were still clearing debris and even though it looked like they had no more than a few days' worth of work left, it should have already been completed by now.

It was obvious her mother was not pushing to get the job done.

Entering the kitchen, she noticed there was still coffee left in the pot and reached for a mug. Out of the corner of her eye, she saw a little face peeking at her from behind the couch.

"You better not pee on the floor."

The puppy whined and pulled her head back and even though she couldn't see the dog, she could tell by the noise that it had crawled under the couch to hide. After dumping the contents of a packet of sweetener into her mug, she walked to the table and took a seat.

And waited for her mother to return.

THE LAST THING Kate expected when she pulled into the driveway was to see Ava's red Jeep parked behind Matt's truck. The last text she had received from her had been four days ago and she hadn't mentioned anything about making the drive up from the City. Something was up. Her oldest daughter was not the type to jump in the car for no reason to visit her parents. Her days were typically planned out weeks in advance and Kate wasn't expecting to see her again until the holidays rolled around, *if* even then. Since she moved out, she only occasionally returned for the holidays and usually it was the day before that she made the decision if she was coming. Over the years, Kate learned to not ask about what her plans might be... if she showed up, she showed up.

Opening her door, Kate glanced toward the house before getting out of the car. While she was happy to see her daughter, she knew there had to be a specific reason that she chose to come by, and that the surprise visit would likely turn into a disagreement. Ava had a strong personality and in many ways was a female version of Matthew with one stark difference... she had always gone it alone whereas her dad was all about the family unit. By her second year in college, even Matt had given up trying to force her to be something she wasn't, but only because he knew she could stand on her own two feet.

As she pulled the final bag out of her trunk, she heard the front door open and looked up. Ava was standing in the doorway. She had a smile on her face, but her body language revealed that she needed to get something off her chest.

"Hi, there," Kate said, approaching the door with her arms full of grocery bags. "What a nice surprise."

Ava stepped out of the way to give her mother room to pass but did not offer to take any of the bags from her. She was surprised at how fresh and awake her mother looked so early in the morning. The last time she saw her, her face looked drawn and pale, and it was obvious that she had lost weight. Today, she looked almost normal.

"Let me put these bags down so I can give you a proper hug," Kate said, moving past her, being careful to not step on Allie Girl who had emerged at the sound of her voice. "Be careful, Allie... I can't see you and you're fixin' to get stepped on."

After setting the paper bags down on the kitchen table, she turned to look for her daughter who had closed the door but was taking her time walking back into the main part of the house. Kate didn't let her daughter's normal stifling mood bring down her spirits... she had too much to get done. Not only did she have to wash the clothes that had piled up over the last two weeks, but she had to get the guest room bedding washed so it was ready for Fiona. Not to mention, she had to get the lawn mowed, hang the sign on the porch all while chasing after an active puppy.

"It's good to see you," Kate said, putting her arms around her daughter and pulling her in for a hug. "Did you hit any traffic coming up?"

Kate released her daughter and stepped back to look at her. Her hair was shorter than it had been when she was here for the funeral and her face looked like she had gotten some sun. Ava had never been what you would describe as outdoorsy and the last time she remembered seeing any tan lines on her body was her junior year in high school when she worked as a camp counselor but only because it would boost her college applications.

"You look different... something has changed."

"Oh, I got my hair cut and colored since the last time you saw me," Ava replied nervously, reaching up to touch the back of her hair.

"I can see that, but that's not it," Kate replied.

"Well, other than my hair, everything is the same," Ava said, dismissing her mother to walk toward the table. "Something has definitely changed here, though... when did you decide to get another dog?"

As if on cue, Allie Girl began to jump up and down next to her empty food bowl. It was then that Kate remembered she was going to feed her when she returned from the store, and she went to the pantry to grab the bag of dog food.

"Sorry, puppy."

Ava rolled her eyes as her mother tended to the dog. With everything going on in her life, the last thing she needed was something else to be responsible for. "What made you decide to get a puppy?"

Standing up, Kate returned to the pantry before responding to her daughter. "It just sort of happened. She was found alone by the dumpster in the alley behind the store... and well, now she's here. I did put up posters to try and find if she belonged to anyone but didn't receive a single call."

"So, you've been to the store then?"

Here we go again.

Something about the way Ava asked if she had been to the store gave Kate the clue she needed as to why she was there. It was because of the store that she came... she had talked with

Charlotte.

"Have you been to the store?" Kate asked her daughter.

"Yes. As a matter of fact, I stopped there on my way to the house and was disappointed to see they were still clearing away the debris."

The debris.

She could feel her defense mechanism kick in as she begun to wall off her emotions to prevent herself from going too far with her words; a familiar reaction when Ava was around. Kate and her daughter were exact opposites. The debris that Ava so coldly spoke about were pieces of her life that had been burned and ripped down, only to be bulldozed into a pile to be carted away to the local dump. Pieces of her very being that she could never get back. Ava held onto nothing. Her apartment was void of any mementos from trips she had taken, awards she had worked hard for or even framed photographs of loved ones. The only attachment Ava had ever clung to, was her career.

"If you would have called me directly, *instead* of going around me to get information from your baby sister... I could have told you that the report from the inspector was just released the other day." Kate paused to wait for her daughter to look at her and stop pretending to care about what the puppy was doing. "Other than turning off the gas and the electricity, they couldn't begin to clear away what was left of the store until the inspector released the site."

"Yes, I talked with Charlotte, but I don't see why you have to make a big deal out of that."

"I'm not making a big deal out of it, Ava." Kate replied. "I'm just wondering why you didn't bother to pick up the phone and call me if you were interested in what was happening here? After all, whatever decision is made is my call."

Behind Ava, she could see Matthew emerge from the bedroom. If she had to guess, it was because he could hear that the tone of their conversation had moved from being a discussion into a confrontation.

"Charlotte mentioned something about that too... that you are thinking about not rebuilding. I don't understand your logic. Without that business, how are you going to support yourself?"

Kate wanted to believe that Ava's interest in her financial status was out of compassion, but she knew better. For Ava, it was all about the numbers and the status of being a business owner.

"I can support myself just fine. I'm not exactly destitute, Ava."

"I'm sure that Dad left a good amount of money in the bank, but you're still relatively young and whatever the number is... it won't go as far as you think it will."

Matthew could see in her face that Kate had moved past being defensive to being pissed off. But what troubled him even more were the words coming out of his oldest daughter's mouth. Listening to her, it sounded like she believed the store and their financial success had come from his actions and that her mother had been along as a passenger. She was so misguided in thinking that. Matthew may have opened the doors every day and been the face of the business in the community, but it was Kate working quietly behind the scenes who kept things running.

She managed the employee schedules, payroll and all the banking, kept track of and ordered all the inventory, organized the financials for tax filings, kept the computers and software up to date... she really did all the work that kept the doors open. She just didn't talk about it.

"You know, Ava... you *think* you know everything, but you don't, and I could say a few things right now to set you straight, but I won't. Instead, I'm going to remind you that I'm your mother and have managed to survive my entire adult life without your input or advice when it comes to your father's and my financial stability."

"You don't have to get defensive-."

"Oh, I'm not being defensive. I'm trying to stear this conversation away from turning into a fight. I have your sister and Ben coming tomorrow for supper and grandma is also flying in again and staying for *however* long... I just don't need this today."

Kate turned her back on her daughter to open the patio door so the puppy could go outside and mouthed to Matthew to please go outside with her. There wasn't anything he could do inside to help the situation and in fact if he started to chime in... she might just go off on them both.

"How about we change the subject," Kate suggested turning back around. "You haven't said anything about the new paint."

"What did you paint?"

"The house! The *entire* house."

Ava began to scan the room and even turned around in her chair to look behind her. "It looks the same as it did when I was here for dad's funeral."

"The *outside*, Ava," Kate said, as she walked back toward the table. "I spent the last week painting the trim, the shutters, the foundation, the siding, the doors. Well, technically, Charlotte painted the doors... why would I have painted the inside of the house when we just completed a total renovation?"

She looked at her daughter in amazement more so because of the blank stare she received in response than her failure to notice, and decided to drop it and change the subject once again.

"Let me get the puppy... I'll be right back."

She walked outside and waved off Matthew

who looked like he was about to say something. "Allie Girl, come on, time to go inside."

The puppy was busy trying to dig a hole by the fence and ignored her, so Kate walked over to pick her up. When she turned around, she saw Ava step outside onto the patio and then turn around to look the house.

At least she's making an effort.

As she approached her daughter, the puppy began to wiggle in her arms to get free and Kate placed her on the ground and watched her little brown butt disappear into the house. She stood next to her daughter and wondered how in the world they had grown so far apart. She couldn't even pinpoint when it happened. When she was first born, they had spent every waking moment of every day together. Kate and Matt didn't take vacations without her or even drop her off at Fiona's for a date night. Wherever Kate went, little Ava was with her. While she couldn't say exactly when things began to change, it was probably sometime after Jackson was born.

Ava would have just turned five around the time her little brother began to crawl, and Kate could remember having to shift much of her focus to the little boy that got into everything. He was a completely different experience from raising Ava. Where she would stay occupied for hours coloring or making clothing out of tissue for her dolls, Jackson had an attention span of about ten minutes on any activity.

"It looks good... I like the green trim."

Kate smiled as she sensed her daughter was attempting to lower the friction level between them. "That was your dad's choice... well, actually, he tried to convince me to paint the house *crimson and cream* but settled for what you see."

Ava chuckled at her mom's obvious attempt to mimic the way her dad used to refer to the colors of his favorite college football team. "I miss him."

For the first time in a long time, Kate felt genuine emotion coming from her daughter and it broke her heart that it was sadness. But she knew better than to make a big deal of it by hugging her or lingering on it... Ava would hate it and flip the switch again.

"Me too," Kate replied. "Hey, I haven't had breakfast yet and have bacon in the fridge I need to get rid of... can I interest you in some French toast?"

"If you make it extra crispy... I'm in."

"Extra crispy it is."

Kate followed her daughter into the house.

Behind her, Matthew watched the only woman he had ever loved and the child who made him a father work through a disagreement without him having to play mediator. His family was figuring it out and moving forward.

Smiling, he drifted toward the yard next door. The familiar landscape conjured up images of the older couple who lived there, but as he stared at the back of the house, he realized that he couldn't recall their name.

Wherever he was going next... the process had begun.

AFTER THE BREAKFAST dishes had been cleared from the table and Allie Girl had once again been given time to run around on the grass, Kate began to search the pantry for the long ago emptied glass baby jar now full of nails she knew was in there.

"What do you need a nail for?" Ava asked, pouring herself another cup of coffee.

"To hang the sign your father had made," Kate replied. "Grab it for me... it's on the mantle."

Ava walked into the living room; her focus pulled toward the polished piece of metal shaped like an egg that had been placed dead center above the fireplace. She reached out to touch the surface and was surprised by how cold it felt beneath her fingertips as she traced the engraved letters. *M.C.* Her mind told her that he wasn't there, but her heart whispered hello to him anyway. She had fought the urge to look at it when her mother carried it home with her the day of the funeral. It looked smaller than she imagined. Her father was seventy-six inches tall and had to duck his head when he walked through the office door at the store; how did he fit into a container no more than eight inches high?

"Did you find it?" Kate asked, walking out of the pantry holding the small glass jar in her hand.

"Yes," Ava replied quietly. "Dad ordered this?"

Kate walked over to the table and watched as Ava picked up the black sign and carefully lifted it over the urn. "He did... a few weeks before the accident. Do you like it?"

"I do," Ava said, handing it over to her mom. "Won't it feel strange... hanging it up now?"

"You know, I wondered the same thing the other day," Kate replied, a smile forming on her lips. "But I was reminded of something your dad once said to me, that this will still be known as the Chapman house long after we leave it."

"It does sound like something he would say," Ava replied, looking back toward the fireplace.

When her stare lingered, Kate looked over

her shoulder and found Matt standing there, staring back at his daughter. For a moment, she thought Ava could see him but a few seconds later, Ava turned and said she needed to get going.

"Well, I'm glad you decided to drive up this morning, and I'm sorry that it started off a little contentious."

"Me too," Ave replied. "And I don't want to start up again... really, I don't, but Charlotte did mention that you heard from Pete about the cause of the fire."

"I'm sure she did," Kate replied, placing the piece of stone carefully down on the table. "I suppose that she also revealed that I wasn't sure if I wanted to rebuild or not."

"She mentioned something about it."

"Pete said he'd buy me as much time as possible, which is why the cleanup took a bit longer than it probably should... but time runs out on Monday."

"You really don't know if you want to rebuild or not?" Ava asked.

"I really don't, but as soon as I decide I'll let you know."

"Well, maybe it's a good thing that Fiona is coming tomorrow. You can bounce your thoughts off her."

"I can't wait," Kate said, faking a smile and following her daughter as she walked toward the front door. "I'll text you a picture of the sign after

I've hung it up."

"I'd like that." Kate was surprised when her daughter was the first to lean in to embrace her. "Enjoy your visit with Fiona and remind Charlotte to decide on a day to come to the City."

"The City?" Kate asked, pulling back.

"She's coming down to look for a crib she saw in a magazine... I told her I'd help."

"That was nice of you... you should try and convince her to make a day of it and spend the night. I'm sure Ben wouldn't mind and soon enough her ability to get away will be limited."

"See ya, mom."

Kate waved and blew her daughter a kiss as she backed her Jeep out of the driveway. She continued to watch until her vehicle disappeared, waving to Ed across the street as he got into his own car. She looked to see if Lilly was also in the car, but the passenger seat was empty.

Allie Girl.

She quickly turned to look to see if her puppy had escaped through the open front door and when she didn't see her, she hurried inside to find her asleep in her bed under the coffee table in the living room.

Matt was still standing in front of the fireplace, and he smiled when he saw her.

"That ended much better than it started."

"Yes, it did," Kate replied, walking over to the table to pick up the sign. "I might as well get this hung up before I start on the laundry."

She glanced back at Matt, who remained where he was. "Any idea where the hammer might be? I couldn't find it in the garage."

She studied his face as he tried to remember the last time that he might have used it, but when he shook his head, no, she walked into the kitchen and opened the junk drawer. After pulling out a pair of plyers, she looked at him and smiled.

"Then this will have to do."

HE COULD HEAR her hammering on the porch, but he didn't go out with her to watch. He could remember pulling the hammer from the toolbox, but he couldn't remember where he had left it. And it was bothering him.

He tried to retrace the actions of his last few days in his mind. He was sure that was when he had used the hammer. Saturday after closing the store, he had made a run to the ball field to fix the netting that protected the stands behind home plate, but he hadn't needed the hammer for that. There next ballgame was the following Tuesday and he needed to make sure they didn't have a repeat of what happened the game before when a foul ball nearly hit the mayor in the head after it slipped through a frayed part of the net. After he finished that, he had stopped by Charlotte's house to drop off the paint fan deck she had asked for, but they hadn't been home, so he left it in a paper bag on her porch. On Sunday, he remembered pulling the final shutter off the house when Kate started yelling about the stepstool that he forgot to bring home. He had the hammer in his hand and the last place he put it was on the passenger seat.

It's in the truck.

He needed to tell Kate.

As he moved through the living room the porch door opened, and he stopped when he heard footsteps. A few seconds later, Kate emerged from the small mudroom with a smile that stretched across her face.

"I remembered where I put the hammer... you'll find it on the front seat of my truck."

"No longer necessary," she said, holding up the plyers and waving the tool in front of her. "I made do with this."

"How does it look?"

Pushing the junk drawer closed, she looked up, her expression soft with eyes that smiled back at him. "I love it." Rushing past him, she called out over her shoulder. "I have got to get started on the laundry, but you should go take a look at it."

Matthew stayed where he was. Sooner or later, he would find himself on the porch again and he'd see for himself how it looked, but for now he felt like he needed to rest and recharge his batteries. He didn't feel like he needed to sleep and knew that he couldn't physically do it, but still... he felt like he needed to be still. Retracing his path back to the fireplace, he positioned himself in front of the mantle. Somehow, being in this spot seemed to help when he felt like this. In the bedroom he could hear Kate as she wrestled with the hampers that had been pushed and stuffed well beyond their capacity.

Closing his eyes, he focused on the house next door and tried to remember the name of his neighbors.

AFTER PUTTING THE final load of bath towels into the dryer, she grabbed the wicker basket on top of the washer and maneuvered through the narrow doorway of the mud room toward the kitchen table. She didn't have to look for Allie

Girl because she could hear her munching away at her food bowl. Kate knew she was starting her off with bad habits by keeping food in the bowl almost all the time, but she didn't care. That bowl full of brown nuggets was helping to maintain her sanity by keeping the puppy occupied so she could get her work done. Her mother would be annoyed enough finding a dog in the house so everything else had to be perfect.

She had cleaned up the guest room which still had left-over knickknacks peppering the room from when Charlotte had occupied it. Fortunately, she had found a few empty cardboard boxes in the garage that she was able to use to pack away the last of the CDs, stuffed animals, books, and shoes she found after she opened the closet. Those boxes along with the brown suitcase full of clothing her youngest daughter had decided to leave when she moved out were now neatly stacked by the front door. Tomorrow when Charlotte came over for supper, she could take the pile of stuff home with her and decide for herself what she wanted to keep, donate, or toss. The room actually looked fresh and inviting by the time she was finished with it. The final touch of moving the round cream faux fur rug originally purchased for the master bathroom into the room had completed the vision she was going for.

After reaching into the basket, she held her breath. Even without the benefit of seeing the article of clothing, she knew what it was. Her chest tightened as tears brimmed her eyes and as the first tear spilled over and rolled down her cheek, she turned to look out beyond the closed screen door into the yard. Closing her eyes, she could feel more tears trail down her face as she tried to focus on the fragrance in the room, the next task needing to be completed, the vet appointment she had to make for Allie Girl... *anything* to pull her focus from what she was holding in her hand.

"What's wrong?"

"Nothing is wrong," she replied, opening her eyes as she pulled the gray plaid pajama bottoms from the basket.

"I'm sorry."

"What about exactly?" she asked, her voice barely above a whisper.

"I forgot they were in there."

She hadn't noticed them before when she was loading up the washer and honestly wasn't expecting to find any of Matthew's clothing at all. Saturday was wash day and the day before he died had been no different. When he got home their last evening together, he was sweaty and gross from fixing the net at the field and it had been later than usual when they finally sat down together to eat. He was supposed to pick up hamburgers on his way home but forgot, and rather than delay eating any further, while he showered, she put a frozen pizza into the oven and the last load of laundry that included what he had been wearing into the washer.

They had spent their last night together, watching Netflix and eating pizza.

"Are you thinking what I'm thinking?" he asked.

"That I need a drink," she replied, picking up the folded clothing to return it to the basket.

"Not quite," he replied. "But don't you find it strange that we spent our first and *last* night in this house eating the same thing."

She couldn't find the words to respond. She was afraid that if she said too much, the dam that so far had only sprung a leak would break open, and she needed a few more minutes to patch up the holes.

"Is there any-."

She shook her head and closed her eyes, and he stopped. She had been so strong over the past week that the reaction she was displaying seemed to come out of nowhere and he was reminded of how fragile emotions could be for the living. While his emotions had remained flatlined since returning, he struggled to find the balance in communicating with his wife who was still clearly riding the rollercoaster. He should be able to help her more than he was, but so far had failed at putting together the winning combination of thoughts into words.

Kate walked to the refrigerator and opened the door finding the spot where she kept the wine empty. The bag full of wine and a bottle of whiskey was still sitting on the floor in the pantry. She glanced at the case of beer pushed to the back of the fridge and sighed. She just couldn't do it. Beer was Matthew's thing and no matter how many times she tried to acquire the taste, he always ended up finishing her beer along with a few of his own. Closing the door to the fridge, she walked to the pantry and initially grabbed one bottle but before she left the room, she spun around and picked up another. Fiona was coming tomorrow, and Kate anticipated she would be needing the extra bottle and was going to be ready.

He observed her fill the wine glass half full and then drink a significant portion of the liquid in one gulp, only to fill the glass again. Even then, she didn't move from the spot but stood there tapping her fingers on the counter staring at the bottle in front of her.

"Did you want me to do anything in particular with your clothes?"

He waited for her to turn and look at him before he replied. "I don't think you should hang onto them, if that's what you're asking."

"Don't take this the wrong way... but I wasn't going to."

"Ask me?"

"No," she replied. "Well, yes... I guess." She set her glass down on the counter. "My point is, neither one of us would have imagined a scenario where the other comes back and we could have a discussion like we're having now. I have to let Allie out... come on, let's continue this on the patio."

Picking up the glass of wine, she walked to the door and pushed the screen door open. After Allie Girl bolted out in front of her, she stepped out and walked over to the bench on the other side of the planters so she could sit and keep an eye on her. She glanced back and saw that he had followed, so she waited until he was next to her before she continued her thought.

"Number one, when we added the main bedroom, we didn't plan out the best use of the space. And number two, most of your clothes are in excellent condition and the church or even Goodwill would really benefit from having them donated."

They were all good points.

When they met with the architect to draw up the plans for the remodel, a walk-in closet hadn't made the wish list. Kate had wanted to use the extra space in the corner of the room as an open sitting area; a place she could go to escape when Pete was over watching whatever game happened to be playing. But at the last minute, Matt had thrown out the idea to use the space instead as a walk-in. She ultimately gave in because she was gaining the sunroom but after the framing and drywall were up, it become apparent that the new closet space was going to be a tight fit for two people to share. But it was too late to turn back, and Kate settled for a chair in the corner by her side of the bed and a dresser for her clothes that wouldn't fit in the closet.

He also agreed that donating his clothing was a good idea and something he should have done himself some time ago. In addition to what was in their bedroom, he had at least six boxes and bags full of jeans, cargo shorts, shoes, winter coats, and jackets stored up in the attic.

"I agree," he replied. "Have a garage sale or donate it all."

"A garage sale? No thank you," she replied. Just the thought of people she knew poking through the pieces of their lives sent a shiver up her spine. "Victoria is coming home for the fourth... I'm sure she'll help me sort through everything."

In the distance, Matt could hear that a train was approaching, and he turned toward Allie to watch her reaction. The first short burst of the whistle got her attention and she sat up in the grass and cocked her head to the side, looking at him. When the second, longer whistle sounded, she threw her head back and howled at the sky.

Just like Birdie.

"Good girl!" he shouted above the whistles.

"Oh my, *God.*" Kate said, walking over toward the puppy to grab her. "Don't encourage her."

He was still laughing as he followed Kate

into the house.

CHAPTER EIGHT

THE NEXT MORNING, Allie Girl had already figured out that the ottoman pushed toward the bed was meant for her. Unfortunately, by the time Kate pushed herself to her feet and made her way to the kitchen, there was a puddle in front of the sliding door and the puppy was hiding under the couch. After grabbing a handful of paper towels from the kitchen, she pulled the patio door open as she cleaned up the mess and watched as Allie Girl tried to squeeze herself out from the now tight space.

"It's okay, you can go out." She looked over at the puppy who sat down three feet in front of her. "Don't look at me like that. I know this was my fault and I'm cleaning it up, but you have to promise to not make a habit out of this." The puppy whined and laid down, placing her head on her paws. "Aww, come on... it's not that bad," Kate said, standing up. "Let's get you breakfast."

She didn't turn back to look for Matt. The last few days, he had been disappearing more than he was staying put and while she could tell that something was on his mind, she didn't press him to get it off his chest. If he wanted to talk about what might be on his mind, he knew where to find her. Before she fed the dog, she started a pot of coffee. Fiona would be here in less than three hours and Kate needed to get moving.

As she was finishing putting food into Allie's bowl, her phone rang but by the time she ran to the bedroom to pick it up, the call had gone to voicemail. Looking at the recent call log, she was surprised to see the call was from Fiona. But before she could push the right buttons on her phone to get to the message, the doorbell rang, and the puppy began to bark.

"Who in the world," Kate whispered as she left the bedroom, still trying to access the message on her phone. "Allie! No bark."

The voicemail finally began to play when she reached the door, but as soon as she opened it, she let her arm drop to her side without listening to the complete message.

"Did you just get out of bed?"

"Mother, what are you doing here?"

"What am I doing here... you knew I was coming," Fiona replied as she turned around to tip the Uber driver who had removed the very large bag from the back of his van.

"Yes, but your flight wasn't supposed to land until eleven."

"I know, but I caught an earlier flight... I left you a message."

"Thirty seconds before you knocked on my door," Kate replied, stepping aside so her mother could enter the house.

She stood on the front porch and watched the Uber driver return to his van and back out of the driveway, and after he disappeared her focus turned to the large bag he had left at her door; her mother would be staying longer than she thought. By the time Kate had drug the heavy suitcase into the front hallway, her mother had helped herself to coffee and was making herself some toast.

"Mom, why are you here so early?"

"You're making something out of nothing," Fiona replied as she reached into the refrigerator to grab the butter.

"The drawer to your left."

"Thank you," Fiona replied, pulling the drawer open and removing a butterknife. "I always forget where everything is."

"*That* drawer has been the silverware drawer for thirty years, mother."

"Well, get in here and make yourself a cup of coffee... there's room for both of us and I'm almost done."

Kate remained where she was, waiting for her mom to finish buttering her toast before she moved from her spot next to the luggage. While she had hoped to have a few more hours of peace and quiet to psych herself up, there was nothing she could do about it now and walked to the kitchen to reach for her mug.

"We could sit in the sunroom if you prefer."

"Doesn't that room get sun in the

afternoon?" Fiona asked, taking a sip from her cup.

"Yes," Kate replied.

"Then, what's the difference between this table or the one over there?"

"The view, we could look out into the yard."

"I can see the yard from here," Fiona pointed out, looking through the glass patio door to her right. "Get your coffee and come have a seat."

Kate could see the puppy's tail sticking out from underneath the couch, but she didn't think that her mother had noticed the bowls on the other side of the patio door, yet. She was not looking forward to the conversation about her getting another dog. Fiona was not a fan of having pets in the house. When Kate was six, she had found a stray kitten and while her mother had let her keep it, it was not allowed in the house. On cold nights, though, Kate would sneak it into her bedroom through the window and that routine went on for years. But, when Kate was eleven, the cat disappeared and she never found out what happened to it.

"So, what made you change your flight?" Kate asked, joining her mother at the table.

"I actually changed it right after we got off the phone," Fiona replied. "My neighbor stopped by to inform me that she was having her carpets replaced. She apologized in advance for the disruption, and I arrived yesterday evening and stayed at a hotel in the City until this morning."

"You've been here since yesterday?" Kate asked, placing her mug on the table. "Why on earth didn't you tell me? I would have come and picked you up."

"It's really no trouble. Besides, I figured that you would need the extra time to get my room ready... did you?"

"Get it ready?" Kate asked. "Yes, your room is ready, mother."

"See, it all worked out then."

Kate picked up her mug to take a drink as a soft whine could be heard coming from the living room.

"You should let that dog out before it *shits* on your floor."

Kate set her coffee down and got up from her chair. She should have known she hadn't fooled her mother. She always seemed to know everything.

"Come on, Allie Girl... let's show *grandma* how you can go potty outside."

A FEW HOURS later, Fiona was almost settled into the room she would be staying in for the length of her visit. Kate had managed to fit the large suitcase into the closet by moving a few things around. Initially, Fiona had argued against the idea of having her go through the extra trouble to find a place for her luggage; she thought it would be fine placed along the wall with the window. But Kate knew that within two days, her mother would be complaining about being crowded in the ten by twelve room and had pushed back. In the end, it had worked out; the suitcase was out of the way and Fiona had the space she needed.

"Here," Kate said, returning to the room. "I got these extra hangers for you."

"You didn't have to do that."

"Just use them," Kate replied, placing the hangers on the bed. "If you are able to hang up everything, I won't have to hear about your wrinkled clothing."

"You have an iron, don't you?"

"Yes, mother" Kate replied. "Do you want me to bring the ironing board in here? You're welcome to use it and there's room now that we have your suitcase out of the way."

"Oh, just open the hangers for me."

Kate knew her mother would stop arguing as soon as she made it clear that any ironing that needed to be done would not be done by her. "There you go." After opening the second packet of hangers, Kate walked toward the door. "I'll leave you alone so you can finish."

Walking out of the room she found Allie Girl sitting at the end of the short hallway. She had been keeping her distance from Fiona, almost as if she could sense that her mom would never be interested in rubbing her belly.

"I wouldn't," Kate said, looking down at the puppy as she passed her.

Seeming to agree, Allie Girl scampered after her until veering off when she caught sight of her favorite chew toy under the table in the sunroom. When Kate heard the familiar *squeak, squeak, squeak*, she paused for a moment to turn back and look down the hallway toward the room her mother occupied.

She'll just have to deal.

Glancing at the clock, it was already nine-thirty, but still too early to start on the pot roast. Charlotte was coming over around three so they could discuss the truck, but everyone had already agreed that supper would be ready at five. *Dessert.* She had bought a bag of Granny Smith apples and it wasn't until she got home and was putting away groceries that she realized what she had done. They hadn't been on the list, but out of habit she had picked them up anyway. She only liked the tart taste of that particular apple in a pie, but Matt used to take two with him to the store every day as a snack. As he was on her mind, she glanced over toward the fireplace, but he wasn't there.

Maybe he's in the yard?

Pausing to look out the patio door, she craned her neck first left and then right to scan the area, but he wasn't there either. He had been disappearing a lot lately and although she didn't want to draw attention to it, the fact that she was thinking about where he was going made her feel like she was going to have to. But it would be more difficult to have a conversation with him, now that her mother was there.

"What are you looking at?"

Kate jumped. "*Jesus*, mother."

"Is somebody out there?"

"No, nobody is out there... I was just looking at the yard."

"Is there any more coffee?" Fiona asked.

"No, but I can make some. I was thinking about making an apple pie for dessert too."

Fiona glanced at the little dog who remained in the sunroom under the table. When she bared her teeth and pretended to growl, Allie Girl whined and moved to hide behind the thick wood pedestal.

"When did you get the dog?" Fiona asked as she pulled a chair out from under the kitchen table.

At least she didn't ask where.

"A few days ago... she actually is really well behaved."

"That's hard to tell. She always seems to be hiding. And what do you call her?"

"Allie Girl," Kate replied. "One cup or do you

think you'll end up drinking more?"

"Oh, *for Christ's* sake, Kate... just make a full pot," Fiona replied. "I'll never understand how your generation became so hung up on making *just enough coffee.* In my day we didn't worry about left over coffee... it sat on the stove until the next time we were ready to drink it."

Kate turned toward the coffee maker and rolled her eyes. "I know, I know... you had far worse things to worry about."

"Well, that's true," Fiona replied. "I was twelve before my father could get the right equipment out to the farm to dig a proper well close to the house. When we needed water, we didn't just turn on a fancy faucet like the one you're standing in front of... we *walked* almost a mile each way to the creek and prayed for rain."

"I know, mother."

"And *God* forbid you had a sick child... you couldn't just call up the doctor and make an appointment that same day or have a consultation over the computer screen or your phone, like you can now."

"You're right, we have it a lot easier than when you were younger."

Biting her tongue, Kate didn't say anything else. Her mother had a war chest full of stories to pull from and she would never win in a game of who had it tougher. She didn't want to fight. All she wanted to do was make a pie.

"Coffee should be ready in a few minutes.

Oh, and I picked up the items you texted me, so if you're ready for dinner you'll find everything you need in the refrigerator."

"Everything?" Fiona asked.

"*That's* in the pantry."

"Thank you," Fiona replied. "The next time you go to the store, I think I'd like to go with you. I haven't been inside for years... I imagine it has changed quite a bit. Do they still make their own baked goods?"

"No, the bakery closed years ago after Mrs. Prescott had a heart attack, and I guess they never trained anyone else.

"Where do they get their breads and pies from then?"

"I guess they just truck it in from the City, like everything else. I don't *think* they make anything onsite anymore."

"What a shame, but it's probably more likely that she *wouldn't* train anyone... *God* forbid she should share her precious recipes with anyone."

"She was a good baker," Kate replied.

"Yes, she was."

"The coffee's ready, mother."

THE SMELL COMING from the kitchen and moving into each room of the house conjured up the image of falling leaves even though outside the temperature would be reaching into the upper eighties. Kate removed the pie from the oven and walked over to the closed patio door.

"Come on, Allie Girl, time for you to take a spin around the yard."

As soon as she stepped outside it felt like she hit a wall of humidity as she walked toward the grass. The wind had picked up considerably from this morning and must have brought the moist air with it. Or maybe it had attached itself to Fiona and followed her from Florida... either way, there was no way they would be eating supper on the patio.

"How is your visit going?"

She looked behind her to find Matt moving toward her from the direction of the open patio door. Wondering where he came from, she decided to wait until he was standing next to her before she replied just in case Fiona had woken up from her nap and was spying on her from a window.

"Better than I expected, if I'm being honest." She kept her focus on the grass and what Allie

Girl was doing. "Where have you been?"

It was the first time she had questioned his comings and goings since he returned but he didn't know how to explain his movements either. Sometimes he left because he remembered a part of town that he wanted to see again but other times he could feel that he was just *gone*, but he didn't know where he was. Those times reminded him of the void he remembered in the days after his death... before he found himself standing in front of the fireplace.

So, he lied. Now wasn't the time to get into what he felt would be a deeper discussion.

"Just around... exploring my old haunts." He turned to smile at her, feeling quite clever with his wording.

"Have you been by the store again?" she asked.

"There and the ball field, town hall, the high school."

"Well, I have to get back inside... Charlotte and Ben will be here in a few hours, and I need to get the pot roast into the oven."

"I can keep an eye on the puppy if you want to leave her out here for a bit."

"Works for me," she replied. "Fiona will be up from her nap soon and I'd rather have Allie out here than hiding under a table."

"Smart dog," he replied, looking at the puppy trying to eat the grass.

He turned around and watched how the hair bounced off her shoulders as she walked back to the house. It was longer than she had worn it in a long time, and he wondered if she had decided to grow it out or simply was avoiding getting back out into their community. Other than her trips to the grocery store, she hadn't yet resumed her other activities. Although that wasn't being fair... other than the shelter, most of her usual activities involved work at the store.

It was harder for him to keep track of time since he returned. But when he combined the days surrounding his death and the funeral and added them together with how long she spent painting the house... he believed that Kate had almost used up the time she had taken off from the shelter. They would be needing her back even if it were only a few hours a day and he believed it would provide the perfect gateway for her to get back out there. He hoped that she came to realize this on her own... his days of pushing and pulling her, sometimes kicking and screaming, were numbered. Inside the house, he could hear Fiona was awake and complaining that Kate had let her sleep for too long. He had known her his entire life and while she had convinced nearly everyone else that she was a bully, he had figured out long ago that it was all an act.

A defense mechanism to keep her from getting hurt.

She had been married four times, but he didn't believe she had ever gotten over the death of Kate's father. While it had forced her to take on the role of breadwinner when most women were still in the kitchen and raising children, it also forced herself to build a wall around her *and* her daughter to keep them safe.

And it had been fate that he came along at just the right moment to sneak inside the walls.

The summer before seventh grade, he had been out early in the morning having just finished delivering the morning newspapers like he did every day for as long as he could remember. But this morning would turn out different from the others. He came around corner on his bike to find Kate's mother kneeling on the sidewalk behind her car. He back pedaled to decrease his speed and as he passed the car, he saw the lifeless body of Kate's calico cat lying on the gravel in front of her. Kate's mother had always looked mean and scary, and Matthew had kept his distance. But that morning, he witnessed the tears streaming down her face and she looked helpless. After laying his bicycle down in the curb, he walked over toward her and got down on his hands and knees. Even before he put his ear on the cat's belly, he knew she was dead, but he did it anyway.

Somehow, he knew it would help Kate's mother accept what had happened.

Without saying a word, he carefully picked

up the cat and carried her body back to his bicycle where he gently lowered the body into the empty basket that had been bolted over the bumper of his rear wheel. As he was lifting his bicycle off the ground, Kate's mother walked over to him and laid her hand on his shoulder before reaching up and removing the black scarf she had tied around her head. He watched as she gently folded the scarf around the cat, covering the exposed fur the best she could before walking back to her car. She sat there for a moment before turning on the engine and backing out of the driveway, but as she drove past him, her eyes remained focused on the road, whereas his eyes remained locked on her as she continued down the street without looking back.

Not even once.

After making sure that the cat was secure in the basket, he rode his bicycle back to his house where he buried Kate's beloved calico cat in the ground below his tree house. From that moment on, the scary woman who lived up the street from him was no longer so scary and a few years later when he began to date Kate, she tolerated his presence. He never told Kate about the bond they shared; the *never to be spoken of* partnership to spare her pain.

But it had been his way in.

The puppy began to growl, and Matthew turned around to find Fiona staring back at him in the open doorway.

"Come in dog, before you get left out there for the rest of the day."

"Trust me, she means it," Matthew whispered to Allie Girl. *"Come on, let's go in."*

MAKING TIME FOR a quick shower, Kate slipped into the most comfortable cotton dress she owned. She needed something easy. Something that wouldn't feel like it pinched, pulled, or constricted her. She was already feeling enough pressure from her life and decisions that would need to be made. Today she needed a break from even her clothing... *and* the humidity.

It had crept into the house and wasn't helping.

"Is that the dress you bought in the park?"

As she hung up her wet towel, she smiled as the snapshots from her memory flipped through that day. They had spent the morning visiting a cemetery just a short walk from Bourbon Street, strolling through row after row of wall vaults, tombs and ground graves with ornate statues and wrought iron as far as the eye could see. On their way back to the hotel, they stopped off to look through the vendors offering handmade goodies as families, friends and couples claimed their spot on the grass for the start of the weekend Blues and BBQ festival.

"It is," she replied. "That was a good weekend, but as I recall... you hurried me through the vendor tents so you could get over to sample the BBQ."

"As I recall... I didn't have to pull you too hard."

She laughed as he moved to the side so she could pass by him. "You got-."

"Kate," her mother asked, knocking on the door, "who are you talking to?"

Her eyes grew wide but instead of feeling fear, she covered her mouth to stop herself from laughing. She had forgotten that her mother was sitting in the living room just on the other side of her closed door.

"Nobody," Kate said, reaching for her phone on the bed. "You can come in."

Kate pretended to close a video on her phone and smiled at her mother who came into the room, her eyes darting around not believing that her daughter was alone.

"I heard voices in here."

"Just watching a video," Kate replied, letting her phone drop to the bed. "Did you take your bath already?"

"No, I decided to wait until after supper," Fiona replied, walking farther into the room to have a peek inside the bathroom. "I'm hoping it will help me relax before bed."

"I think that you'll find the bed comfortable," Kate replied. "The mattress is the same brand you have at your condo in Florida."

Spinning around, Fiona stared at her daughter. "Now, how could you possibly know that?"

"Matthew ordered that bed for you... remember?" Her mother still looked puzzled. "Before you moved, he took you to the furniture store in the City and helped you pick out all the pieces for your new place. Don't you rem-."

"I remember, just fine." Fiona replied as she walked back toward the bedroom door. "What I'm wondering is why *you* have the same mattress?"

"Well," Kate replied as she stood up and reached for her phone, "after Charlotte moved out and we made the decision to turn the room into a guest room... you were the person we had in mind. So, we ordered the same mattress."

"Really? How come you never told me before?"

"I never thought about it until now," Kate replied. "And since you are staying for a while... I thought maybe, even if it's only psychologically, it would help you knowing we had your comfort in mind."

"Well, I appreciate that," Fiona replied, as she turned to leave the room. "You can really smell that pot roast now... it'll be ready in an hour."

Kate looked at her phone. "My timer says ninety minutes."

"Mark my words," her mother replied. "When you start to smell the pot roast, you got an hour to set the table, get the bread ready, and clean up any dishes still in the sink."

"Okay, mother."

Behind her, she could hear Matthew burst into laughter and she looked back at him, rolling her eyes but made a mental note to check the pot roast in thirty minutes, just in case.

"Looks like your dog had to go out again," Fiona said as she walked into the living room.

"Why do you say that?"

Kate looked to her right as her mother pointed toward the oblong-shaped puddle on the floor in front of the patio door.

"Allie Girl!"

She hurried into the kitchen to grab a handful of paper towels as her mom moved out of her way and took a seat on the couch. "What time is Charlotte and her husband coming?"

"Should be any time now," Kate replied as she cleaned up the pale-yellow liquid. "Ben, mother... her husband's name is Ben."

"I'm aware of that," Fiona said, reaching forward to grab a magazine off the coffee table. "Are you aware that he is the only *husband* left in the family?"

As Kate turned to look at her, the doorbell

rang and a moment later, a smiling Charlotte opened the door.

"*Oh*, it smells wonderful in here!" she exclaimed, leaving the door open as she walked forward to greet her mother. "Hi, mom."

"Grandma is here too," Kate replied, giving her daughter a quick hug, and nodding her head toward the living room.

"Fiona!"

Kate waved to Ben and watched her youngest child maneuver around the furniture to get to her grandmother. After a short embrace, her mother stepped back to look at her youngest granddaughter who most resembled Kate as a child. "Why you're beginning to show!"

Charlotte stepped back and smiled, putting her hands on her lower abdomen. "Just a little."

"Enough that you should think about shopping for some maternity outfits," Fiona replied.

"Mother, women don't try to hide it like they used to," Kate replied. "A pregnant woman's body is beautiful."

"Oh, my *God*," Fiona replied, a horrified look on her face. "Tell me you aren't going to be one of those women who take naked pictures are you?"

"Probably not, grandma," Charlotte laughed. "But if I do, it wouldn't pictures that I share with anyone except for Ben."

Desperately wanting to change the subject, Kate moved her daughter toward the kitchen.

"Look, there's even a pie for dessert."

"You made a pie?" Charlotte asked. "Oh, I can't wait."

"It's good to see you finally excited about food again," Kate replied.

"Morning sickness was no joke and that syrup they had me take was so gross... even if I could eat, I didn't want to."

"I'm just glad you seem to be past it now," Ben said as he came behind her, placing his hands on the top of her shoulders.

"Then why did you complain when I asked you to go get me some *Doritos* last night?" she asked playfully.

"Because it was ten o'clock and I had one foot under the covers!" he replied. "But I did it, didn't I?"

"Yes, you did." She leaned back and puckered her lips to invite a kiss.

They are so cute.

Kate noticed Allie Girl peeking out from behind the couch to investigate the new people who had invaded her space. She could see her little tale moving a hundred miles an hour and called for the puppy to come out of hiding.

"It looks like someone else wants to say hello," Kate said, stepping toward the couch.

Charlotte turned to scan the floor, spotting the dog slowly edging her way out into the open. "You decided to keep her, huh?"

"Nobody called, so I didn't really have a

choice... right, Allie Girl?"

"I like the name... it fits." Charlotte sat cross-legged on the floor and called for the puppy who immediately ran up to her and climbed on her lap. "Are you being a good girl?"

"Careful she doesn't pee on you," Fiona said, as she pulled a chair out from under the kitchen table.

"Grandma, why would you say that?" Charlotte asked, laughing as she lifted her chin in the air as the puppy jumped at her face. "You're a good girl, aren't you, Allie Girl."

"Does anyone want or *need* anything to drink?" Kate asked. "I have iced tea, beer and wine if anyone is interested."

"I'll take a whiskey Coke," Fiona shouted out.

Charlotte laughed again at her grandmother's words. She definitely marched to the beat of her own band. For as long as she could remember, her grandmother's free spirit that occasionally bordered on being raunchy and inappropriate intrigued her. By the time Charlotte came along, her grandmother had already begun to step away from the store and out of her four grandchildren, it was Charlotte who spent the most time with her. But Fiona would be the first to point out she should not be considered a babysitter. She would make sure the child didn't die and that was about the only commitment she would make when Kate had no choice but to leave her youngest child in the care of her mother.

By the time Charlotte started school, Kate had begun to volunteer at the shelter early in the morning before the store opened, and on mornings when Matt wanted to get in some sunrise fishing trips, Fiona would come over to the house to make sure her youngest child was dressed and dropped off at school. It was those days that Charlotte would point to that sparked her unique sense of style. Fiona would let her wear whatever she wanted, but she drew the line at letting Charlotte pull dirty clothing out of the hamper.

To this day, Charlotte was usually ahead of trends, wearing fashionable items of clothing that she found at thrift stores or garage sales and redesigning and tailoring them to fit her small frame. Her unique perspective and love for fashion was the primary reason Kate had been so disappointed when Charlotte decided not to go to college but to get married as soon as she graduated. Last summer, she made a custom, sleeveless wedding dress and veil for Ben's sister that had been fashioned out of some white curtains and a white pool pull-over they found at a mall in the City. The bride-to-be had requested something simple that was made from repurposed material, without a lot of frills... and something she could afford. What she got was a beautiful, one-of-a-kind gown that kept her smiling the entire day and most of the women asking where she bought it. From that day on, Charlotte had enough work to keep her as busy as she wanted to be.

"Here you go, mother," Kate said, setting the drink with ice that her mother requested in front of her.

"Charlie, can I get you anything?"

"No thanks. But is now a good time to talk about the truck?"

"Sure," Kate replied. "Did you make a decision?"

"Well... we've talked about it and as long as you're okay with us trading it in for something that'll work for our growing family," Charlotte said, reaching to grab Ben's hand, "we would love to have dad's truck... it would help us a lot."

"Oh, hunny," Kate replied, holding back the tears. "Like I said before... I don't expect you to keep the truck. That was your dad's vehicle, his style... and I'm sure if he could be standing here," she paused to look over toward the fireplace, "he would be saying the same thing."

"Are you sure though? Dad really loved that truck."

"But he has no use for it anymore." Fiona watched as her daughter turned to look at her, shaking her head. "Why are you looking at me like that? I *support* your decision to give Charlotte the truck and her decision to trade it in for something else."

"Have you found a vehicle that you want?" Kate asked, returning her attention back to her daughter and son-in-law.

"Not yet... but if we could keep the truck here until we do? I don't want-."

"That'll be fine. Tomorrow, I'll find the title and we can go downtown and have that taken care of so when you're ready for it, all I'll have to do is hand you the keys."

"Since we're talking about things that move us forward... have you decided yet, what you're going to do about the store?"

Kate scanned the faces that were intently looking back at her waiting to hear her decision. "I *have* decided, but I want to sleep on it one more night... just to make sure I feel the same way in the morning."

"When do you meet with Pete again?" Ben asked.

"It's not Pete I have to meet with. His job is done now that the inspector has submitted his findings." Kate walked over to the counter to finish pouring herself a glass of wine. "Tuesday, I have to go down and talk with the mayor... and probably the rest of the town council."

"Wait, you heard back from the fire inspector?" Fiona asked, surprised to hear she seemed to be the only one not be up to date on the latest developments.

Kate spent a few minutes, telling her mom what happened the day Pete stopped by. Her mother had actually taken it better than she thought, considering she had spent more time building the store than she had raising her own daughter.

"I think it's good that you are being forced to make a decision and I'm willing to keep my opinions to myself until you tell us what you're thinking... but then I can't promise that I won't speak my mind, even if it hurts your feelings."

"Mom, since we're all here, can you at least give us a hint which way you're leaning?" Charlotte asked.

"Nope, I want to sleep on it first."

And speak with your father.

The timer that she had set earlier on her phone to double check the pot roast according to Fiona's timeline went off, and she got up and went to the oven. As soon as she lifted the cast iron lid, she could tell that her mother had been right... supper was done.

After turning off the oven, she called out to the group. "Who's ready to eat?"

HANDING THE BAG of leftovers to Ben as he got into their car, Kate waved at them until she could no longer see the vehicle as the dark street swallowed up the red taillights. Walking into the house, she thought about the day and how it had started out so nuts by the early appearance of her mother but ended quiet... *almost* making her feel like things were getting back to normal. Matthew had hung around longer than she thought he would, but it hadn't escaped her that he had been staying in front of the mantle much more than usual.

When her mother went to bed, she'd have to ask him what was going on.

As she passed the red truck, a positive feeling washed over her reinforcing that she had made the right decision in parting with it. When she got to the bumper, she walked around the front of the truck and opened the passenger door. Feeling around in the dark, she smiled when her hands touched the leather handle of what she was searching for. Matthew had been right again. Backing away from the truck, she closed the door and carried the hammer into the house. It was as she closed the door to the pantry, that she heard the familiar sound of her mother's slippers shuffling across the wood floor.

"Ready for your bath?"

"Just about," Fiona said as she moved across the living room to the kitchen island. "I wanted to ask what time you were going to town hall tomorrow?"

"Why?"

"Well, two reasons." Fiona placed her hands flat on the counter and met her daughter's stare. "I need to speak with that woman from the social services office about their plans for my house, and two... I want to be there when you discuss your plans."

"Mom, I don't need you to hold my hand."

"That's not the reason I'm going." Fiona replied matter of factly. "I want to be there because I've been there from the beginning... and whether you choose to give up the space or fight to keep it, I want to be there for that too."

"Mom, I wouldn't have to fight to keep it... *if* that's what I decide."

"Don't be so sure, sweetie pie. The people who run this town are still very much a part of the *good old boys' club* and while that building was mine to give to you... the town owns the lot and just because a Thompson has occupied it for the past almost sixty years, doesn't mean you won't have to fight for it."

Kate hadn't thought about that before. It had always been Matthew who dealt with the town and while he seemed to get whatever he asked for, she had not cultivated the same relationships.

"Okay, mom. I'd love to have you go with me." Kate observed her mother stand a little straighter. "My meeting is at eleven."

"I'll be ready." Pulling the top of her robe tighter around her neck, she stepped back from the counter and turned around. "Night dog."

"Enjoy your bath and don't forget to close your door so the puppy doesn't try to come in and bother you."

"Oh, I'm not worried... that dog won't come into my room," Fiona called out over her shoulder. "See you in the morning."

Out of the corner of her eye, she saw Matthew enter the bedroom and after shutting off the lights in the kitchen, she scooped up the puppy and walked in that direction. Making sure the door was closed behind her, she put Allie Girl on the chair and pushed the ottoman over toward the bed.

"Did you hear any of that conversation?" Kate asked, turning on the television in her room. She wasn't in the mood to watch anything, but the local news would create the ambience she needed to have a conversation without worrying about Fiona overhearing them.

"Enough," he replied, moving over to crouch by the chair to look at the puppy. It was remarkable how much she had changed in just a couple of days. "It does sound like you've made a decision about what you want to do."

When she didn't respond, he looked behind him to search for her, but the room was empty. A few seconds later, he heard running water and knew that she was washing her face. A nightly routine she had done as long as they had been married; clip her hair on top of her head, brush her teeth and wash her face followed by a thin application of original formula *Oil of Olay*. Her medicine cabinet was not cluttered with the latest jars of serums and potions that *claimed* to have the power to turn back time... the pale pink plastic bottle was her only beauty regimen. She took care of her skin but didn't fuss about her appearance and usually could get dressed and be ready to go before him.

One of the *many* things he loved about her.

After the water shut off, he waited for her to return to the bedroom rather than try to start a conversation by shouting into the other room. He didn't have to wait long. Less than a minute later, Kate emerged dressed for bed, her mostly blonde hair mixed with a touch of gray still clipped up off her neck.

"You'll think it's stupid."

"What?" he asked, rising before moving closer to her.

"I don't want to rebuild the hardware store."

"What? But Kate, this town and others in the area depend on us. We're the only hardware store for fifty miles."

"I just don't want to do it anymore and

people will find other options... they already have. The store has been gone for a month now and by the time it's rebuilt... what, a year from now, a lot of them won't return."

He studied her face while he thought of the words to counter the point she made, but she was right. People will always move forward and find new ways to keep going.

"But what will you do? Retire?"

"I was thinking about that too. What would you say if I told you I wanted to open an art gallery... somewhere people can come to learn to paint and where local artists can display their work?"

"An art gallery? Where did that come from?"

"I've had a lot of time to think about what I want to do." She sat down on the bed and Allie Girl quickly jumped from the chair to the ottoman and then to the bed to join her. "I kept going back to that little introduction to painting class I took while you went fishing and... ah *hell*, now that I'm saying it out loud, I'm realizing how stupid it all sounds."

"Kate, I've known you almost your entire life and I have never seen you jump into anything without thinking long and hard about it." He watched as she reached up to remove the clip, letting her hair fall to her shoulders. "I think you should give it a shot."

She looked up at him and squinted her

eyes. "Really? Just like that, you're okay with me letting the store go to try something completely insane."

They talked into the early morning hours about how the store was not really something she had been passionate about... just some place she was comfortable with. He had pushed her like he always did to take on more of a role than she wanted. The store had been *his* dream and now that he had time to think about it, she had done all the work to keep his dream alive and he liked the status it gave him and his family in the community. Sure, he had been there every day just like she was, but his job really was to complete the chore list she had laid out for him for the week. Find room for this new line of products. Pull out the older rolls of carpet and either mark them down or donate them to the church. Reinforce shelves and display cases before they fell on the customers. Load the flat bed and make the deliveries of mulch and gravel.

She was the one who kept the store running all the while never wanting to do it but doing it anyway... for him.

By the end of their discussion, when she could barely keep her eyes open, they both had been on the same page. She had a plan on what she wanted to try to do and with the insurance money easily covering the few business debts that remained she'd have enough to cover that and pay the salary of their four employees for a year. And with his life insurance money, she would be able to support herself for the rest of her life and be able to take a risk to do something that she was passionate about.

It was time for her dream.

CHAPTER NINE

DESCENDING THE STEPS, Kate wished she had chosen a different pair of shoes. She didn't come to town hall often and forgot about the two flights of solid oak steps that would be her way out if she couldn't find the patience to wait for the elevator.

The meeting had not gone as well as she thought it would. The mayor and two members of the town council voiced concerns about the type of business she wanted to start. She had not yet met with an architect and none of them had the vision to imagine what it was that she was trying to explain. And when she left the room, they were not on board with her plan. Her mother and father's original building had been grandfathered into the bylaws that all new businesses since the seventies had to abide by them. The land and the buildings were now all owned by the town. Since the grandfathered building had been destroyed, the new structure would have to follow the same rules and regulations set forth for all new construction, and the mayor and the town council had the final say on what kind of new business inhabited the historical downtown district. They reminded her that there was still plenty of land on the outer edges of their growing town and she would have fewer restrictions if she decided to build her new project out there.

But Kate didn't want to build anywhere but downtown. That was where her store would get the most foot traffic from both the people who lived there and visitors. Ten minutes into the meeting she knew she was in trouble. Her mother had sat quietly beside her... taking it all in, but not sharing her feelings. That only further frustrated Kate. She thought her mother would at least be an advocate in her corner, helping her fight to keep the spot. The meeting had been over twenty minutes after it started and while Kate couldn't wait to get back to the car, Fiona had stayed back to speak with the mayor for a few minutes about her other property.

Kate felt better as soon as the *click-clunk* sound of her shoes striking the hard surface stopped echoing through the empty corridor and she was able to push open the door to breathe in the fresh air from outside. She turned around briefly to look at the two-story red brick building behind her and hoped that Fiona wouldn't take long.

She wanted to get home.

SHE WAITED UNTIL she could hear Kate's footsteps fade away before she removed her eyes from the mayor; a man of short-stature, a bad comb-over and a personality that could bore even a nun. Fiona never liked him. He slipped into the position riding on the coattails of his father's reputation who died at the age of ninety-three after holding the position for nearly forty years.

"Fiona, it's so nice that you were able to accompany Kate to the meeting today and while I am sorry that we weren't able to come to an agreement, I do hope that you and I can still do business together."

"Aww, yes. My house that you want to turn into some kind of a community afterschool house."

"It would be ideal to meet the needs of our growing community," he replied, leaning back into his chair. "It's across the street from the school, the perfect size and not to mention it's in excellent condition and of historical significance as one of the oldest structures in town."

"I already know all of that," Fiona said, snapping her purse closed. "What I need to know is how much cash you're willing to part with so you can realize your dream."

"*My dream?*"

Fiona leaned back in her own chair and smiled. "A little birdie told me that you want to put your name on a brass plaque outside the front door when you name the house after yourself... already got the plans drawn up for some fancy dedication ceremony too, as I hear it."

"The naming and the ceremony are insignificant. What matters is the good we will be doing for the children of our comm-."

Fiona began to laugh. He was such a turd, and so predictable. "I have a proposition for you. I have something you want, and you can give me something that I need."

"I'm listening," he replied.

"My daughter wants to make a go of some sort of art gallery, and she wants to do it where our family business stood for nearly sixty years. If you can convince the other members of the council to agree to let her build, I will *donate* my house to the town."

"*Donate?*" he asked.

"Yes, donate."

"The town will own the building... I can't do anything about that, I'm afraid. But I can convince the others to allow Kate to hold the lease for the first year."

"The first two years," Fiona countered.

"I believe I can make that happen," he replied. "But she will have to pay rent at the current rates and provide her own insurance, furniture, etc. She will be a tenant like all the other tenants downtown."

"And since I'm donating my house which we know will more than cover the town's cost of the building, she gets to help design it... so that it will suit her needs."

"I can agree to that."

Fiona stood up and stretched her arm across the desk. "Well then, Melvin the Mayor," she said, shaking his hand, "we have a deal. I'll be in town for a few weeks, so when the paperwork is ready, have it sent to Kate's house." Reaching for her purse, she turned back to look at him. "And I trust that none of our private conversation will leave this room?"

"You have my word," he replied.

"Whatever that's worth," she muttered under her breath as she turned and walked toward the closed door. "Oh, and I won't say anything to Kate... I'll let you do that tomorrow when you call her with your decision."

He watched as she walked through the open door toward the elevator, foolishly believing he had gotten the better end of their deal.

IT WAS VERY strange to be driven through the town she had called home for almost seventy years. While so much had changed in the fifteen years since she moved to Florida, much had remained the same. After touring the third new neighborhood, Fiona had instructed her daughter to stop; streets lined with similar homes began to blur and bore her. While the grocery store still carried the same smell of steel, insulation and cement, the owner had added two large sections so he could bring in more product, but the aisles remained narrow with barely enough room for two carts to pass each other. Except for the large industrial sized air conditioners installed on the roofs, even the schools still looked the same.

"Let's go downtown... I want to see the store."

"Mom, I'm sure it's mostly gone by now."

Fiona turned to her daughter. "Are you telling me that you haven't been down there for yourself yet?"

"Not yet" Kate replied, keeping her focus on the street in front of her.

"Elaborate on *'not yet'*?" Fiona asked.

Kate took in a long, deep breath through her

nose as she gripped the steering wheel. "I haven't been down to the store since it happened."

"Well... no time like the present," Fiona replied, "let's go there together."

"Okay, but we can't stay long. I need to get home to let the dog outside."

Turning left onto Main Street, Kate drove below the speed limit to give herself a few extra seconds to prepare. Glancing over at Fiona, she witnessed her clenching the leather straps of her purse with both hands revealing she was also anxious about what was about to happen.

"Would you look at that," Fiona whispered.

A few seconds later, Kate focused in on what her mother was reacting to. About three hundred feet in front of them was an empty space where their store had once stood, the gaping hole changing the familiar landscape of downtown Linvalle that had been there for more than half a century. After making a quick U-turn, Kate pulled over and parked in what had previously been *her* spot. There was no such thing as a reserved parking space downtown and while the occasional tourist pulled into the spot, most of the residents left the space empty out of courtesy.

"It looks *so* different. I want to get out and take a closer look... you coming?"

"I'm game if you are," Fiona replied.

Leaving the keys in the ignition, she opened the door and stepped out onto the street. Leaning forward, Kate placed her hands on the roof of the car and continued to stare at the space. A small pile of wood and broken cinder blocks could be seen in the back corner of the lot and except for the electrical box and a few capped sewer and water lines, there wasn't any evidence that a building had ever existed.

In front of her, Fiona stood with her feet shoulder width apart, her back straight and her hands on her hips as she glanced first left, then right and then straight up as she surveyed the nearly empty space. The sun was directly overhead and even though the wide-brimmed hat that she wore shielded her eyes, she did not remove her sunglasses. Closing the door, Kate stepped up onto the curb to join her mother on the sidewalk. As she stood next to her, it was as if everything else around them disappeared. The sound of traffic moving behind her, the chatter of passerby's... even the Mourning Doves perched on the overhead wires had become muted.

"It's such a strange feeling," Fiona said. "I almost feel as if I never existed."

"Of course, you exist, mother," Kate replied, surprised by her statement. "Why would you say that?"

"Well, think about it," Fiona said, turning to her daughter. "Other than you, evidence that I *ever* lived here, ever made a mark on this community is gone. Up in smoke, in that pile over there or currently at the dump... scraped up off the ground we're standing on and carted away along with the dirt, burnt wood and shattered glass."

"Maybe it wasn't a great idea that we came here," Kate replied, reaching for her mother's elbow. "How about we go back to the house and make something to eat?"

Fiona reached into the front pocket of her jacket and pulled out a tissue. "I've seen what I came for." Turning around, she said, "Let's go."

Kate could hear the crunch of gravel under her shoes as she took a few steps forward to look at the place where she had spent more waking hours than any other place on earth. No matter what the mayor or the town council decided, the next time she saw this place it would look different. It *already* felt different. Whatever it was that had made this place special was gone or maybe it was still there, but becoming something else... something not yet decided.

"Kate, come on... let's get a move on."

As she pivoted, she looked down and something green and half buried under the gravel caught her attention. Bending down, she picked up what was left of an old plastic keyring. Wiping the dirt away with her thumb, she saw that although faded and scratched, the gold lettering was still legible. *Thompson Hardware.*

"Coming, mother."

AFTER MAKING SURE the side gate was secure, Kate left the puppy playing in the grass and returned to the house. A quick scan of the empty kitchen and living room had her guessing Fiona was in the bedroom.

She's probably lying down.

During dinner, her mother had been unusually quiet and other than commenting that she preferred Miracle Whip to mayonnaise, it was the sound of chewing and *The Weather Channel* that filled the room. Unsettled. That is how Kate would describe the mood since returning to the house. Opening the dishwasher, Kate transferred the plates from last night's supper carefully into the cupboard; the stack one dish shorter than it had been the day before. Last night, while rinsing the plates, Kate had been distracted by the conversation going on at the table and dropped a plate, watching in slow motion as it caught the edge of the heavy cast iron pot soaking in the sink. The plate with the painted rainbow trout had cost no more than fifty cents at a garage sale, but sentimentally it was priceless. It was the one Matthew always reached for.

"How did it go downtown?"

While she had grown accustomed to him starting a conversation out of nowhere, she had been lost in her memories and this time he startled her.

"Jeez," she replied, closing the cupboard door. "Could you start by clearing your throat or something? You almost gave me a heart attack."

"Shhh. Fiona will hear you." He moved closer to her so they could continue their conversation. "How did it go?"

She leaned forward, placing her elbows on the kitchen island. "I'm not very optimistic that I convinced anyone."

"But it'd be a great location... tell me what they said."

"That the library already offered painting workshops every other month and they couldn't see an art gallery with local artists generating any buzz or income for the town."

"When are you supposed to hear back about their decision?"

"Sometime tomorrow." She watched as he pressed his lips together. "Trust me... I knew that it was over even before he announced they needed only the one night to sit with it."

"Then forget about downtown," Matthew replied. "There are plenty of other locations where you can buy a building or even build one."

"Yeah, that's what the mayor said."

"He did?" Matthew asked.

"Yep."

"The little worm had already made up his mind before you got there," Matthew said, turning to move toward the door.

"That's what I figured too. What's the dog doing?"

Kate walked around the island to move in front of one of the windows. When she didn't find Allie Girl on the grass, she began to search the yard, her breathing becoming fast and shallow.

"Look on the chair," Matthew whispered. A few seconds later, he could hear the pattern of her breathing return to normal. "Am I crazy or has she doubled in size?"

"She's definitely bigger. Pretty soon she won't need the ottoman to get on and off the bed." Kate walked over to the table to sit down. "Now... if I could get her to stop peeing in front of the door, things would be great."

"Hey, at least it's the door that leads to outside and not the rug, the bed or one of the twenty pair of slippers you have laying around the house."

"Ha, ha," she replied. "Three pairs... I have *three pair* of slippers. The brown pair, the pink pair and the leather ones with the grease stain from when you dropped the piece of chicken on the floor."

"It was hot!"

"That's why I told you to wait five minutes," she replied, smiling.

"But it smelled so good," he replied. "I can still remember what a perfectly seasoned and grilled piece of chicken smells like."

"You really can't smell anything?"

"Nothing," he replied.

"Not even when Allie Girl...," she began to laugh, unable to finish her thought.

"*That* I don't need to smell ever again."

"What's so funny?"

Kate leaned over to see Fiona exiting the short hallway that led to her room. "Did you have a nice nap?"

"What time is it?" Fiona asked.

As she turned around to look at the clock in the kitchen, out of the corner of her eye she saw Matthew move through the patio door. "It's two-thirty."

"Only two-thirty?" Fiona repeated. "*God*, it feels like it should be later."

"Can I get you anything?"

"I know where the kitchen is," Fiona replied, taking a seat at the table and softening her tone. "I don't expect you to wait on me."

Kate saw her phone sitting on the table and while her instincts were to reach for it, she knew it would only give Fiona something smart to say about how people have lost their ability to have a conversation in person. Her gaze shifted to outside. She could see Matt move over toward where the puppy was still sleeping on the chair. He seemed *normal* today, but last night he admitted to her that it felt like things were changing. His ability to recall events and places were flickering in and out, and there were periods that he was aware of only total darkness... like after the fire and before he found himself in the living room.

"Where's the dog?" Fiona asked.

"Asleep on one of the patio chairs," Kate replied, tilting her head in the direction of the patio doors. "Mom, can I ask you something?"

"Shoot."

"After my father died, did you ever see him again?"

"Well, I saw him at the funeral home. You have to remember that back then, everyone belonged to a church and had a wake followed by a funeral with an open casket."

"How about *after* the funeral... did you ever think you saw him or hear him talking to you?"

"Oh, sure. Sometimes I would see him walk into a room at the house or even at the store."

"You *did*?" Kate asked, leaning forward in the chair.

"I think it's perfectly normal to imagine that you see someone who has died or a pet who you were used to seeing around all of the time. Your eyes can play tricks on you that way." Fiona looked at her daughter's curious expression on her face. "Why are you asking? Are you seeing Matthew?"

Kate reached for her phone and began to pick at the edge of the silicone protector. "Oh, you know, just like out of the corner of my eye or something... I'll think that I see him go into the bedroom or I'll hear his voice."

"I think that's perfectly normal," Fiona replied. "He was in your life for longer than he wasn't."

After a few seconds of awkward silence, Kate changed the subject. "I forgot to ask. How did your meeting about your house go? Have you decided to keep it or are you going to sell it?"

"We came to an understanding," Fiona replied. "The town will get the house and use it for some sort of after school gathering place. I didn't ask about the details because honestly, I'm not interested."

"Well, when you need to go back downtown to finish any paperwork... or whatever, just let me know. I'd be happy to take you."

"Oh, I won't have to be going down there again. No, we agreed that any paperwork for the transfer that needs to be handled, would be brought to the house."

"At least your meeting went better than mine," Kate replied. "I'll have to start thinking about a backup plan."

Outside, Kate heard a loud crash followed by short, sharp yelps coming from Allie Girl.

Scooting her chair away from the table to investigate what happened, she moved past her mother who hadn't even flinched. As soon as she stepped out onto the patio, she discovered one of the patio chairs and the table next to it had been upended but when she stepped in between the planters to get to the grass, she couldn't see the dog.

"Allie Girl," Kate called out softly. She stopped to listen for a bark, a yelp or even a whine in response to her calling for the dog, but the yard remained silent except for the Purple Finch darting between branches above her head. "Allie, it's okay, you can come out."

A few seconds later, Kate noticed movement to her right as a small a brown tail moved back and forth across the grass. After taking a few additional steps forward, she found her hiding behind one of the large planters. As soon as she made eye contact with her big brown eyes, the puppy scampered to her feet and ran over to take shelter between Kate's legs, plopping her butt down in the grass between Kate's bare feet.

"You were trying to get that bird, weren't you?" Kate asked, looking down at the puppy who still seemed unsure if it was safe to come out. "Come on, let's go inside."

As soon as Kate took a step toward the overturned chair, the puppy bolted forward, racing toward the open door. Shaking her head,

Kate picked up the metal chair and small metal table and began to wonder if she needed to invest in more solid furniture that would be able to hold up to a sixty-pound dog. From inside the house, she heard the doorbell ring and as she walked around the planters, she noticed Fiona walking toward the front entrance. As she entered the house, her mother was closing the door and when she turned around, Kate saw the large white envelope with purple and orange lettering.

"FedEx came... it's for you."

No kidding.

After taking the envelope, Kate squinted to read the label to see who it was from before she opened it. She wasn't expecting anything, but perhaps Matthew had ordered something else he had failed to mention. Unfortunately, without her glasses, she couldn't even read her own address.

"Looks like it's from an insurance company," Fiona volunteered.

Kate looked at her mother. "How did you read that without your glasses?"

"I couldn't, so I asked the driver to tell me." Fiona glanced down at the dog sitting next to her empty food bowl. "Not my problem."

Placing the envelope on the kitchen island, Kate entered the pantry to retrieve the bag of dog food. But even after she heard the crunch of nuggets between Allie's little teeth, she left the envelope where it was and proceeded to the refrigerator. She knew what she would find inside, and needed something that would take the edge off before opening it.

"I'll take some of that," Fiona said, as she watched Kate pull out a bottle of Riesling.

Don't expect me to wait on you, huh?

Placing two wine glasses on the counter, Kate filled both half full before returning to the kitchen table to join Fiona. Before she sat down, she reached back and slid the envelope across the island and picked it up.

"Do you know what that is?" Fiona asked.

"Yep," Kate replied, leaning the envelope on the table against the napkin holder and reaching for the glass in front of her.

"And are you going to open it?"

"In a minute."

The two sat at the table staring at the envelope and drinking their wine for several minutes before Kate finally reached for it. Having been in her position more than once, Fiona knew what it was before her daughter opened it... the payout of her husband's life insurance.

But the dollar amount inside would be a shock to them both.

Kate placed the wine glass down on the table and broke the seal of the mailing envelope only to reach inside to find another smaller, sealed envelope. She glanced at her mother before slipping her finger under the flap and carefully pulling it towards her. Letting the empty envelope drop to the table, she slowly opened the crisp white paper that had been neatly folded into thirds and began to read the canned text.

While Kate read the letter, Fiona recalled the year her first husband died. She received two hundred and twenty-six dollars from Social Security to pay for the funeral. The check went directly to the funeral home, and she never saw a penny. But her daughter's experience would be different. Her children were grown, and Kate would have made sure the insurance for the store was sufficient to cover a loss. The only uncertainty was the choice Matthew had made when it came to their own personal policies. The day before the funeral, the first and only time she discussed this with her daughter, they had gotten into an argument. She had been disappointed that Kate had left the management of their personal life insurance benefits solely up to her husband and her anger hadn't relented after Kate informed her that the policy had been in a file cabinet in the store. Fiona had been the one to ultimately walk away and end the discussion but only because Charlotte had returned to the house to bring her back to the hotel so she could go lay down.

Across the table, Fiona observed her daughter's eye grow wider and wider, but she wasn't saying anything. For a moment, she wondered if Kate was having a stroke, or some other kind of medical emergency and it wasn't until Fiona extended her hand toward her daughter that Kate shifted her gaze to stare into her mother's eyes.

"What is it?" Fiona asked, quickly pulling her hand back to her chest.

"A check."

"I know that! For how much?" Kate's only response had been to sit there, slowly shaking her head back and forth while she held the check, so Fiona reached across the table and gently took it from her. *"Jesus, Mary and Joseph!"*

Kate reached across the table and took the check back. This time it was her mother's turn to sit there in shock.

"Seven digits and six zeroes," Fiona whispered as she reached for her glass of wine and drank what was left in one gulp. "Is that what I saw on that check?"

"Yep."

"Holy *shit* bird."

"You can say that again," Kate replied, reaching for her own glass and finishing her wine.

For the duration of their marriage... even the years before the big box stores opened in Oklahoma City when the store was doing exceptionally well, they had never managed to save more than a few hundred thousand dollars.

"That money is for you Kate... for you and in

case the kids need help."

She looked over her mother's shoulder to see Matthew standing in front of the fireplace again.

"The insurance check for the store should be coming soon now that the investigation is over and that's the money you use to build your art gallery and get it running... promise me."

Tears brimmed her eyes, and she nodded her head up and down. "Promise."

"Well, I'm gonna need some more wine," Fiona said, standing up and grabbing her glass. "Want some?"

Kate blinked and wiped the tears from her cheeks and looked back at her mother as she made her way into the kitchen. When she turned back to look for Matthew, he was gone.

"Yes... and bring the bottle."

AFTER THE WINE, followed by cheese and then fruit, there hadn't been a need to make supper and by eight o'clock Fiona had gone to her room to turn in for the evening. Even Allie Girl was fast asleep on the bed earlier than usual, tuckered out or perhaps still traumatized by what happened in the yard. For Kate, the numbing effect of the alcohol had begun to wear off about thirty minutes before and rather than wake up to a messy kitchen, she decided to tidy things up before heading to bed herself. As she watched the last of the bubbles swirl around the sink drain, movement caught her eye.

He was back.

She nodded her head in his direction but chose to wait for him to move closer before she began to speak. Fiona was in the bedroom, but she could see a dim light at the end of the hallway, so she hadn't yet turned off the lamp. It was also quite possible that she had fallen asleep on top of the covers, still wearing her skirt and stockings but Kate wasn't going to take any chances.

"Did the shock wear off yet?" he asked, as he neared the island that separated them.

"Mostly."

"You're a millionaire," he said, smiling.

"I didn't remember the amount being that high."

"It was actually higher a few years ago, but when some of our business started to fall away it decreased and then when I hit sixty a few months back, it went down again."

"Millie will just love me when I send her the tax stuff for this year."

"You'll only have to pay on the interest you

earn... and she's been our accountant for years, she'll know what to do. I'm not worried and you shouldn't be either."

"Well, it'll make Ava feel better when *she* finds out," Kate replied, turning off the faucet and pushing the start button on the dishwasher. "Ever since she learned I was thinking about not rebuilding the store; I think she's worried that I'll become destitute or even worse a financial drain on her."

"Your art gallery is going to be a smashing success and you won't have to worry about money... just finding the talent to display on your walls."

"If there ever are any walls," Kate replied. "They're gonna say no, I can feel it."

He watched as she covered her mouth to stifle a yawn. She looked tired. Not the same kind of tired that he witnessed in the days after the funeral... the kind of tired after a long day. He felt his own energy was low again too. It had been several days since he had tried to move anything. That and passing through any solid object seemed to zap his energy down to nearly empty and he would disappear for hours.

"You should go to bed. Isn't Charlotte coming by with breakfast for the three of you tomorrow?"

"That's right," she replied. "I completely forgot."

He watched as she moved around the

house, turning off the lights and checking to make sure that all the doors were locked. Another task that had once been solely his to complete, now seemed like second nature to her.

"Are you coming?"

"You go ahead," he replied. "I'll see you tomorrow."

Even as he said the words, he didn't know for sure how much longer that would be true.

CHAPTER TEN

BY THE TIME she made her way out of the bedroom, Kate was already having her first cup of coffee out on the patio while Allie Girl played in the yard. Fiona hated using the shower because it always felt like she was drowning, but the thought of waiting for the tub to fill to an acceptable level hadn't been appealing either. Especially given the marching band parading around inside her skull this morning, but thankfully the hot water had done wonders.

Today she would stay away from the wine and go back to her whiskey Coke; the tried-and-true combination of bitter and sweet that never left her feeling less than human the next day.

She needed to be sharp.

If the mayor held up his end of their bargain, he should be calling Kate by ten o'clock and if he didn't... she wouldn't leave town until he fully realized how miserable consequences could be.

"There's plenty of coffee," Kate called out after Allie Girl alerted her to movement inside the house.

"When is Charlotte supposed to get here?" Fiona replied.

"What time is it now?"

"It's seven," replied Fiona.

"Then I would imagine in about an hour... she always arrives around eight."

Lifting her feet off the small table in front of her, Kate placed her slippers back into the wet grass and stretched her arms above her head to the sky. It was time to stand up. The coffee had done its job and now she needed to get moving. Inside the kitchen, Fiona had turned on the television and was slamming cupboards looking for her mug.

"Check the dishwasher." Stepping over the puppy, Kate walked toward the patio and stopped to rub her feet on the rug before entering the house. "Come on Allie, let's go in. Hey, Fiona, will you toss me that dishtowel hanging by the oven?"

After stepping onto the rug just inside the patio door, Kate pulled the screen door closed behind her so the dog would not try to sneak back outside. The rain shower that had rolled through last night had left the grass wet and until the sun reached the back yard, Allie would not be going outside again.

"Here you go," Fiona said, handing the towel to her daughter. "Why is she all wet?"

"Didn't you hear the rain last night?" Kate asked, as she rubbed the towel over the wet puppy who seemed to think it was a new game to play and tried to catch the material between her teeth. "Allie, stop."

"It rained?"

"I'm surprised you slept through it with the skylight in your room," Kate replied as she made her way to the mud room to throw the wet towel in the hamper. "Charlotte always complained about the noise when it rained."

"Santa Clause *himself* could have landed on the roof and I doubt I would have heard a thing." Fiona sat down with her coffee and looked down at the dog who had moved to sit next to her chair. "And *you* smell." Fiona chuckled as the little dog, whined but stayed where she was.

"Are you gonna need a ride to your old house today... to do a walk through or something?" Kate asked, as she poured herself a second cup of coffee. She looked at the carafe, debating if she should dump out what was left and start another pot or wait to see if Charlotte remembered to bring coffee.

"*Hell,* no," Fiona replied as she gently tapped the spoon against the top of her cup. "I haven't had any personal items stored in there for years and the town is getting the house in the condition it stands."

"I thought maybe you'd like to take a final walk around the property," Kate replied. "I could even take a few pictures for you with my phone."

After swallowing the hot liquid in her mouth, Fiona cleared her throat. "My mind works just fine, Kate. *Hell,* I still have memories of that place that I'm trying to forget. I sure as *hell* don't want to go back there and risk even more resurfacing."

The word *hell* was a favorite of Fiona's, and the only one that Kate could tolerate without cringing. Growing up, her mother had a reputation for having a very colorful vocabulary that Kate attributed to a life spent in the home improvement industry surrounded by men in what was, and still is considered by most, to be a man's business. It had taken Kate years to finally get her mother to curb her language around the children but along the way she had made a few concessions too. Fiona could use *that* word as freely as she pleased, and Kate was never to question how her mother lived her life.

In the end, their mutual understanding had worked out.

"Okay, okay... it was just a thought." Sitting down at the table, Kate heard an alert from her phone and realized she had left it in the bedroom again. "That's probably, Charlotte. I'll be right back."

"Well, I'm going to get dressed," Fiona replied. "Oh, speaking of clothing," she said, turning around in her chair, "where do you want me to put the ones that need to be washed?"

Kate stopped just outside the bedroom door and turned around. "There is a hamper in the hall bathroom... feel free to use it."

"Perfect," Fiona replied before finishing her

coffee and placing the empty cup down on the table. "And leave my cup where it is. I'll be back for a second cup."

Kate continued to her room and found her phone where she had left it on the nightstand. She had been right. There was a text from Charlotte making sure they were still on for breakfast. Rather than respond to the text, she decided to call her daughter instead.

"Hi hunny... yes I got your text and yes we are still on for breakfast... I know but you know how I feel about texting... okay see you soon... hey wait... are you bringing coffee... no problem I can make more...okay... bye."

Tossing her phone on the bed, Kate walked to the closet to get another summer dress she hung in there for days when she didn't feel like ironing. Like today. After next week, though, finding space to hang her clothes shouldn't be a problem. Victoria was coming home for a few weeks, and she promised to help go through Matthew's things so they could be donated.

Finding the dress that she was looking for, Kate hung it on a hook in the bathroom and turned on the shower.

THE DOG WAS the first to alert them that Charlotte had arrived. As much as Kate had originally fought the idea of having another pet, the benefits were beginning to grow on her. It also amused her to see how Fiona's attitude toward the puppy who was no longer so small had changed over the past few days. Growing up, Fiona had been one hundred percent against having an animal but when Kate came out of the bedroom, she found her mother sneaking the dog a treat. Although she walked past the scene of affection as though nothing had occurred, she couldn't contain the smile spreading across her face as she opened the front door.

"What are you smiling about?" Charlotte asked, handing her mom the newspaper she had picked up on the driveway.

"And good morning to you."

"It's about time, I'm half-starved," Fiona called out from inside the house.

This time it was Charlotte's turn to smile as her mother stepped back, opening the door wide enough for her to pass.

"Morning, grandma. I couldn't remember exactly what you liked so I got one of everything."

"Oh good, you remembered… it's the one with everything that I like," Fiona replied. "Well, come on, get over here so I can see how big you've gotten."

Behind her, Charlotte could hear her mother stifling a laugh. "You just saw me a day ago, Fiona... I doubt that anything has changed since then.

"I'll be the judge of that."

Charlotte turned back to look at her mother, opening her eyes wide so Fiona wouldn't see but had nothing but smiles when she turned back to give her grandmother a hug. Although the older woman sometimes said shocking and inappropriate things, she loved her very much.

"I'll get the plates and silverware," Kate said, closing the door. "Charlie, you'll find the mug you like in the cupboard... creamer is in the fridge."

"Got it," Charlie replied, putting the two paper bags on the kitchen table. "Fiona, your bagel should be in the white bag and Mom, I got you the cinnamon raisin one you like and hopefully they put it in the brown bag with the plain bagels."

"Have you and Ben started looking for a car yet?" Kate asked.

"Funny you should bring that up," Charlie replied. "Someone came into the shop wanting to put up a poster for a car they were selling, so we went to take a look at it. The car was in great shape, but the inside smelled like an ashtray, so we passed."

"Good call," Kate replied.

"But next week I'm going into the City to

meet with Ava to look for a crib and I *think* Ben is planning to come with so we can check out the inventory up there."

"Well, Victoria is coming home on Monday... I'd be happy to tag along."

"Oh, I forgot she was coming home," Charlotte replied. "Ava already moved her schedule around to have Wednesday off and I don't really want to ask her to move things around again."

"Enough said," Kate replied bringing the plates and silverware to the table. "Better to keep to the original plan then. Mom, did you want another cup of coffee?"

"Just top me off," Fiona replied.

Returning to the kitchen, Kate was reaching for the carafe when she heard her daughter's shrill voice behind her.

"Oh, my *God*!"

Kate turned around to find Charlotte staring at the insurance check on the freezer door.

"Yeah, that was about the reaction we had," Fiona said, holding her cup in the air.

Squeezing past her daughter, Kate returned to the table with the coffee. "Mom, put your cup down so I don't spill."

"Oh, sorry."

"Mom, when did this come?"

"FedEx brought it yesterday," Fiona answered.

Kate shot her mother a look. "Is your name, mom?"

"Sometimes," Fiona replied, grinning at her daughter.

"Is it for the store?" Charlotte asked.

"No, that is from your dad's life insurance policy," Kate replied, returning to the kitchen with the carafe. "Get your mug."

"*Holy moly,* mom... that's a lot of money."

"Yes, it is."

"Your mother is a millionaire."

"Fiona, please," Kate said. "Yes, it's a lot of money, but let's not talk about it outside of this house please. People will get weird."

"My lips are sealed, but you know when Ava finds out... she'll want you to invest it and oh my, *God*, she's gonna go nuts."

"Can we just sit down please and enjoy the wonderful breakfast you brought for us?" Kate asked.

"Yeah, sorry... hey, where's the dog?" Charlotte asked.

"Sleeping under my chair," Fiona replied.

"Would you look at that... she's getting big, and she's so well behaved. Mom, you have a magic touch with animals," Charlotte said, pouring her coffee. "Are you ever going back to the shelter?"

"Oh, I don't know," Kate replied, pulling her chair away from the table to sit down. "I called there yesterday and apparently the lady I found to fill in for me is doing a really good job and wanting to stay on."

"But wouldn't you miss it?" Charlotte asked.

"Yes, and I'm sure no matter what I decide, I can still be of use to them from time to time, but if I move forward with the art gallery, I don't know how much extra time I'll have on my hands... for a while anyway."

"So, you've decided to let the store go?" Charlotte asked, glancing over at her grandmother to see if she had a reaction to the conversation.

"What are you looking at me for?" Fiona asked. "It's up to Kate what she wants to do with her life. I've wanted her to leave this town for years, but I think the second-best option would be for her to start doing something she wants to do... since it looks like she's staying."

"Mom, you were thinking about leaving town?"

"No, never. That's something your grandmother has wanted for years... even when you kids were little. I *think* what grandma is trying to say is that since I've finally convinced her that I'm happy here, I should stop doing things that make other people happy and worry about myself."

"Exactly," Fiona chimed in, agreeing.

"Which is why I went down to town hall yesterday with grandma and we talked to the mayor and a few town council members to pitch my idea about the art gallery."

"Really," Charlotte replied, returning to the table with her coffee. "And... what did they say?"

With the help of side commentary from Fiona, Kate spent the next ten minutes relaying what happened during the meeting, and the options she would have if things didn't work out. While Charlotte seemed to be happy for her, Kate could see the reservation in her eyes but didn't push her daughter to be honest about how she felt. There would be plenty of time in the future to have those difficult conversations, but Kate wanted to wait until what was just an idea became a reality before she had to defend her position.

As they were finishing breakfast, Allie Girl crawled out from under the chair and began to search for crumbs that had fallen to the floor. While she was sniffing around under Kate's chair, Fiona reached into the bag for a second plain bagel and casually ripped off a small piece and dropped it to the floor. Under the table, she could hear *tippy-tap* of the dogs' nails as she hurried through the legs of the chair to claim her prize.

"Mother, I'm sitting right here."

"Oh, *fine*. Just one more piece."

Kate shook her head but didn't scold her mother too harshly. It was like she was seeing a transformation before her very eyes of a hard, rough-edged stone being tumbled around in a river, all its sharp edges being smoothed away even though her tongue remained sharp.

"Tell me, Charlotte... have you done one of those scans that tells you what the sex of the baby is?"

Kate looked at her mother and once again felt like she hadn't been paying attention. Matthew was the first to notice that Charlie had begun to show under her clothing and now her mother was being bold to ask if they found out the sex. A question that hadn't even entered Kate's mind.

Charlotte glanced at her mother as she twisted the napkin in front of. "Yes, we know what the sex is... we found out last week."

Kate reached across the table and covered both of Charlotte's hands with her own. "Why didn't you tell me? Unless you want to keep it a secret, that's okay too."

"Oh, *hell*," Fiona replied. "You're not going to keep it a secret and do one of those silly magic shows where blue balloons or pink smoke comes pouring out of a box, are you?"

Charlotte laughed. "Reveals... they are called gender reveals, grandma. No, we weren't waiting to do something like that."

"Then spit it out," Fiona stated.

"We are having a girl."

"Good luck."

"Don't listen to, Fiona," Kate said, pushing her chair back. "Oh, baby, I think that's wonderful news... a little girl."

Kate crouched down and hugged her youngest daughter. Part of her secretly had been hoping for a little boy, but she couldn't explain why. Maybe it was because it just seemed easier to raise Jackson compared to his three sisters. Maybe it was because the females in this family severely outnumbered the males. But it was more likely, because a little boy to tag along after him would have been what Matthew wished for.

"We actually have a name picked out."

"A name," Kate said, relaxing her hug and pulling back to look at her daughter. "Already?"

"We both love the name Matilda or Matty for short."

"I think that sounds perfect."

Without warning, Charlotte covered her face with her hands to hide the tears that had begun to flow; the combination of excitement to become a mother and the heartache she felt for missing her dad too much to hold in. Seeing her daughter break down caused Kate's wall to reveal a crack and she began to cry. They stood up and held each other, sobbing while Fiona drank her cold coffee and remain seated. The crying soon turned to giggles and then fully belly laughter after Allie Girl began to whine and then howl under the table.

"Oh my, *God*! Would you *all* just stop." Fiona shouted, which only caused the dog to howl louder causing Fiona to push back her chair and march into the kitchen.

Unable to control their laughter the two women released each other, and Kate walked to the kitchen to grab a stack of napkins. It was after they both gradually calmed down that Kate realized how badly she needed that release of emotion. She felt almost as if she had been cleansed; having been caught out in a summer rain shower and she felt lighter for it.

Kate turned toward the kitchen after she heard a loud *psst-crack* sound to find her mother had opened a can of Coke before disappearing into the pantry again only to emerge a few seconds later holding a bottle of whiskey.

And the laughter started all over again.

SEVERAL HOURS LATER, she was still waiting for Matthew to show up to tell him the news about the baby. She had expected to find him in the living room or perhaps even in the yard. She had told herself early on that she would not get into a habit of actively seeking him out. That behavior would only ensure she had more pain in her future, yet she found herself doing it.

After breaking out the whiskey and Coke before nine o'clock in the morning, Fiona had gone in for a quick nap shortly after Charlotte left for home.

Even though Kate took her time, the cleanup had taken only a few minutes and by nine thirty she found herself wondering what to do with herself. She could mow the grass, but that would likely wake Fiona and she was enjoying her alone time. She could rearrange the pantry, but she had already done that at least three times in the last four weeks. She could clean the windows, but that had been done the day she finished painting the house. She could dust but she hated that task more than cleaning the bathroom. Suddenly, she knew exactly what needed to be done.

She would clean out Matthew's truck.

Allie Girl was laying quietly on the rug in front of the closed screen door but as soon as Kate made eye contact, her tail instantly began to swish back and forth, and she sat up ready for an adventure. Kate walked to the pantry and grabbed the dog tie out she had purchased the day after she knew the puppy would be staying. There was a small strip of grass in the front yard, but the area wasn't fenced so she needed to make sure Allie Girl would be safe while she was distracted working in the truck.

Going out into the front yard might be viewed as an invitation by Lilly, but it was a risk she had to take. She also wouldn't mind a quick chat to catch up with her neighbor; it had been several days since she had even caught a glimpse of her. Kate assumed it was because of the potential closure of yet another store in town, but hopefully when she found out what Kate had planned, things would go back to normal.

"Come on, Allie," Kate whispered as she bent down to pick up the puppy. "We've got work to do."

With her hands full, she reached for the keys hanging on the wall and carefully opened the front door. The puppy in her arms instantly began to squirm wanting to get down but Kate held on firmly until she got to the patch of grass. Securing the clip to Allie's collar, she quickly twisted the spike into the ground, making sure it was snugly in place before releasing the puppy allowing her to test the limits of the leash.

"There," Kate said, stepping back to once again make sure the stake was secure before leaving.

The length of the leash would allow Allie to reach only the truck area, but Kate hoped she would prefer the soft comfort of the grass and let her get some work done. After feeling confident the puppy was safe, Kate walked toward the back of the truck to start in the bed, but she was surprised by how clean it was. Other than a vinyl tarp, weighted down by a metal toolbox, the back of the truck was empty. Climbing onto the open tailgate, she grabbed the edge of the blue tarp and began to drag it toward the open end. As she began to climb back out of the truck bed, she heard a familiar voice approaching from behind.

"Well, aren't you the *cutest* little thing."

With her feet firmly back on the driveway, Kate looked toward the grass to find her neighbor down on her hands and knees, scratching Allie's belly.

"She's adorable," Lilly said, brushing the grass and dirt from her knees as she stood up to face Kate. "Wherever did you find her?"

"Actually, she found me."

"How's that?"

"A longer story than I have time for, I'm afraid," Kate said, crossing her arms in front of her. "But I am glad that you came by... I wanted to tell you something."

"Oh, I already heard the news, silly! That's why I came over."

"News?" Kate asked. "What news?"

She found out about the money.

"Why, the new art gallery that you're building downtown... what else would I be talking about?"

"How did you-."

"Mary heard it from Kelly who I think found out from Kurt after he heard the mayor talking with your-."

"Kurt... from Mayor Murdoch's office?" Kate asked.

"That's the one," Lilly replied, smiling from ear to ear. "I have to tell you; this is the most exciting thing to happen to Linvalle since Subway came to the gas station."

Kate was speechless and unsure how to respond. When she left the mayor's office, he had been *very* clear that the town wasn't interested in supporting her idea of an art gallery... not in the downtown area, anyway.

Looking at the confused expression forming on Lilly's face, Kate realized she needed to say something. "*Wow,* I'm surprised how fast the word is getting around town."

"*Right*! But that's a small town for you."

"When did you hear, exactly?" Kate asked.

"Last night at the softball game," Lilly replied, taking a few steps closer to Kate. "Oh, I wish you would have been there. They renamed the field... in honor of Matthew."

"What?" Kate whispered, more confused by this news than hearing from her neighbor about the mayor changing his mind."

"The field... they changed the name to Chapman Field." She could see the surprised look on Kate's face and lowered her voice to almost a whisper. "There's a new sign and everything. Are you okay, Kate? I'm sorry... I thought someone would have told you."

Taking a moment to quickly gather her

emotions, Kate took a deep breath and forced a smile. "You know what, they probably did. I have a pile of unopened mail in the house that didn't seem important. I'm sorry I missed it."

"I'm sure the guys would be happy to dedicate another pitch... hey, just talk to Pete about it and-."

"Lilly, it's okay, really. It sounds like it was a great night and that makes me happy." She continued to force the smile until she could see that her neighbor began to believe her. "I'm glad you were there to tell me about it."

Without warning, Lilly leaned forward and put her arms around her and squeezed her tight for a few seconds before letting go.

"You know I'm always here if you need anything." She smiled and turned to look at the house. "The house looks great by the way."

With the subject changed, Kate felt like she had been given room to breathe again and she turned around to look at it. This was the first time she had walked out to the street to see what the new paint looked like from the road.

It does look great.

"Hey, sugar plum!"

Kate and Lilly turned to the sound of Ed shouting from across the street.

"I think he means me," Lilly giggled. "What it is, sweetie pie?"

"Your mother is on the phone." Her husband began to wave a cordless phone above his head.

"Gotta go… I'll talk to you again soon, Kate."

She watched her neighbor cross the street to take the phone from her husband. The obvious excitement that she felt to speak with her mother evident in the way she almost skipped across the street. Kate couldn't recall a time when she ever felt that way about a conversation with her own mother who wasn't three states away, but sleeping in one of the bedrooms less than one hundred feet away from her.

The bedroom.

She was reminded that she still needed to get the other room cleaned up before Victoria arrived. It had been years since they needed to use the smaller of the kids' rooms but with the unexpected visit of her mother, her middle daughter would have to settle for the same twin bed she slept on as a teenager. Jackson had taken the smaller of the two rooms when they were home for the funeral. He said both the bed and the size of the room were better than the base housing he had grown accustomed to. Fiona would not be as generous, and Kate would never ask her elderly mother to swap rooms.

Turning her attention back to the truck, she lifted the heavy toolbox up and carried it the short distance to the side gate. When she turned around, she noticed Allie Girl had left the grass to walk under the truck to see what she was doing.

"Get out from under there," she said, bending over and waving at the puppy to move back.

Walking toward the back of the truck, she opened the door and climbed onto the seat. A few seconds later, the puppy had moved to sit on the driveway next to the open door so she could watch her once again. Looking around, she found an empty plastic shopping bag tucked into the pocket of the door.

This will work.

Opening the middle console, it was empty except for a few receipts, some loose change, and a power cord to charge a cell phone. Surprised by how clean he had kept his truck; she opened the glove compartment. That was empty too except for the registration, insurance card and the manual that came with the vehicle. After closing the door to the small compartment, she glanced around the inside of the vehicle a final time to make sure she hadn't missed anything and looked up.

Tucked into the visor above the driver seat were Matthew's sunglasses.

She hesitated for a moment before reaching across the cab. Holding them in her hand and closing her eyes, she tried to remember the last time he wore them, but she couldn't. They rarely rode in the truck together and Matthew rarely used them outside of driving in bright sunlight. Taking a breath, she opened the glasses and placed them on top of her head rather than shoving them into the plastic bag to be scratched by the loose change floating around. When she got inside, she'd find somewhere put them... somewhere to keep them safe. After swinging her legs toward the open door, Kate stepped out of the truck and bent down to grab the plastic bag.

"Come on Allie Girl... time to go in."

IT WAS THE thuds and thumps coming from the next room that woke her up. Fiona wasn't interested in finding out what was going on as much as she wanted it to stop.

"What are you doing?"

Without turning around, Kate replied to her mother. "Getting the room ready for Vic."

Fiona looked around at the piles of clothing, rolls of Christmas paper and stacks of magazines, books, and puzzle boxes. "I hate to tell you this, but it looked better before."

"*I know*," Kate sighed, pushing the assortment of plush animals off her lap so she could stand up. "I started with that stupid bin at the back of the closet and then couldn't stop... and now I have a mess everywhere."

"Well, pass me the basket with the bedding," Fiona instructed. "I'll throw it in the wash but you're on your own for the rest."

"There isn't room for the both of us in here anyway," Kate replied, stepping over the pile of magazines to get to the laundry basket. "It's a good thing I have a few days to clean this up. Most of it is worth donating... it's a shame that I've left it shoved into the closet all these years."

Handing the basket to her mother, Kate waited until she was sure Fiona had a firm grip before she let go. The last thing she needed was for her to drop the basket and trip. Even though Fiona still did all of her own housework back home in Florida, she was still getting up there in age and needed to take more precautions than she was willing to admit. After watching for a few seconds until Fiona exited the hallway, she turned back toward the mess she had made and got back to work.

FOUR HOURS LATER, Kate felt good about the

progress she had made. The room had been thoroughly dusted and all the clothes being donated were in plastic bags and stacked next to the front door. When she put the tool box away, she had even found a few empty plastic crates in the garage for the books, puzzles, and stuffed animals. After rinsing them off with the garden hose, all she had left to do was wait for them to dry so she could fill them up and carry everything to the car. The new mattress pad she ordered from Amazon wouldn't be there until Saturday, so the items that Fiona washed would remain where they were, neatly folded in the basket on top of the bed until then.

Her mother had eaten another bagel while Kate continued to work, but she had been determined to finish and *now* she was starving. Grabbing a cold Mountain Dew from the fridge and a packet of saltines, Kate picked her phone up off the kitchen table and walked out into the sunroom to join her mother.

"That rocker is comfortable, isn't it?"

"It is," Fiona replied. "Where did you find it?"

"A local guy makes them." Kate sat down, put her feet up on the chair across from her and opened the package of crackers. After placing a whole cracker in her mouth, she cracked open the can of coke and drank half of it before placing the can back down on the table.

"That stuff will kill you."

"Right... because drinking Coke and

whiskey for breakfast has really shortened your life span."

Fiona laughed. It was rare that Kate said anything that amused her to the point that she couldn't contain her emotions. She liked to keep what she felt under control; a baseline that kept people guessing, without ever revealing what she was truly feeling.

"Did you hear back from the mayor?"

"Nope," Kate replied, reaching for another cracker.

"Really? Your phone was ringing before."

"What?" Kate replied, sitting up and putting her feet back on the floor. "When?"

"When you out throwing stuff away in the trash bin."

Picking up her phone, she looked at her missed calls and saw that someone had left her a message. After giving her mother a look, she shook her head as she accessed her voicemail.

Hi, Kate. This is Mayor Murdoch calling. I am sorry that I missed you and hate to do this over the phone, but I wanted to let you know that me and the rest of the town council had an emergency meeting yesterday afternoon and after much discussion and contemplation, we have decided to allow you to rebuild in what has been considered your family location downtown. Now, as we discussed in my office the town will cover the material cost, but you will have to cover the labor of the new structure.

And to remind you, the town will own the building outright, but you will be entitled to one year of free rent and lot lease fees since you paid for the labor. Because of your family's special standing in our community, we are willing to extend this offer into a second year, should you decide to stay. Of course, at the end of the second-year term, the monthly fees will kick in. All of this will be in writing and properly documented when you come in with your lawyer to sign the agreement. Once that's settled, well, we can begin building. Oh, I almost forgot. The council has also agreed that you may design the building as long as the exterior meets our downtown aesthetic guidelines. Do please call my secretary and set up an appointment so we can discuss next steps. Say hello to your lovely mother for me. Have a good day. Bye now.

"I don't believe it," Kate said, putting down her phone.

"What?"

"They changed their mind... I got the spot downtown if I want it."

"And do you?" Fiona asked.

"Do I what?"

"Still want it?" Fiona asked, stopping her rocking motion. "It seems that the tables have been turned and now *you* have a choice to make."

For the first time since she got the idea, she was afraid or perhaps uncertain was a better way of describing how she felt. This was the first time in more than forty years that she had decided something on her own and would have only herself to rely on to see it through.

Stop it!

She could feel herself already beginning to come up with a list of reasons why she shouldn't. But it wasn't because she never made decisions solely on her own before. Throughout her life there had been plenty of decisions that she had made on her own. She found the kids pediatrician and made all the appointments. She decided on what gifts for birthdays and Christmas would be purchased and made sure they were wrapped and ready when needed. She decided what meals would be made for supper every night. She made the decision on how the house would be decorated and picked out most of the furniture and artwork. And at the store, she made sure everything ran like a well-oiled machine.

But Matthew had always been there. Letting her borrow his strength when she needed it and being her sounding board when she had an idea. Like the new layout of the store, she had been thinking about, the pet adoption carnival she thought would be a good idea to organize but didn't know where to start or helping her narrow down twenty versions of the same white paint so she could finally choose one. She worried now that if he hadn't been there, she would have become lost in the options, unable to chip away until there was only one to choose from.

And she didn't know how she would do this without him.

THE NEXT SEVERAL days left her feeling like a tornado had touched down in the middle of her life. Allie Girl had her first vet appointment and was given her first series of shots and a clean bill of health. Fiona had signed the paperwork transferring ownership of her house to the town and Kate's contract was with her lawyer who was giving it a final review before she signed on the dotted line.

After she finally had a chance to speak with Matthew, things had moved very fast.

It was obvious that something was going on with him, but he continued to downplay it, refusing to get too far into a discussion before changing the subject or disappearing altogether. But she had managed to keep him around long enough to discuss her fears about jumping into something completely foreign to her. While he didn't tell her what choice to make, he helped her clear away the clutter that was making it difficult to see the path. He reminded her that she was the one who made the store function as a business; without her, it was just a building with stuff. While it was true that the foundation was already built by her mother with a customer base and the bones of a business model, that business no longer existed. Over the years, she had reimagined it into what it had been. And while she would have to reimagine what this new business would look like; she had already built the foundation in the towns people who would be behind her one hundred percent, but it would still be up to her to get them excited about it.

"What time do we have to leave for the airport?"

"We?" Kate asked. "You want to go with me to pick up Victoria?"

"What else am I going to do?"

Kate glanced toward the living room where Allie was asleep on her bed under the coffee table. The thought of leaving her alone for three or four hours wasn't something she wanted to do, but if she couldn't convince Fiona to stay with her, she wouldn't have another choice.

"I was hoping that you'd stay here and help me with the puppy. You know... keep her company and maybe let her outside every hour or so."

Fiona stared at her daughter without responding. If she replied to quickly, Kate would know that she had done her mother a favor. She had never intended to return to the airport until she was ready to return home. Fiona didn't mind flying, but she disliked the process of checking her luggage and required a valium to tolerate being so close to so many people.

"So, I'm to be a pet sitter... are you going to pay me? People usually get paid for this sort of service."

"You want me to pay you?" Kate replied, not entirely shocked by what her mother was asking.

"Yes, and for payment of services rendered, I will settle for a few of those pretzels I like."

"Auntie Anne's pretzels... that's what you want?"

"That'll do it," Fiona replied, walking over to the kitchen table where she had placed her nearly empty tote on the back of a chair.

"Any particular kind?"

"I like the cinnamon raisin and the almond one is pretty good too." Fiona reached into her bag and pulled out her book of crossword puzzles. "What time do you have to leave?"

"Victoria's flight lands at one-thirty, so I'd like to be on the road in about thirty minutes."

Fiona lifted her wrist to see what time it was. "Will that give you enough time?"

"Yes, Fiona. I'll get the pretzels after I get

Victoria... just in case she wants something too."

"Are you sure that's a good idea?" Fiona asked, looking up at her. "I thought she mentioned something about watching her weight when she was here for the funeral."

Shaking her head, Kate walked into the kitchen to empty the dishwasher. "And I'm sure if she decides she doesn't want one, she will tell me."

"Mother, promise me that you won't start anything when she gets here... please."

"What?"

"She's coming here to help with the festival and to help me go through Matt's things... she doesn't need you to add to her stress by jabbing at her weight."

"What stress? She hangs out in bars all day, writing songs and playing a guitar. That doesn't sound like a stressful existence to me?"

"She doesn't just hang out in bars... she works too." Kate replied.

"Since when?" Fiona asked, putting down her crossword.

"Since she broke up with her girlfriend... she lives in a *shitty* little studio and waits on tables to pay the rent." Kate slammed the dishwasher closed. "*Shit*."

Returning to her crossword puzzle, Fiona softened her tone. "Don't worry... I won't tell her you spilled the beans."

"Thank you," Kate replied, opening the

dishwasher again. "I'm sure she'll tell everyone when she's ready, but you know Victoria, she's very private about what goes on in her life."

"No need to say anything else... I get it."

Kate glanced toward her mom as she proceeded to put the dishes away. She wasn't worried about Fiona. If anyone could understand the choice to keep your personal business private, it was her mother.

CHAPTER ELEVEN

TWO MORE WEEKS. She just had to get through the next two weeks. That's what Kate kept telling herself as she pulled out of the parking lot with the payment her mother had requested. She expected a mixed bag of emotions when they started to go through Matthew's closet, and she wasn't looking forward to it. She also wasn't looking forward to having to talk with the kids about the contract she was about to sign or the new business she was going to build either. She decided to wait and not say anything to Victoria until they got home. It appeared to her that Fiona was on her side and it would be good to have an ally to help defend her plan.

"How has it been having Fiona staying there?"

"Not as bad as I thought it would be," Kate replied. "She's actually been quite pleasant."

"How long is she staying?"

"You know... I don't know. She came back to deal with her house, and she signed the papers last Friday, so I guess she could go home at any time."

"Wait... Grandma sold her house?"

Shit.

"Umm, yeah," Kate replied. "The town got it and have plans to turn it into an afterschool teen or daycare center... I'm not really sure which one." Kate looked in her side mirror as she moved her vehicle into the center lane of the interstate. "You know how Fiona is... she didn't ask about what they were planning to do because she couldn't care less. She just wanted it not to be her problem anymore."

"But won't she miss the extra income from renting it out?"

Kate shot a quick glance at her daughter when she heard the concern in her voice. "My mother? Worry about money." Kate shook her head. "No way. Fiona would never have given up the house if she was worried about money. Don't worry about grandma. She saved almost every penny she ever made and invested it well. Heck, she probably has more money than I do."

Well, maybe not anymore.

"Really?" Victoria said, returning her focus to the windshield. "Well, that's good to know."

"Wait until you see your little sister," Kate said, a huge smile spreading across her face. "She has the cutest little belly starting to pop out."

"Already?"

"Yes, she looks so good."

"Is she coming over today?"

"I'm not sure, but I don't think so," Kate replied, shaking her head. "Her and Ben are driving to the City tomorrow to do some shopping with Ava."

"Better her than me."

"I really wish the two of you would give it a rest."

"Well, maybe when she stops trying to run my life and telling me how I'm throwing it away with the choices I'm making... I will stop believing that she's the biggest *bitch* on the planet."

"Victoria Anne, that's your sister you're talking about."

"And maybe you should be reminding her of that," Victoria replied, raising her voice. "She's the one acting like my mother instead of my sibling. You know what, it's probably better you don't get into the middle of it... we're not in high school anymore and I don't need you to fight my battles."

"I don't want to fight with anyone," Kate replied. "But I hate it that you two always seem at odds with each other."

"It's a personality thing... I have one and she doesn't."

"Victoria," Kate replied, looking toward her daughter as she stifled a giggle. "That wasn't nice... it was true, but it wasn't nice."

As her daughter put her bare feet up on the dash and burst into laughter, Kate returned her attention to the road and moved back into the right lane when she saw the first sign for her exit. It would be good to be back home again, and she couldn't wait for Victoria to meet, Allie Girl. Out of all the kids, she had been the only one who asked for a pet and the reason they adopted, Birdie. It was at that moment that Kate decided she would wait a few days before they began the task of going through Matthew's things. She felt like she needed a few days where there wasn't a plan. No house to be painted. No meetings to attend. Nobody to drop off or pick up from the airport.

Nothing to do but chill and relax.
Enjoy a summer day.
That is what she needed.

THE FIRST NIGHT Victoria was home, Kate was very restless. She couldn't put her finger on it, but something felt *off* and she laid in bed awake most of the night listening to the sounds of the house, trying to figure out what it was. At first, she thought it was because her daughter was home, and she felt bad about having to put her in the room big enough for only a twin bed. But if Victoria was upset about it, she didn't show it and even Kate had to admit that the room looked twice as large once all the junk was cleaned out of it. Even after Victoria tossed her oversized duffle bag into the corner, she still had plenty of room to move around. She didn't even seem to mind that she had to share a bathroom with her grandmother.

Having her daughter home wasn't the problem.

Then she thought, perhaps it was her mind trying to tell her that she had made a huge mistake in giving the mayor a verbal yes about taking the lot downtown. Her lawyer had called and left a message that the contract looked good and that he could meet her down at the mayor's office the day after tomorrow to sign it if that worked for her. But it hadn't taken her long to realize that what she was feeling was excitement. In fact, she was having a hard time not blurting out to Victoria what was going on, but she wanted to wait until the lot was locked in and not jinx the positive thing that seemed to be happening to her.

The art gallery wasn't the problem.

It was only after she felt the bed move as the puppy shifted positions to snuggle against her back that she realized what it was.

It had been four days since she last saw Matthew.

The same restless feeling she felt in the days

after he died, was very similar to how she was feeling now. Not identical, but definitely related. The last time she saw him was early Friday morning, just after midnight. He had been disappearing more and more and staying away for longer periods, but he had never stayed away for more than twelve or fourteen hours, let alone an entire weekend.

He hadn't even returned to see Victoria.

Something must have happened.

Maybe his visitors pass or whatever it was that brought him to her had expired and he was gone for good. She tried to rationalize in her mind that if that is what happened, then it too was meant to be... but that didn't make sense either. Shouldn't this second chance to say goodbye if that's what it was, come with some kind of warning, like the beep of a microwave when your food was ready?

None of this made any sense.

As her eyelids began to feel heavy, she stopped fighting and let them close; maybe she would get lucky and her brain would shut off too. A few minutes later, she heard Allie begin to softly snore behind her and her mind finally began to relax as she drifted into her dreams.

SHE HAD JUST finished making the pancakes when her phone began to buzz on the table. She ignored it, believing only a telemarketer would call before nine o'clock in the morning. But when it began to buzz again only a few seconds later, she turned her phone over to see who it was.

Charlotte?

"Hello... did something happen... well it's just that you rarely call you're more of a texter... yeah she's here... just after three... as far as I know she just got out of the shower... today... sure what time were you thinking... no it's fine... I cleaned out the truck already too... okay well just have him come in and get the keys... yes there is still insurance on the truck... drive safe and have fun... yeah you too... bye."

"Who was that?" Victoria asked, exiting the bathroom dressed but with a towel wrapped around her head.

"Your sister... don't you dry your hair anymore?"

"Which one?"

"What?"

"Which sister?" Victoria asked again.

"Oh, Charlotte... Ben's going to stop by and

get the truck. He thinks he found the car they are looking for in the City."

"Umm.... I forgot to pack my blow dryer," Victoria replied, pointing to her head. "Do you still have that extra one you used to keep around?"

"I do... it's in my bathroom, left cabinet below the sink. Eat first... the pancakes are getting cold."

"Not a problem, I'm starving."

Kate pulled three plates out of the cupboard and looked toward the hallway. "Is Fiona up?"

"I don't think so."

A few seconds later, Kate heard a door open and then close. "I think she just went into the bathroom. She's been sitting in that chair," Kate said, pointing to the one closest to the patio door. "I'd avoid it if I were you."

"Did Charlie say what time Ben was coming by?"

"Should be any minute," Kate replied.

"Well, how is she not coming with him? Won't she have to drive their car back to their house?"

"No, she asked if they could leave it here for the day... just in case they don't find the car they want."

"I don't get it?" Victoria asked. "Why don't they just take the truck over to their house."

Kate watched her daughter load up her plate with pancakes. "I think because it reminds her too much of your father."

"It's probably the hormones," Victoria said.

"I recall a few years ago when you told me that word was *ignorant*... I believe that is what you said."

Kate and Victoria turned toward Fiona, shuffling across the hardwood floor in her slippers.

"*What* are you talking about?" Kate asked.

"Oh, I'm sure I'm right about this," Fiona replied as she made her way to the kitchen to grab her coffee. "You were telling me a story that involved your two friends back in Nashville... the ones that lived together."

Kate looked at her daughter with a confused look on her face and a few seconds later, Victoria began to chuckle at the memory. "I said *hormones*, grandma... we were talking about Charlotte."

"Oh." Fiona replied, picking up two pancakes with her fingers and transferring them to her plate. "What's wrong with Charlotte?"

"Nothing is wrong with her," Kate replied as she carried a cup of hot coffee to the table for Fiona. "Ben is coming by today to get the truck... they're driving it to the City to maybe trade it in."

"But I thought they were going to buy a crib?"

"They're doing that too."

"Better them then me... where's the syrup?"

"On the table," Kate replied, stepping over

Allie Girl who was asleep on the mat in front of the stove. "There's a sugar-free bottle in the pantry if you want it."

Fiona ignored her daughter and walked to the table to join Victoria. She sat down in what had become *her* chair as the revved-up engine of a muscle car could be heard pulling into the driveway.

"I don't understand why he doesn't keep Matt's truck and trade his car in," Fiona said. "It sounds like the engine is about to blow up."

"It's meant to sound like that, grandma."

"Then I don't understand why anyone would want to drive a car that makes that much noise?"

"Because he's twenty-five... you remember being twenty-five don't you, grandma?"

"I was never twenty-five," Fiona replied, taking a sip of her coffee. "In my day, you got married at fifteen, skipped ahead to your thirties and if you were lucky, lived to see your fifties."

"Or in your case at fifteen, and then again at twenty, thirty and thirty-eight," Kate chimed in. "Right, mom?"

"Only because I had a child to think about," Fiona replied, over-chewing the pancake she had in her mouth but still managing to get it stuck in her throat. As she reached for her coffee, she avoided looking at her daughter.

"Are you saying that you would have never married again, if it hadn't been for me?"

Fiona finally looked at her daughter. "They were different times, Kate."

Thankfully, the knock at the door interrupted the awkward silence that filled the room. Kate turned around and walked toward the door. After she opened it, the smiling face of Ben looked back at her, and she reached for the keys on the wall.

"Hi, Ben," Kate said, greeting him. "Here you go... and remind Charlotte she needs to bring the title and maybe even the bill of sale we filled out."

"I will." Ben took the keys from his mother-in-law and leaned across the doorway to wave at the women sitting at the kitchen table.

"Morning!"

"Hi, Ben," Victoria waved back.

"I wish you guys a lot of luck today," Kate said. "What kind of car are you going to look at... wait. Forget I asked, I don't need to know."

Ben chuckled. "There are a few options. I gotta get going or we're going to be late. Thanks again for letting me keep my car here. You sure you're not going anywhere today... I can move it to the street?"

"No, it's fine where it is. I'm staying put."

"I'm sure Charlie will text you with updates... see ya."

Kate watched as he climbed into Matthew's truck and began to slowly back it onto the street. Across the street, she noticed Lilly waving to her, and she waved back and when she looked back,

Ben and the truck were gone.

THE REST OF the day had gone pretty much as Kate had hoped it would. Uneventful. After Ben left, she had thought about picking up the conversation with her mother but decided against it. What would digging into the past and trying to understand the logic behind Fiona's actions get her? After deciding it would be nothing but aggravation, Kate decided to let it go and leave the past where it belonged for now.

Fiona had disappeared to her room shortly after Ben left, but Victoria let her hair air-dry and offered to clean up the breakfast dishes. After they were done, she joined her mother in the yard where the puppy was busy exploring.

"Remember what happened the first night we had Birdie?"

"I do," Kate replied, looking over at her daughter and smiling. "In fact, I was reminded of it the first night this little girl entered my life."

"I forget… did the keys belong to you or dad?"

"Oh, they were your father's… I always hang

mine up."

As the puppy began to sniff the grass and turn in a circle, both women burst out laughing.

"How long... did it take... for the keys to show up again?" Victoria asked, struggling to get the words out between bursts of laughter.

"Sometime the next day." Kate regained control and used the sleeve of her sweater to wipe her eyes, but one look at Victoria leaning forward on the bench, clutching her knees to her chest and she lost it again.

"Stop!" Kate said, putting her hand on her daughter's knee and pushing her away.

After she finished her business, Allie Girl came galloping over to investigate what was happening. After flipping over the metal chair, she was still skittish about jumping up on the outside furniture so with her paws firmly on the ground, she went after Kate's slippers instead.

"Allie, no bite." Kate leaned over, pushing the sharp little teeth away and gently held the puppy's mouth closed. "No bite."

"You still have a long way to go with this one," Victoria said.

"Tell me about it."

"What made you want to get another dog?" Victoria asked. "You didn't even hint about it when I was home for the funeral."

"Your father-." Kate stopped. "Your father always wanted to get another dog and although I hadn't really thought about it... when this little one came into my life, I figured it was meant to be."

"Well, I for one am glad that you have the company. It felt a little weird leaving... knowing you would be all alone in the house."

"I'm definitely not alone now," Kate replied, smiling.

Without warning, Allie jumped up and ran into the house. Kate looked back to see Fiona had gotten up and was walking into the kitchen.

"Do you think she's okay?" Victoria asked.

"Yeah, she's fine."

"Did you want to get anything done today? It's not even noon yet... we could start in the bedroom or the attic?"

Kate turned back to look at her daughter. "You know what." Kate stood up. "How about we just enjoy the peace and quiet? Besides, my car is blocked in so we can't drop off anything today at the church so why make a mess that we can't get rid of? We can play cards, put a puzzle together or do none of that and just watch something on Netflix?"

"A day off?"

"A day off," Kate repeated.

"Works for me."

"Let's go see what grandma's doing and ask if she wants to take the day off with us."

Victoria followed her mother, but as she stepped off the grass and onto the patio, she thought she heard someone call her mom's name. But after scanning the area by the garage for several seconds, she assumed it was the wind she had heard and continued into the house, closing the screen door behind her.

THAT WAS IMPOSSIBLE. Up until now, only Kate had been able to hear him even if he was standing only steps away. Yet he would have sworn that Victoria had heard him too… she had turned back to look in the exact area he had been standing.

He had been searching his way through the dark, looking for a way back, but he had no sense for how long. Like his sense of smell and taste or need to sleep or eat, *time* no longer held any meaning for him. How he ended up standing outside in front of the garage instead of returning to the fireplace, he couldn't explain either.

He was also surprised to see Victoria.

When he found himself in the back yard,

he saw who he thought was Kate walking back into the house, but after he called out, it was his daughter who had turned around. He didn't remember Kate mentioning that she was coming home, but he was happy to see her. As he moved toward the patio door, he was careful to stay off to the side, just in case he had been right. If she had in fact *heard* him, maybe she'd be able to see him too.

And the last thing he wanted to do was to freak her out.

Getting closer to the screen, he could hear voices coming from the area of the kitchen. That's when he remembered that Fiona had returned from Florida. Straight ahead, he could see the puppy eating out of her food dish and he quickly passed through the screen and didn't stop until he had moved through the living room to the back corner; the shadows would give him the cover he needed until he was sure it was safe to move around.

He needed to speak with Kate.

She would be able to help fill in the gaps.

HE CAME BACK. She noticed him as soon as she turned around, but it wasn't the first time that he seemed to appear out of nowhere and she was able to hide her surprise. They were about to make popcorn and sit down to find a movie, but it was clear that he was trying to get her attention.

"You know what, I'm going to take a quick shower before we start the movie," Kate said, as she left the kitchen and moved toward the bedroom. "Why don't you guys sit down and find something... I'm okay with really anything. Just keep an eye on Allie and give me fifteen minutes."

Before they could voice their objection, Kate walked into the bedroom and closed the door. When she turned around, Matthew was standing at the edge of the bed. She put her index finger to her mouth and walked past him to turn on the shower.

"Where have you been?" she asked. "I thought maybe you were gone... like *gone, gone*."

"How long?"

"What?"

"How long since you last saw me?" he clarified.

"Friday morning." It took her a minute to realize that the day of the week meant nothing to him. "You've been gone for almost four days."

He moved away from her and turned

toward the bedroom door. "Four days? That's impossible."

"Where were you?"

"That's just it. I have no idea. But wherever I was, it was harder to get back this time."

"What's Victoria doing here?"

This time it was her turn to look confused. She remembered that he mentioned he had been forgetting things... he must have forgotten that she told him Victoria was coming back too. She could see that he was confused, and she didn't want to add to it, so she said nothing.

"The timing worked out with her vacation and the music festival the town is putting on, so she came back to help."

"Music festival?" he asked.

"As part of the fourth of July celebration... she had some artists in Nashville sign some of their CDs and t-shirts and is going to give them away and put a few items up for auction."

"Sounds familiar."

It should.

She could tell that whatever was happening to him was definitely getting worse. The fact that he couldn't remember an event that was his suggestion in the first place, was further proof of that. His memory gaps were getting bigger and not only were they impacting things that happened in the past, but also the present. Glancing at the clock, she knew she had to get back. Leaving the water running in the shower, she turned on the sink faucet and bent over so she could get her hair wet.

"Hand me that towel," she said, pointing to the one directly to his right.

He tried to pick it up, but his hand passed right through it. He tried again with the same result.

"It's okay... I can use this."

He watched as she turned off the water and reached for the hand towel hanging on the wall next to her. She quickly rubbed the towel over her head and then reached behind him to grab the towel hanging on the hook. Bending over, she wrapped the towel around her head and stood up, moving toward the closet where she quickly removed her clothes and grabbed another summer dress.

"Look, we can talk about this lat-."

Kate stepped out of the closet and looked around the room, but he was gone.

THE MOVIE HAD just finished when Kate heard first one and then another car pull into the driveway. At first, she thought it might be Charlotte and Ben returning, but the sound of the second car parking outside her house, didn't make sense. Pushing herself out of the chair, she was on her way to the door when she heard a key in the lock.

What the heck?

A few seconds later, the door opened, and Ava marched through followed closely by Charlotte and then Ben. Her oldest child had that *look* that she gets, so Kate quickly moved past her face to focus on Charlotte who refused to even look her in the eyes. That left Ben and the best he could do was shrug. He looked like an unwilling participant who given the choice, would rather be somewhere else... *anywhere else* but walking into her living room.

"Hi guys!" Victoria said, getting up from the couch. "I didn't think you were stopping by today."'

"Greetings are going to have to wait," Ava said, pulling her phone out of her bag.

"Okay, who's going to tell me what's going on?" Kate asked, moving away from the couch to take a position in front of the kitchen table.

Charlotte began to speak, but Ava raised her hand in the air and pointed in her little sister's direction, motioning for her to stop. "Jackson... okay we're back at mom's house... yes we're all here... just shut up and listen then... I'm putting you on speaker."

"Has everyone lost their *damn* mind?" Kate asked, beginning to lose her patience with what was happening.

Ava ignored her mother, walking straight for the kitchen and stopped in front of the refrigerator. After staring at the freezer door for a few seconds, she reached up and yanked the check off the fridge, sending a magnet flying across the kitchen.

"This... is *part* of what's going on," Ava shouted, as she walked out of the kitchen to stand in the middle of the room by her little sister. "This and the fact that you are planning on building some sort of midlife crisis, hippie art commune in the middle of downtown."

Hippie art commune?

"What are you *talking* about?"

"Mother, are you going to deny that you have decided to *not* rebuild the store?"

Kate looked around the room at the faces staring back at her and took a slow, deep breath in. "No."

"And do you think that it was fair of you to make that decision on your own... without consulting us?" Charlotte asked.

"Why would she have to consult us?" Victoria asked, stepping over Fiona's outstretched leg as she went to stand next to her mother.

"Because that store is a part of our family and the only thing that dad left behind for us," Charlotte replied. "She didn't even ask how we felt about it."

"Charlotte, I didn't think to ask because none of you ever asked about the store when it was open. You never asked how business was going. You never asked if we had any trouble filling open positions. You never asked if the town was giving us any trouble about the *huge* white bass your dad put on the sidewalk by the front door. My point being... you never asked. Why would I think you'd have a problem if it didn't exist?"

"I for one think it's *hilarious* that you're the one making a big deal out of it," Victoria shot back at her younger sister. "Out of all of us, including Jackson who I think is still on the phone... you're the only one who never actually worked there."

"Still here and Vic has a point," Jackson shouted through the speaker.

"Oh, shut up, Jack!" Charlotte shouted back. "You hardly worked there either."

"That's because he was involved with sports," Kate replied, defending her son who was at a disadvantage.

"I played sports too," Ava said. "That didn't seem to matter, but we all know that Jackson is your favorite and you baby him."

"What?" Kate shot back. "I don't have favorites."

"I pushed you, because I knew you were mature enough to take it on and we needed more help back then. Dad and I had just taken over the store and we didn't have the money to hire more staff... we *needed* you to help. But if you didn't want to, Ava, you only had to say something, but *God* forbid you actually open your mouth to let other people know what you're feeling."

Kate regretted saying the words as soon as they came out. She hated confronting her children, but it seemed like no matter how she tried, their personalities were always at odds.

"I'm not the one who needs therapy," Ava replied, her tone controlled and cold. "I'm not the one who thinks it's appropriate for a middle-aged widow to take a gamble. But I guess dad's life insurance is making it easier to drop that life and start a new one, isn't it?"

"Ava, stop it," Charlotte said, taking a step to stand in between her oldest sister and her mother. "We didn't come here to say hurtful things... we came here to have an honest discussion about why mom thinks she can open an art gallery, and we should give her that chance."

"Okay," Ava replied, walking into the living room to turn on the light in the corner. "Let's talk about that."

The minute the light came on, Kate saw Matthew standing in the back corner behind the lamp. He was the one with a look of surprise on his face as he quickly looked around at everyone standing in the room. Everyone seemed to be looking in his direction, but not reacting.

"They can't see me."

Kate watched as he moved to the other side of the room to position himself in front of the bedroom door and when he turned back to face her, she could see he looked more relaxed than before. But when she returned her attention back to the other people standing in the room, they were the ones with a strange look on their face.

"What are you looking at?" Ava asked, still annoyed.

"N-nothing," Kate stuttered. "Didn't you have some questions for me?"

"Why do you think you know anything about painting or about art for that matter?" Ava asked. "I mean, before you brought home this seascape painting that you bought on what I think was your last trip to Nantucket, I *never* heard you or dad mention anything about being interested in art."

"Well, it's a beautiful painting, so she does have a good eye," Charlotte replied, trying to defend her mother.

"Why are you all of a sudden on her side?" Ava asked questioning her sister. "If it wasn't for you opening your mouth, I wouldn't even know what she was up to or that she received all that cash."

Charlotte glanced at her mother. "I wasn't trying to start trouble... honest, it just came out when we were looking at the cribs."

"Oh, you said more than that," Ava fired back. "You practically started crying when you talked about how it wouldn't be the same with the store gone and that you didn't think mom was thinking clearly."

"Now that was probably the hormones talking," Fiona said, finally getting up from the couch and joining the discussion. "Maybe it's time for your mother to follow her dream... don't you think she's put it on hold for long enough?"

"Grandmother, stay out of this," Ava said, dismissing her.

"Hold on there, little missy," Fiona replied as she marched over toward her granddaughter. "You might get away with talking to your mother like that, but you try it with me again and I'll smack that smirk right off your face."

"Grandma!" Victoria exclaimed, shocked by the words coming out of her mouth.

"Don't you grandma, me." Fiona replied. "Your mother has been supporting you financially your entire adult life, so you can chase after your dreams of writing songs about cowboys pining over lost loves, but do you have her back when she's being attacked? The answer to that is no."

Fiona turned toward Charlotte. "And do you really think it didn't cost your parents anything when you decided working shifts at the store like your brother and sisters did, wasn't your *thing*? Do you think your mom likes driving around that old car? Well, she might… but she also had to hire another part-time person to pick up the shifts you *would* have worked and that's my point."

"Jackson, just because you're not here, doesn't mean you get a pass." Fiona walked closer to Ava to yell into the phone. "Don't think that I didn't notice the extra shifts your mom picked up so that you could go off to football camp every summer."

The elderly woman stepped back and put her hands on her hips as she stared at her oldest granddaughter. "And you," Fiona said, waving her finger in her granddaughter's face as Allie Girl began to bark. "The big shot, fancy city lawyer of the family. All those years of education under your belt but you're still too ignorant to realize that your mother didn't *buy* that piece of art," she said, moving her finger to point toward the fireplace, "she painted it!"

Fiona exhaled as she looked around the room that was silent except for the dog who continued to bark at the closed screen door. As she turned to look at Kate, she caught the gaze of Ben who had side-stepped behind Charlotte.

"You... you I like. But you really should think about fixing your engine," Fiona said, lowering her voice as she looked at the wide-eyed young man. "It's too *damn* loud for someone who's about to be a father and don't you work at a garage?" Fiona continued to stare at Ben until he slowly began to nod his head up and down. "Now would somebody please open the *God damn* door and let the dog out before she pees on the floor."

Victoria was the first to move but only because she was the closest to the patio door. As soon as she pulled the screen open, Allie darted between her legs and ran straight through the large planters to the grass.

"Kate, I could use a drink... would you please? You know what I like."

Fiona walked over to the table and sat down in her chair, suddenly feeling exhausted from all the excitement but relieved that she had said what she said. Her eyes moved toward, Ava who was moving closer toward the painting.

"Mom, why didn't you tell us that you painted this?" Ava asked, turning back toward the kitchen. "It's really beautiful."

"I knew that mom painted it," Jackson said, shouting through the speaker once again.

"She told you?" Ava asked, staring into the phone.

"No, she didn't tell me... I noticed the initials *KC* in the bottom corner when I was home for the funeral. I fig-."

Annoyed with her brother, Ava pressed the option to end the call and cut him off.

"I'm with Ava... why didn't you tell us?" Charlotte asked.

Kate walked over to the table and put a glass down in front of her mother. "Well... nobody asked me. I've seen each of you stand in that living room and stare at that painting at one point or another over the last few years, but none of you ever asked me about it."

Kate walked back into the kitchen and poured herself a glass of wine, drinking half of it before returning to take a seat next to her mother. The quiet and peaceful day that she had hoped for, had come to a crashing end... but at least everything was out in the open. The only thing she hoped for now was that the worst was over and that they could move forward.

"Charlotte, did you find the crib you were looking for?"

"Yeah... we ordered it. Should be here in a few weeks."

"Good," Kate replied, taking another drink from her glass as Ava walked out of the living room to join the group gathering around the kitchen table.

"I'm not going to say I'm sorry," Ava said, her voice back to her normal, controlled tone.
"But I will concede that I could have handled it better."

"Well, I won't disagree with you that it

should have been handled better," Kate replied. "But I am glad it came out. Look, part of what you said is true... what do I know about opening an art gallery? The answer is nothing. But I do know how to run a business, I do know people and I know that when I think about art... it makes me want to get out of bed again."

"She never wanted to work in a hardware store you know," Fiona interjected. "She got into it to help me, and she stayed in it to support your father."

"Mom," Kate said, "thank you, but... just, thank you."

Fiona tilted her head and raised an eyebrow, picking up her whiskey Coke. It was time to let her daughter fight her own battles... she was finally ready.

AN HOUR AFTER the pizza had been delivered, Ava left. It was still a little awkward for everyone when she decided it was time to go home and headed for the door, but Kate went outside to stand in the driveway, waving goodbye. When she turned around, Ben, Charlotte and Victoria were walking out of the house.

"I like the car," Kate said as she walked back up the driveway to meet them.

"It's a different color, but the model that I wanted," Charlotte said.

"Did you get a good deal?"

"We did... even walked away with a few bucks in our pocket," Ben replied. "Thanks, Kate."

She gave her son-in-law a hug and watched as he walked to his car and backed out of her driveway. "Drive safely," she called out before turning back toward her daughters. "Where's grandma?"

"On the couch, sleeping." Charlotte walked up and laid her head on her mother's shoulder. "I'm really sorry about the ambush, mom."

"Oh, stop it," Kate replied, pulling her daughter in for a hug. "No harm done... I'm a big girl." After stepping back, she smiled at her. "You should go home. It's been a long day for you... for all of us. Go put your feet up."

"Bye, Charlotte," Victoria said, as she waved to her sister.

"I'll stop by again in a few days."

Kate walked over to stand next to her daughter and they both watched as Charlotte climbed into her shiny, nearly new Honda CR-V. She could see the smile on her face through the windshield and continued to watch as she slowly reversed out of the driveway. As she began to drive away, Kate took a few steps forward and continued to wave until she was out of sight. She turned to go back into the house but stopped for a moment to stare at her car which for the first time in as long as she could remember, was the only vehicle parked in the driveway.

"I think it's time you trade up, mom." Victoria said, trying not to laugh. "We know you can afford it."

"Oh, shut up and get in the house." Sighing, Kate followed after her daughter and bent down to pick up the puppy running towards her. "And just where do you think you're going?"

After going through the open door, Kate gently kicked the door closed behind her and locked the door.

BY NINE O'CLOCK, both Kate and Fiona had gone to their rooms. Whether it was from the long day of doing nothing, the excitement that followed or their age wasn't clear, but the result was the same; neither could keep their eyes open any longer.

Victoria sat alone on the couch and stared at the television screen as she searched through the movies that had a lot of dialogue. Jackson had already texted her twice and she knew the only way to get him to stop was to call him, but she had to find a good movie first. After scrolling through the options two or three times, she found one that would work and pressed play.

Leaning over to verify that she couldn't see a light under her mother's closed door, she picked up her phone and dialed her brother.

"It's me... they left... a couple of hours ago... they're both in bed... in the living room with the television on... because I'm in the room next to Fiona and if she's awake she might hear me through the walls... no because I have The Breakfast Club playing... great movie... that's why I chose it... so what's up... oh it was crazy but after Fiona did her thing it got pretty mellow... she seemed okay when she left... aren't you going to ask about Ava... I know she started it but you can't deny we all were thinking it... she has to go back downtown tomorrow but I don't think she meets with the architect until next week... Uncle Pete's helping her... someone he knows from college... she seems pretty sure about what she's doing... what's that... no not yet... I will... no I'm not asking her for any more money... because I'll figure it out... stop it that's her money... I'm gonna hang up now... because you're starting to *piss me* off... maybe but it's none of your business... later... you too."

Grabbing the remote, Victoria turned down the volume of the television and settled into the cushions. She was feeling tired herself and knew she should go to bed, but the movie had sucked her in. Putting her feet up on the coffee table in front of her, she let go of the drama of the day and got lost in her favorite movie.

WHEN SHE CAME out of the bathroom, he had been standing next to the bed staring at the puppy sound asleep at what used to be his side of the bed. Earlier, he had stayed in the living room for as long as he could, but it appeared that his family was falling apart before his very eyes and just when he thought that he couldn't take it any longer, the darkness thankfully had swallowed him up.

"I didn't think I'd be seeing you so soon," Kate whispered. "When you disappeared, I thought maybe it was for good this time... and I wouldn't have blamed you. That got pretty ugly."

"I don't know why they're being this way."

Kate put her finger to her lips and carefully crept across the floor to listen near the door. "She started a movie; it should be okay for us to talk if we keep our voices down." Walking across the room, she sat in the chair and looked up at him. "I have got to sit... it's been a day."

"We have to fix this Kate... get them to understand."

She studied his face. Unsure if he had missed the last part of the discussion or if he had forgotten already. "I'm not sure what the last thing was that you stuck around for, but by the time Ava and Charlotte left... things were better."

"Really?" he asked, sounding surprised but relieved.

"Yeah. They're still worried but I think I've at least convinced them that I *might* know what I'm doing."

"Good... that's really good," he replied.

"I can tell you know... that something's going on. You're not as good at hiding things as you used to be."

"I've been afraid to talk about it too much. In part because I don't really understand it so I haven't been able to explain it to you and I also don't really know how I feel about it. All I know is that I seem to be drifting... I can feel myself being pushed or pulled away from the house. Away from you."

She took a deep breath and stared into his face. "Maybe it's time that you stop fighting it. It's got to be a wonderful place that you're going to... a lake as far as the eye can see is what I imagine when I try to picture what it is you might be doing when you're no longer here."

"Now that doesn't sound so bad." He smiled at her.

"No, it doesn't," she said softly.

"Hey, remember that time you went fishing with me."

"You mean that *one* time," she replied.

"You freaked out as soon as you saw the boat," he laughed.

"Umm, hello. It was made of aluminum. All I could picture was my box of tinfoil back in the kitchen drawer."

"Anyway... after I finally got you into the boat, we sat there for like half an hour before you would let me push away from the dock so you would be sure that it would float. After you calmed down and we finally rowed out onto the lake, I think you enjoyed it."

"I did."

"Then... umm, then we-."

Kate witnessed the look on his face transition from joy to confusion... he forgot what happened next.

"*And then* that stupid fish jumped into the boat and freaked me out!" she whispered as loud as she dared, trying desperately to hold back the laughter.

"That's right," Matt continued. "Right before I stood up and fell over the side."

Kate was smiling again, watching him tell her one of his favorite stories. "As I recall, I was the only one who caught something that day... you."

"You've always had me," he replied before getting quiet.

"It'll be okay," she whispered. "You're going to be okay and so will we... I'll make sure of it."

"I finally figured it out."

"Figured what out?" she asked.

"This whole time that I've been back... talking with you, watching the kids, walking around town and revisiting my life. Our life. It's this that I'll miss... the day to day of us."

"I love you Matthew Jackson Chapman... don't you ever forget that."

"But I loved you first," he replied. "You should go to bed... big day tomorrow."

Tomorrow morning, she was signing the contract to lease the lot, and in the afternoon, Pete was stopping by with the name of the architect he recommended she meet with to design the building.

It *was* going to be a big day.

He watched as she turned off the lamp and kicked off her slippers, climbing into bed to fluff her pillow twice before laying down. Even before she flipped over from her right side to her left to face the puppy, he knew it would happen. It was the same thing she did every night. He moved toward the foot of the bed and in his mind, he could envision him lying next to her, his hand reaching out to her. She would cover her hand with his and spin his wedding ring until she fell asleep. The memory of what used to be faded and he looked down to watch her drag her finger on the bedsheet next to the puppy.

"Sleep tight, Kate," he whispered.

It felt like only a moment had passed when she opened her eyes and she sat up in bed. But the blue light from the clock on her nightstand displayed two o'clock and she could no longer hear the noise from the movie playing in the living room. Her chest began to feel heavy when she realized she was alone.

She had forgot to say goodnight.

And he was gone.

CHAPTER TWELVE

SHE HAD MADE a mess again. But lucky for her, this time Victoria was there to help clean it up. After breakfast and after her short meeting downtown, they started in the attic. *Do the worse first.* That's what Matt always used to say and that's what she did.

While Victoria climbed up into the dark space with only a flashlight to guide her, Kate stayed on the floor of the kitchen and waited. Twenty minutes later, after more than a few swear words had been uttered and it sounded like something broke, she heard the instruction she was waiting for.

"Okay, try it."

Looking at the small white remote she held in her hand, Kate found the *on* button, looked up and then pressed her thumb down.

"Hey, it worked!"

A second later, she looked up at her daughter's smiling face staring out of the open space in her ceiling. "And it's going to keep on working for how long?"

"Well, I attached the solar pad just outside the window and ran the wire up to the ceiling where I found a nail already there, so I hung the light on that... theoretically, as long as the solar thing outside keeps working, the light should work."

"And this remote will last for how long?"

"There is an extra battery in the junk drawer. Don't lose the remote or drop it and it should outlast the LED light... which might just outlast you considering how often I expect you to actually come up here after today."

"Very funny," Kate replied. "Okay, I'm coming up."

After placing the remote on the kitchen island, she carefully crawled up the wooden ladder. It was sturdy, like she remembered, but it didn't make her feel any better about where they were leading to. But once she stuck her head up into the space, she realized that it no longer looked as scary as it had in her mind. The light revealed all the dust that was evident but at least now she could see the entire space.

"Okay, let's get started."

Working together, less than an hour later, all the boxes, duffel and plastic bags that they could identify as belonging to Matthew were stacked neatly in the open space between the living room and the kitchen. After sorting through everything, most of the items found their way into the donate pile and only a few things were too well worn, even for the church donation box.

"Well, that didn't take as long as I thought,"

Victoria said. "Want to start in the bedroom now?

"Might as well. What time is it?" Kate asked.

Victoria leaned back so she could see the clock in the kitchen. "Almost noon. What time is Uncle Pete coming by?"

"Not until after five," Kate replied, pushing herself up off the floor. "How about we stop for a quick dinner. Fiona is in the yard with Allie, why don't you go out there and ask her to come in."

While Kate made everyone a turkey sandwich, some with mustard and one with Miracle Whip, Victoria transferred the boxes and plastic bags out to Kate's trunk. The dinner break was quick, and Fiona waved them away to take care of cleaning the table herself, so they could get back to their task.

Although the closet was more organized, Kate knew it would take her longer to go through the items. The memory of Matthew wearing these clothes was fresh in her mind and it was harder for her to put them into a plastic bag. Thank, *God* that Victoria was there to help her keep on track... reminding her this is what he would have wanted.

"This was always my favorite," Victoria said, holding up a blue down vest.

Kate watched her daughter slide her fingers down the puffy segments. "Take it... it should fit you."

Victoria smiled and opened the zipper,

pulling the vest free of the hanger before slipping her arms through it. Kate could see the tears glistening in her eyes, but it was the smile on her face she would never forget.

A few hours later, the two women stood in the middle of the small closet, now empty except for a single article of clothing; a cream-colored cardigan Kate couldn't part with. While it was officially Matt's, she had worn it many nights while walking on a beach or leaving the theater after a late movie.

"I put the things you wanted to save for Uncle Pete on the bed," Victoria said.

"Thanks... it looks so big now that it's empty."

"Just think about how many new pairs of slippers you could fit in here."

"Very funny," Kate replied. "Come on, let's take everything to the church... Pete will be here soon."

ON THE WAY home, she turned off Main Street

and saw the back of Pete's truck two blocks ahead of her right before it turned onto her street. She continued the route she was on and by the time she turned into her driveway, Pete was standing in her driveway leaning against his truck waiting for her.

As soon as Kate parked the car, Victoria threw the door open and jumped out of the car. She waved at Pete through the windshield and removed her keys from the ignition. A few seconds later, he was standing alone again, and her daughter was talking on her phone as she walked into the house.

"I thought that was you," Pete said as he stepped away from his truck.

"You're very observant, but I make it easy driving the same car for almost twenty years."

"True," Pete replied, reaching into his pocket. "I have that card for you."

Kate walked over to the passenger side of her car. "Thanks, I appreciate it."

"An art gallery, huh?"

"Oh, don't you start," Kate replied, taking the card from him.

"Not starting... just curious."

"I'll tell you about it sometime," she said, a smile crossing her face. "I have something for you, too."

Pete watched as she walked to the back passenger seat and opened the door to reach inside. After she stepped clear of the door, he noticed the brown plastic bag she held in her hand and as she used her hip to close the door, he noticed that the smile remained on her face.

"Victoria and I were going through Matt's things... I thought you might find good use for a few things."

Pete opened the bag to glance inside and immediately recognized the green fishing vest, neatly folded on the top. Clearing his throat before his eyes met Kate's, all he could manage was a choked, thank you, before he turned away to put the bag into his truck. She could see him wipe his eyes before he turned back around, and was reminded of how Matthew was loved by almost everyone he met.

"Umm, my friend," he said, pointing to the card she still held in her hand, "lives in the City... but, he's expecting your call. If you want me to be there when you meet him, I'd be happy to clear my calendar."

"Thank you, Pete. I appreciate that very much... and just might take you up on that."

"Well, I should get going... tell Fiona I said hello."

She stepped back and watched as he left, giving a quick wave before turning toward the house. As soon as she opened the door, she could hear the chatter coming from the living room where Fiona and her daughter were watching the evening news.

"When do you have your meeting about the

music festival?"

"Day after tomorrow," Victoria replied. "I'll be gone most of the day... even for supper."

"You'll need my car then?"

"Oh, right... yeah, if that's okay?"

Kate looked at the cheesy grin her daughter had on her face as she leaned over the back of the couch. It reminded her of when she was five years old and had just flushed her brother's pacifier down the toilet.

"Fiona, are you planning on still being here on the fourth of July?"

"*Hell,* no... I'm going home on Friday."

"This Friday?" Kate asked, surprised.

"That's the one."

"And when were you going to tell me?"

"I'm telling you now," Fiona replied, continuing to stare at the television.

"And what if I didn't ask you?"

"Well, then I guess you'd have figured it out when you went into the bedroom and saw it empty. Oh, and that reminds me... think you can have my clothes washed by Thursday? I have to pack."

Kate walked to the fridge and pulled out the bottle of wine and behind her, Victoria's laughter grew louder and louder.

"Fiona, you crack me up!"

GRABBING THE KEYS on her way out the door, Victoria waved at her mother standing in the kitchen but didn't turn around. The scene had Kate flashing back to her daughter's high school years. At least this time, she offered to fill the car up with gas before returning.

"Mom, I made a fresh pot of coffee if you're interested," Kate called out.

Pouring herself a cup, Kate debated if she wanted to sit outside or in the sunroom. When she left Allie earlier, she could feel the humidity in the air and decided indoors with the conditioned air was the better option.

As she took her seat, she could hear her mother return the carafe to the coffee maker and pushed the chair to her right out with her foot. She was hoping they'd get a chance to talk, alone before she left and now seemed like the perfect time.

"Victoria left already?" Fiona asked, as she entered the room.

"A few minutes ago. The sky looks like it might open up so maybe she'll be home sooner than she expected though."

"Days like this remind me of Florida," Fiona

said.

"I would hate it... dealing with humidity every day. Yuck."

"You say that now, but wait until you get past those hot flashes and your skin becomes as thin as paper then you'll appreciate the weather Florida offers."

"I'm not moving to Florida," Kate replied, taking another sip from her coffee. "I'm not leaving my kids... I'm not you."

"Only time will tell if that statement stays true."

Kate felt something fall on her foot and when she looked down, Allie had dropped a squeaky toy at her feet. Leaning over, she picked it up and tossed it as far as she could.

"Mom, can I ask you something?"

"Sure."

"The other day, you made a comment about marrying again after my father died... because of me." Kate waited for her mother to look at her. "Was that true?"

"Oh, Kate... why are you asking me this now?"

"Was it true?" Kate asked again.

"The answer is, yes. I married because a young girl needs the influence of a father figure in her life... someone with the personality to handle the things that I didn't have the skillset or the patience for."

"Like what?"

"Take you to soccer practice, teach you to drive a car, tell you what to watch for with young men and to walk you down the aisle. I was a terrible mother, Kate... I realize that. But I did try to make up for it."

It was the last thing she said that helped Kate to understand who her mother was. For her entire adult life, she had tried to understand what made Fiona Thompson tick, but she was like a jigsaw puzzle missing key pieces that connected the image. All along, she never guessed that *she* was the missing piece... the one piece that no matter how you turned it, fit into every open space bringing the other pieces together.

"You know what I wish I would have gotten before I left?" Fiona asked.

"What?"

"One of those twisted cones... you know, the ones that are half chocolate and half vanilla."

"Well, unfortunately unless it rains, Victoria is going to have my car all day," Kate replied. "I wish you have said something earlier."

"It's only four blocks from here, unless they moved their location." Fiona said. "I can walk if you can... we could even bring the dog with us."

"The shop is in the same spot, but mom... it's four blocks up and back," Kate replied. "Are you sure you could make it that far?"

"I walk farther than that to get my whiskey when I'm at home."

"Why do you walk-," Kate held her hands up in front of her. "You know what... I don't even want to know. Okay, if it's not raining, we'll go get ice cream."

"Oh, and I found the folded clothes on my bed when I came out of the shower," Fiona said as she picked up her coffee cup. "Thank you."

"You're welcome... mom."

CLOSING THE GATE behind her, Kate bent down and unhooked the leash from Allie's collar and watched her run across the patio pavers as she made a beeline toward the back yard. Never again. She knew before they reached the end of the driveway that the puppy was too young to try the leash, but Fiona seemed to be unusually happy about getting out of the house. Thankfully, they hadn't passed any other dogs, but Allie Girl went crazy when she saw her first kid on a skateboard. She weighed only sixteen pounds but had lurched forward with so much energy that Kate nearly dropped the leash.

She was better by the time they made it to the ice cream shop, and Kate had been able to keep her under control by asking for an extra cone and feeding it to her bit by bit. Fiona had only gotten through half of her treat before tossing it in the garbage because it was melting faster than she could eat it. Given that it was eighty-nine degrees outside, Kate had opted for the safer option and gotten a cup instead. All in all, the outing would have been quite pleasant if Fiona hadn't suggested that they bring some ice cream home for Victoria.

Unfortunately, Kate hadn't considered that Fiona might walk more slowly on the way home and by the time they were still a full block away, the cookie dough ice cream had completely melted and began seeping through the thin paper container that was turning to mush in Kate's hand. As the sweet cream began to drip out of her hand and onto the sidewalk, Allie caught a whiff of it and began to zig and zag in between Kate's legs trying to lap up every drop before it hit the ground.

By the time Kate had found a trash can to throw away the ice cream, most of it had already melted, landing on her clothing and the dog. With each step, she could feel her hand and the leash grow stickier and stickier as the melted treat began to dry in the warm air. When they finally reached the driveway, she instructed Fiona to go inside while she went through the side gate with the puppy.

They both needed to be hosed down.

She examined the leash she held in her hands and decided she could salvage it; if the water from the garden hose didn't do the trick, she'd soak it in the kitchen sink overnight. Turning the corner, she found Allie rolling around in the grass and by the time she reached her, she looked like a Chia pet with grass sticking to her entire body.

"Come here you little *shit*."

She started at the top and worked her way down. Surprisingly, the puppy tolerated the cold water pretty well, but the hard part was stopping her from rolling around in the grass. After Kate was sure that all trace of the ice cream was gone, she grabbed Allie by the collar and brought her to the patio where she finished cleaning off the debris from the grass from her coat. Behind her, Fiona stood with a towel and as soon as Kate shut off the water, she tossed it to her.

"I have another one on the floor in here, like you asked."

"Thanks, mom."

By the time Kate rolled up the hose and walked through the patio door, Allie was rolling around on the floor, playing with the second towel. She was positive it would have holes in it by the time she was done, but Kate didn't care.

"I'm going to change… be back in a minute."

Walking into the bedroom, Kate closed the

door behind her and began to pull off her wet, sticky clothing. She needed a hot shower to get clean and to help her wake up. Stepping out of the shower, she wrapped the towel around her and walked into the closet. It was such a strange feeling walking into the space and finding *her* clothes hanging up. Reaching for a t-shirt and pulling a pair of sweatpants off the shelf, she walked back into the bedroom and threw the clothes on her bed. After she pulled the t-shirt over her head, she stared at the empty chair in the corner and finished getting dressed.

Hearing soft scratching at the door, Kate walked across the bedroom and opened it. On the other side sat Allie, her head cocked to one side and her little tail moving a hundred miles an hour behind her.

"'Come on... let's go see what grandma is up to."

PACING BACK AND forth, Kate looked at the

clock on the wall for the third time in ten minutes. The driver that Fiona had booked to take her to the airport was late, yet Fiona sat calm as could be in the chair she claimed as her own and hadn't looked at her wristwatch even once. But why would she? If the driver didn't show up, she knew Kate would take her. Kate was her backup even though she knew that her daughter had arranged to meet with the architect an hour from now.

"Okay, if your driver doesn't show in the next two minutes, I'm putting your bag into my car, and I will take you. What kind of service did you use anyway?"

"Don't worry about it... the driver will be here," Fiona replied.

"Oh, I am worried about it," Kate replied. "For one, I don't want to drive all the way to the City only for you to miss your flight and two, I need to call Mr. Kent and tell him not to bother to waste his time driving here because I won't be here... I'll be driving to where he *was*!"

"You're not making any sense. But, on the off chance you do have to take me... why don't you just arrange to meet him at his office after you drop me off? If he is free to meet you here in one hour, then he should be free to meet you there... and it'd probably be more convenient, at least for him."

Kate stared at her mother. Her reasoning was sound and if Kate hadn't been feeling so much stress and anxiety, perhaps she would have thought about that resolution herself.

"Mom, I could always take Fiona to the airport," Charlotte offered.

"Thank you, but don't you have plans with your sister?"

"This afternoon, but we can always move it to tomorrow," Victoria replied.

"None of that will be necessary," Fiona said, standing up. "My driver is here."

A few seconds later, a car horn honked twice, and Fiona walked to the door where her bag was already waiting. The other women in the room followed her to the door and Kate was the first to reach for her bag while Charlotte opened the door.

"After you, grandma."

Fiona smiled at her youngest granddaughter who held the door open for her and reached up to touch her face. "The next time we see each other, you could be holding a daughter of your own." Fiona could see the tears welling up in Charlotte's eyes. "Do yourself a favor... when they offer you the drugs, say yes."

Charlotte laughed as she watched her grandmother move through the open door and continued to hold the door for her sister and mother, before following behind them herself.

The driver of the sedan opened the driver's door and walked around to the back of the vehicle to open the trunk. At the end of the sidewalk, Fiona stopped and faced the women standing behind her and her gaze settled on Victoria.

"I left something in your room on your pillow. Just this once, *don't be like me*... accept the help. You can text me and thank me later."

Before Victoria could respond, Fiona turned to face her daughter as the driver picked up her single piece of luggage and placed it in the trunk.

"Have a safe trip, mother."

"I'm looking forward to you proving me wrong... that your purpose was to stay in this small town and make it better." Fiona turned to walk toward the rear passenger door that had been opened for her. "And it wouldn't kill you to give that dog some treats every now and then."

The three women stood at the edge of the driveway and watched the sedan drive away. Wanting to see what Fiona had left her, Victoria was the first to turn around and run into the house.

"Victoria, close the-!"

Kate hurried back up the sidewalk to stop Allie Girl from running out the open door and by the time she made it to the kitchen, Victoria was emerging holding something in her hand.

"It's a check!" she said, waving it in front of her. "Fiona left me a check for twenty-five thousand dollars with a note that says, *'take the next year to think about your options'*."

"So, what did my mother discover that you

haven't told me?" Kate asked.

"Jackson," Victoria whispered. "She had to have gotten to him."

"Well, now that the secret is out, why don't you enlighten us all."

Victoria looked at her mother and sister's faces as they stared at her, waiting for her to spill the beans. "It's nothing really... I was just thinking of finding a full-time job."

"But if you do that, when will you find time to write and perform?" Charlotte asked.

"I was thinking, *maybe* it's time I change course and try something different. I mean, how many years am I supposed to waste trying to make something happen?"

Kate looked at her daughter. Her words trying to convince herself and them that it was time to move on, betrayed by the sadness evident in her eyes. "Until it's no longer what you want. Until your heart leads you in another direction. Don't do what I did, Victoria... give up on your dream because you think chasing it will disappoint someone else."

"But I can't keep taking money from first you, and now grandma. It makes me feel like I'm still a teenager with an allowance."

"That's your own hang-up that you need to get over," Kate replied. "I've already told you what I think, now it's up to you to figure it out."

"Vic, why don't you take Fiona's advice and just say, *thank you*. It's not like Fiona or even mom for that matter... can't afford it. They're both loaded."

"That's great advice, Charlotte," Kate replied. "Now, I hope you will take it yourself."

Kate smiled as her daughters looked at her, both with the same confused look on their face... their expression reminding her so much of their father.

"What are you talking about?" Charlotte asked.

"Well, I was going to talk about this with you in private, but this moment seems like the perfect setting to discuss it. After the baby comes, when things have settled down... I want you to think about starting a business of your own."

"A business of my *own*? Mom, what are you talking about?" Charlotte asked.

"I'll rent you a little house or one of the empty shops downtown and I think you should open up your own dress shop or alteration shop or whatever you think it should be. The point is, you have a talent and I have a feeling if you pursue it... you'll find something to balance what you give up being a mom and a wife. Something to keep you anchored so you don't lose yourself while taking care of everyone else."

"Mom, I don't-."

"Oh, stop," Kate replied, reaching across the space between them to take her youngest child's hand. "I just want you both to promise me that you won't chicken out, push aside or give up on what keeps you awake at night."

Releasing her daughter's hand, Kate dumped the now cold coffee down the sink and placed the cup in the top rack of the dishwasher.

"And now it's time for me to meet with someone to talk about what keeps me up at night." Kate walked to the front door and reached for her keys. "Do me a favor and keep an eye on the puppy until I get back... shouldn't be more than an hour."

CHAPTER THIRTEEN

WHEN THE DAYS, weeks and months began to blend into one big blur, Kate gave in to the crazy, but instead of trying to push against it, she found the help she needed to pull and mold it into something that she could manage.

Something she could control.

After the initial meeting and while the architect was drafting his first attempt at her vision, she took a full seven days off to enjoy the fourth of July parade and music festival while Victoria was still in town. But after she dropped her off at the airport and before she even realized it was happening, the balls she had to juggle quickly grew from three, to four and then five. If it hadn't been for Lilly who even from her living room window recognized the signs that something was wrong, she may have dropped every single one. But Lilly called Pete and together they staged their own intervention, one that encouraged Kate to sit down and figure out a way that they could help her.

At first, Kate denied that she had a problem or that she needed any help. Sure, she was busy but who wouldn't be building a business from the ground up? But Lilly and more so

Pete, refused to leave until she made a list of everything pressing that needed to get done and then picked two from the list that she felt were of lower significance that she could trust someone else to complete for her. After that... accepting their help again, came easier.

By the end of the first week, Pete had assumed the role of project manager, working as the primary point of contact with the architect. He would have supper with Kate several times a week so they could discuss the changes Kate wanted to make and every Tuesday and Friday, he would meet with the architect to collect the new drawings and gather any questions the architect might have. His task was relatively easy as the design that Kate was looking for was not architecturally challenging; the design of the building was simple to let the art displayed be the focal point.

Lilly's task was more challenging.

Kate asked her to help with finding local artists from their community who were both willing to display their work in public and more importantly, talented enough to have their art displayed in public. Kate never thought that her neighbor who liked to dress in bright neon activewear from the eighties would ever succeed. But she surprised her by introducing Kate to a friend she had known since kindergarten who painted watercolor portraits of friends and family pets. The portraits were absolutely incredible, capturing the true likeness of the subject with a flare of whimsy. After Lilly proved to be someone she could rely on, Kate felt like she could stop to take deep breaths again and focus on another ball that needed her attention.

Her daughter, Charlotte.

Ben's dad had done some construction of his own and after the new bay opened, business picked up significantly resulting in longer days at the garage. Kate filled in where she could. The crib that was supposed to be delivered two weeks after it was ordered, didn't show up until eight weeks later and while Ben was a mechanic and knew his way around all kinds of engines, the less than adequate crib instructions had him stumped. Kate enlisted the help of Pete and between the four of them, they managed to construct the piece of furniture that started out as a crib, dresser and changing table, but could be converted into a child's bed and dresser when the time came. It was a beautiful addition to the nursery once it was put together, and Ben and Charlotte repaid them by getting Chinese takeout and nonalcoholic wine.

And it was one of the best ways that Kate had spent a Sunday in a long while.

BY THE TIME the holidays rolled around, the first and second floor of the art gallery had been framed and the construction crew was beginning to work on rough electrical and plumbing. With the help of Pete and Ed, steady progress continued to be made. It also helped that when you lived in a small town, everyone was connected to someone who was working on the project, and nobody wanted to be the one who let Matt Chapman's family down.

Victoria had finally settled into her new two-bedroom apartment and had taken a few days off from work to spend Thanksgiving with her family. Fiona was also planning to come back but two days before the flight, twisted her ankle walking to the corner store and decided being wheeled around two airports was not something she was interested in doing. Instead, they would have to settle with her joining the video chat with Jackson. Ava decided to come at the last minute, even though Kate was sure that she was more interested in seeing the progress of the new building than sitting down for a loud meal around a crowded table. Charlotte even volunteered to bake the pies. That job had previously fell on Matt's shoulders, even though all he had to do was order the pies at the store and remember to pick them up by five o'clock the day before Thanksgiving. The kids even convinced Kate to invite Uncle Pete, to thank him for everything he had done to help.

At the end of the day, after all the dishes had been washed and put away, all the goodbyes had been said… and the house was once again quiet, with Allie Girl asleep on the bed, she sat in the chair in her room, wearing the cream cardigan from the closet and thought about how different this Thanksgiving had been.

The first without Matthew.

The last before she would have a grandchild to hold in her arms.

The first without having to go to the store after the meal to get ready for Black Friday.

The last time Charlotte would try to bake a pumpkin pie from scratch.

The first time they had eaten left over mini-marshmallows and Cool Whip for dessert.

The day that had been everything she hoped it would be… and more.

TYPICALLY, WHEN THE phone rings in the middle of the night the news is never good. But as Kate pulled on her jeans and reached for a sweater, all she could feel was excitement. The baby was coming. She pulled her hair up into a ponytail and opened the screen door so Allie could go to the bathroom before she left.

She didn't know how long she would be gone.

"Come on, Allie Girl... I don't have all day."

Even as she said the words, Kate knew that was probably not true. This was Charlotte's first baby and even though she was being admitted, it was probably going to be hours and hours before their little one made her grand entrance. As the dog came running back into the house, Kate locked the patio door behind her and walked into the living room to turn on the Christmas tree lights. A soft white glow filled the room and a sense of peace replaced the anxious feeling that was growing in the pit of her stomach.

A few seconds later, her phone rang.

"Hello... did he call you too... well make sure you're awake before you get behind the wheel... yes I'm going to the hospital now... if it's anything like what I went through with you it'll be hours... no I haven't called them... because what are they going to do... I think we should at least wait until six or seven... yep I'm heading out now... okay... see you there... drive safely."

Walking to the door, she turned around to find her dog following. "Allie Girl, you can't go with me this time... I'm sorry."

Closing the door behind her, Kate unlocked her car and after climbing into the front seat, sat there for a few minutes before putting the car in reverse. From this point forward, everything was changing. She would no longer be referred to by her family as mom or Kate... she would be grandma, and this would be grandma's house.

Smiling, she put the car in reverse and drove the short distance to the hospital.

EVERYTHING WAS READY. Everything on the to do list had been completed and the mayor's office had called to confirm the time of the ribbon cutting ceremony. Everything that could be done, was done and the doors were opening.

Some days it felt like today would never come and other days it felt like she needed more time. Another month. Another week. Another day.

Kate had picked up Fiona and Victoria yesterday, and Jackson's flight landed forty minutes ago. Ava had picked him up and was under strict instructions to come straight to the house. There would be just enough time for them to drive out to the lake and then get back to the gallery to meet the mayor at noon.

Everything was ready except for Kate... she couldn't find her other shoe.

"Mom, coffee's ready."

She heard Victoria call to her as she looked under the bed for the third time. "Coming." Letting the bedspread fall to the floor, Kate stood up and looked around the room.

Oh, hell!

Walking out of the bedroom holding only one shoe in her hand, she could feel herself overheat and pulled off her sweater, throwing it over the back of the chair as she passed by the living room.

"Has anyone seen my other shoe?"

"You mean this one?" Fiona asked, pointing to the black leather mule in the middle of the kitchen table.

Sighing, Kate reached for the shoe and put them both by the front door, hoping that when she needed them, she would remember where they were.

"Is Pete coming here or are we meeting him somewhere?" Victoria asked.

"Coming here," Kate replied. "That reminds me, text Charlotte and remind them to pull all the way up into the driveway... Ava needs to be able to park behind them when she gets here."

"You want me to text her?" Fiona asked.

"No, mom... Victoria will take care of it."

A few minutes later, the doorbell rang, and Allie began to bark.

"It's open," Kate called out.

"Hi, Vic." Pete said as he waved to Kate on her way back to the bedroom. "I didn't see Ava's car."

"She's not here yet, but they should be here any minute," Victoria replied.

"Coming through!"

Recognizing Charlotte's voice behind him, Pete stepped out of the way to make room for her, the infant seat she was carrying and Ben, trailing closely behind.

"Did you get my text?" Victoria asked.

"Yep," Charlotte replied as she carefully placed the carrier onto the floor. "When is Jackson supposed to get here?"

"Any minute... I hope," Kate stated, returning to the room as she closed the clasp of the gold bracelet on her wrist. "Oh, I love that dress."

"Thanks, I just finished it this morning."

"Pete, did you text Ben and Ava the instructions in case we get separated?"

"Taken care of," he replied in a cool and controlled tone. "Everything's set."

Kate stopped suddenly in the middle of the room. "Everyone, make sure that you go to the bathroom before we leave... there aren't any bathrooms where we're going. Right?" she asked, looking toward Pete.

"Right, no bathrooms."

"Just two hundred acres of woods," added Fiona. "One of the many reasons I always have a pack of travel tissues in my purse. If a bear can shi-."

"Mother! There's a child present."

"What?" Fiona asked, looking at her daughter. "Oh, *please*... she's four months old."

"I think she's grown since the last time I saw her," Pete said, crouching down to grab Matilda's little hand as she laughed and cooed back at him.

"Uncle Pete, you saw her yesterday," Charlotte replied.

Kate walked toward the door and slipped into her shoes only to return to the kitchen a few seconds later to look at the clock. She could feel the anxiety building just below her ribcage. They needed to leave but she felt like she was forgetting something. Something important.

Shoes, clothes, makeup, hairspray, rings, bracelet... purse is hanging on the door... phone, speech and keys are in my purse... Allie's leash is already on her... that's everything.

"Mom, are you okay?"

"What?" Kate turned toward Victoria who was standing next to her. "Yes, sweetheart... just running through the list in my head." Behind her, she heard the distinct sound of a car engine and smiled. "They're here. Everyone let's go! Me and the dog are riding with Pete. Mom, you ride with Ben and Charlotte. Victoria you are going to ride with Ava and Jackson."

Kate stepped aside and ushered her mother and children out the door while Pete walked over to Allie and picked up her leash trailing on the floor beside her. As he stood alone with Kate in the house, he watched as she scanned the room.

"That's everyone, Kate. Time for us to go, too."

"I feel like I'm forgetting something," she whispered. Scanning the room one final time, Allie barked when Kate's focus moved to the area in front of the fireplace. "Oh, my *God*."

Pete watched as she maneuvered around the furniture to get to the back of the room and only when she reached toward the mantle, did he understand. When she turned around, she gently cradled the gold urn to her chest, and he could see tears begin to brim her eyes.

"Ready?" he asked.

"Now I am."

THE DRIVE TO the lake took twenty minutes and Kate spent most of it staring out the passenger window enjoying the scenery and thinking about what she was about to do. She couldn't have asked for a more beautiful day. It was when she felt the truck come to a stop, that she finally turned to look at Pete.

"We're here. That's the trail," he said, pointing out the windshield. "It will take us right up to the dock."

"Would you take Allie for me?"

"You bet," he replied, getting out of the truck, and moving his seat forward. "Come on, Allie Girl, you're coming with me."

Kate took a slow breath in and touched the top of the urn sitting in her lap as she exhaled. After opening the door, she stepped outside and breathed in the clean, fresh air that surrounded her.

"It's beautiful here." Victoria said, as she stepped out of the Jeep behind her.

Kate looked back to find the other two vehicles parked in a single file behind Pete's truck and as Jackson walked toward her, she could feel her eyes fill with tears again.

"Hi, mom," he said as he embraced her.

"How was your flight?"

"Good. Early… but good."

"I'm sorry you have to sleep on the pullout," Kate said, reaching up to touch the stubble rarely found on his face.

"That's okay. Hey, it's only for a few days until Victoria goes back to Nashville… then you'll be stuck with me for a week."

"There will be plenty for you to do at the gallery," Kate replied.

"Mom," Ava interrupted. "I'd like you to meet, Paul."

Kate turned her attention to the man standing next to her oldest daughter. "Paul, nice to meet you. I'm Kate." As she shook his hand, the smile on her daughter's face said everything she needed to know. "I hope you'll be hanging around today, so we can chat later… after the opening?"

"We're planning on staying for supper, if that's okay?" Ava asked.

"Perfect."

"Kate," Pete said. "We should get going if you want to get back in time."

"Right... let's do this."

The group followed Pete through the woods on the short trail that led to the body of water that only a select number of people knew about. Several years ago, Matthew and Pete had spent an entire month building a small dock large enough for them to sit with a few beers enjoying the sunset and to tie up their small boat.

Today it would be used to say goodbye.

Staring out onto the lake that Kate had only visited one time, she finally got it... why Matt always made time to come to this place. After the sound of approaching footsteps stopped, she turned around to face the group that had gathered behind her.

"Ready?" she asked, turning to face her family staring back at her.

After looking into the tearful eyes of everyone present, Kate turned back toward the water and began to slowly unscrew the lid. She focused on the task as she moved the urn back and forth across the water and watched as the coarse ash, almost without a sound, mixed with the water and gradually disappeared. Behind her, she could hear throats being cleared and the sound of her mother blowing her nose, but Kate's eyes remained free of tears.

"What's that?" Jackson said.

"What?" Ava asked.

"Over there," Jackson replied, pointing toward their right.

Kate scanned the area to look for what her son was seeing and immediately found the surface of the lake where it looked like the water was boiling."

"Surface feeding," Pete said. "Probably white bass feeding on a school of minnows."

"Gross," Charlotte whispered.

Kate's attention was then drawn to the shoreline, where she noticed someone standing along the bank wearing a green vest and hat. She was about to turn to Pete to tell him that his lake was not so secret, when the man in the vest began to wave at her as he smiled, and her words caught in her throat. A moment later tears flooded her eyes, blurring her vision and by the time she blinked to force them away, he was gone.

And she was okay.

They all were.

"What time is it?" Kate asked.

"Time for us to be going, I'm afraid," Pete replied.

The group retraced their path back to the vehicles and drove the twenty minutes back into town. As the caravan drove past the Little Flower Catholic Church, Kate could feel the nerves begin to bubble to the surface again. There were spaces reserved for management along the side of the building, so she wasn't worried about finding a place to park, but she wasn't looking forward to standing next to the mayor, even though it would only be for a few minutes. She removed her phone from her purse and texted Ava and Ben where to park.

"Look at all the cars," Pete said, as they approach the downtown area.

"You can park along the side of the building," Kate instructed. "There." Pointing to the left, she put her phone back into her purse and straightened the pendant hanging from her necklace.

"Kate, I've been here before... I know where to park," Ben replied, smiling over at her.

"Sorry."

"At this point, you might as well just enjoy the ride. The caterer is set up in the conference room and ready to go. The flyers are stacked on the table by the door. All the art has been hung up *and* lit or put on an easel... and even your desk was delivered last night. I had them move it into your office, but I'm not sure if I put it in the right spot."

Kate looked over at him and knew he was right. Everything so many people had worked hard for over the past ten months to make this happen had been done. And at this point, whatever still needed to be completed would have to wait.

"Are you ready?"

"As ready as I'll ever be," she replied, opening the door and stepping out onto the pavement. "Oh, can you-."

"I got the dog," he replied, smiling at her through the open door.

One by one, the other car doors opened and closed as her family gathered at the back of Pete's truck, waiting for her next instruction.

"Now what?" Jackson asked.

"Now, we go cut that ribbon and welcome whomever wants to look around, I guess," Kate replied. "Come on, let's go and get this over with."

Less than ten minutes later, the brief ceremony was over, and she watched as her friends and family casually walked around the space looking at the work of the local artists who had been showcased for the grand opening. She couldn't help but smile as she watched Lilly glide around the room completely in her element, chatting up the guests about the artists and explaining how easy it was to purchase what was displayed.

After spending some time, making the rounds herself, greeting the friends and neighbors who had taken the time to show their support and visit the gallery, she asked Pete to take Allie home. It was when she walked him to the entrance that she remembered the small wooden sign hanging in the display window.

Waving again to Pete, she flipped the sign over.

The gallery was open.

OTHER BOOKS BY THIS AUTHOR:

Grace Discovered, Book One
Grace Destined, Book Two
Grace Hunted, Book Three (coming Nov 2021)
Grace Banished, Book Four (coming Spring 2022)
One Step At A Time: Breaking Free

ABOUT THE AUTHOR

Emmaline Givens

Haunted: A Love Story is my fourth published novel. Emmaline Givens is the pen name I use as my real name is somewhat of a tongue twister and often misspelled or mispronounced. The name Givens, comes from one of my absolute favorite characters ever written, from the TV Series, Justified.

Originally from the upper midwest, my husband and I now call the beautiful state of Arizona home. Our three adult children have left the nest but our rescue kitties still keep us company. I love to write and put the stories in my head down on paper, and I enjoy hearing from my readers.

I WANT TO HEAR FROM YOU

Good or BAD - reviews are important for an author...

Share your opinion of each book that you read to help the author and other readers who are looking for the next book to read...

Reviews are Important!